AN IRRESPONSIBLE AGE

Also by Lavinia Greenlaw

Mary George of Allnorthover
Night Photograph
A World Where News Travelled Slowly
Minsk
Thoughts of a Night Sea (with Garry Fabian Miller)

LAVINIA GREENLAW

An Irresponsible Age

FOURTH ESTATE • *London*

First published in Great Britain in 2006 by
Fourth Estate
An imprint of HarperCollins*Publishers*
77–85 Fulham Palace Road
London W6 8JB
www.4thestate.co.uk

1

A catalogue record for this book is
available from the British Library

ISBN-10 0-00-715629-4
ISBN-13 978-0-00-715629-0

Typeset in Sabon by Palimpsest Book Production Limited,
Polmont, Stirlingshire

Printed in Great Britain by Clays Ltd, St Ives plc

'Here,' he thought, 'is where we differ from women; they have no sense of romance.'

Ralph Denham in Virginia Woolf's
Night and Day

He had stylised himself – life was easier that way.

Graham Greene, *The Ministry of Fear*

ONE

'So of course there was nothing for it but to leave.'

Juliet Clough had been about to sit down at her desk but now felt that although this was her room, she had interrupted something and ought to wait. She remained in the doorway while the voice coming from the other side of the wall continued: 'Yes . . . well, thank you . . . No, absolutely. Of course . . . She's just so . . . All the time these days . . . I do try but it's just . . . You're absolutely right . . . If only she could see it like . . . It's just that I . . . You know . . . You do understand . . . Thank you . . . thank you . . .'

Juliet crept to her chair and lowered herself into it. The conversation appeared to have finished but she sat for several minutes, concentrating on staying still. Whoever he was, he must not hear her listening.

A telephone rang. Juliet tensed and leant towards the wall, only this time the man did not pick it up. Her own telephone rang so rarely that it took her a moment to realise that it was hers and not his that was ringing now. If she answered it, he would hear her and then he would know that she had been listening. She grabbed the receiver and moved across the room as far as the cord would allow.

'Hello. Yes, it is. The Shipping Office, yes.' She was crouching on the floor. 'No, I can't speak up. The opening? She'll be delighted. I'll tell her. Yes, I know who you are. Yes, I can spell it. Goodbye.'

So as not to have to speak again, she went outside to have a cigarette. She slipped out through the firedoors at the back of the building and hurried along the path by the river, relieved that she had not had to encounter him.

She stretched over the broad stone wall, trying to see the mud whose smell oozed in under her office door at low tide, only she wasn't tall enough to manage it. The roll-up she had cobbled together with cold fingers kept going out, but she needed to smoke and to shake off the effect of the man who had turned up on the other side of the wall. So of course there was nothing for it but to leave. The line was familiar. Had she read it? Heard it? Never said it, though. That sort of thing hadn't come up.

It was nothing, just something she wasn't used to. Tania had had an odd corner at the back of the gallery turned into a self-contained unit to be rented out. Juliet had forgotten about it and could not imagine who might want it. Most of the nearby offices were unoccupied still – spice warehouses hastily converted for lease as work spaces, as if all it took was a rearrangement of letters.

Some of these streets were lined with blind walls while others were overlooked by tall windows and jutting iron hoists, suggesting such a scale of effort and industry that Juliet imagined the spices had once arrived here by the ton, in great sacks and chests that had to be heaved up and in. What surprised her most was the romance of the air, always a little stormy, into which the walls leaked the scent of nutmeg, coriander and cloves after rain. She was too wary and proprietorial to tell anyone about that.

It was January 1990, the end of a pugnacious decade

and the tail end of a particularly long century. The city experienced a loss of tension and with it, a loss of momentum. Much that had been started had been set aside, but London was not a place to abandon an idea just because it proved to be a bad one. Attention wandered until no one could remember who had begun what or why, but sooner or later things would fall into place, although this usually took longer and cost more than anyone had predicted.

This in-between area east of the Square Mile and south of the river was now a blank space in the *A to Z* marked 'under development'. It was being reconstructed in an optimistic mirroring of the Docklands project which was transforming the river's north bank. The sidestreets around the hopeful, isolated gallery in which Juliet worked had been built for barrows and carts and did not encourage traffic, and so the cars belonging to the few who lived there got stuck negotiating tight corners. Juliet never saw these people in the streets, where there was nothing for them. They drove away early and came back late to sit behind glass and gaze across the river at the homes they had really wanted.

Juliet didn't notice what was happening on the river because it was all so routine. Police launches veered waspishly about while barges slunk up and down, so low-lying they might be about to go under. What lay beneath their tarpaulins? What was left for them to transport? Dingy sightseeing cruisers ploughed back and forth, the wind garbling their amplified commentaries: 'HMS Belfast . . . battle of . . . Elizabeth . . . The Tower . . . Docklands . . . Boom . . .' Someone always waved and someone on shore, though never Juliet, always waved back.

On the north bank, the tallest office block in Europe had just been built on a redundant wharf. The roads that would lead towards it were as yet unmade. To the west was Traitor's Gate where water splashed against an iron grid. Juliet could imagine those who acted against the state being taken through on a boat, blindfolded, hands tied, gagged; terrorists, perhaps.

A city with so little space and so much history that it had become its own obstruction. Juliet had wanted to study in London because she believed herself to be solitary, unknowable and footloose, and that this was the place most likely to confirm that for her. She could not say that it had, but nor did she care. She looked down into a swirl of rotten timber, industrial froth and brick-pink stain. She couldn't care less about her stupid job in this gallery where she had to put up with things like the man through the wall. She was going to America.

'I had no idea you could be so boring.'

For a moment Juliet thought it was a different voice: it was as light as before but needle sharp.

'Calm down. I know you're not shouting, Bar, but you need to calm down. And do stop swearing all the time. It's not terribly attractive . . . I know . . . We must . . . we will . . . of course, sweetie . . . try to understand . . . Buck up, why don't you . . . That's better. Good girl. Now you've got work to do, haven't you? Good girl. I'll drop by and see you tonight . . . No, it was a triumph. You were a triumph. What do you mean let you down? What on earth would you need me there for when you were surrounded by all your . . . I'm going to put the telephone down if you start. You really can be very stupid . . . The reason I got this place was to be able to . . .'

Juliet heard a click and a curt laugh. *Buck up?* She felt appalled on behalf of Bar, or whatever her name was, to whom this man was speaking like a lion-tamer, games

4

teacher and dentist all at once. He must be driving her mad.

For the rest of the afternoon, Juliet typed lightly, opened her filing cabinet smoothly and held sheets of paper by their edges but her computer bleeped and clicked, the printer growled and everything she touched crackled, whispered and whirred. She coughed twice. The first time without thinking and the second time on purpose, just to see what she could provoke. She hadn't heard him leave but couldn't hear what he was doing, which meant that after all he probably could not hear her. Juliet relaxed a little.

Tania was at a board meeting and so the gallery was empty. Quiet rolled back from the two locked front doors, whose original designations, 'Upstream' and 'Downstream', were still visible, carved into the lintels. It rolled through the fresh white space with its stacks of wrapped and sealed exhibits, along the corridor and into her office; it stopped at the wall.

She knew by his tone that this time it wasn't Bar.

'Yes, this is Jacob Dart . . . yes . . . really? You'd like me to . . . ? Well, gosh, I mean . . . me? No, I'd be . . .' His voice ran on in these bubbling, unfinished phrases with such sincerity that Juliet regretted writing him off as a creep. She thought now that he was a boy, nervous and strange and perhaps not in charge of himself.

Juliet chose this moment to leave. She dropped the padlock and chain on the cobbles, but he did not react to the clatter. Jacob Dart. It had been like listening to three different men and she was annoyed to find that she was three times as interested.

She cycled along the embankment path to London Bridge, where she dragged her bike up the steps and rode north on the crowded pavement, tilting and jinking, braking and back-pedalling. With her mind elsewhere, she could size up the slightest gap and guess where a foot would fall. She might lean a little too far over and brush the sleeve of a man in a heavy coat who would jerk and swing out his arm, his briefcase almost catching in her rear wheel. She would hear him grunt and then mutter something that might be 'How' or 'Cow', perhaps even 'Wow', as he realised that she had swooped past him and that he had had no idea she was there. What if he had moved this way or that? He might want to shout after her, but she was long gone.

Juliet Clough was twenty-eight. She looked like an Italian boy and sounded like an English girl. She had grown up in a village where she refused to make friends and had passed through her childhood landscape as she passed through the city now, removed from the drama but affected by the backdrop. She was young and immune and fond of her family, none of which encouraged her to find out more about what was going on around her.

In any case Juliet conserved herself because there was a slight hitch in her body, which had so far manifested itself in the stiffening of her lower back and a tendency in conversation to run out of steam. You may notice that she does not reach as freely as she might and that her gestures are economical, but you might also assume, as did her three brothers, her sister, her parents and friends, that this was characteristic.

There were more straightforward routes home. At Blackfriars Bridge, Juliet rode back to the south side where the beginning of an official river walk was broad enough for her to skim past the clumps of tourists taking photographs of a skyline flushed with a polluted sunset. When she had begun to travel to work this way, she made detours or waited for the tourists to take their shot, but there were so many of them that now she just rode through. She supposed that sometimes she must have got caught in the frame and would appear as a blur like that of a finger in front of the lens, spoiling the view – a notion that pleased her.

As far as Lambeth Bridge there were white walls, swagged chains and cast-iron railings. Then the path gave way to four lanes of traffic edged by an intermittent yellow line which was supposed to designate a cycle path. Half a mile ahead, this line ended as the road crossed from a borough which supported cycle paths into one that did not. Here, Juliet concentrated on being predictable. The last stretch took her through the backroads around Battersea Park, past the mythical white chimneys of the condemned power station and the overloaded mansion blocks, and on across an estate where Juliet had worked out a route along water-logged walkways, ending with a bump down a stinking spiral staircase and out onto a road of sorts lined with corrugated-iron fencing behind which was wasteland.

This had once been a grid of terraced streets named after military victories. Some had been bombed and the rest, except for two rows of six houses, had been knocked down. Over the last ten years, the tower blocks of the estate had been supplemented first by maisonettes offering a sliver of balcony or garden, and then by what were almost terraced houses again, except that they looked like broken-off chunks of the flats. One row of the old houses belonged to the railway and had been leased to the housing co-op Juliet belonged to. She lived at the end of the road, on what used to be a corner, between the newest houses and the wasteland.

On the stairs, she met her brother Fred who asked, 'Going to change out of your uniform?'

'I have to look smart. It's a gallery.' Juliet wore either neat shirts and narrow trousers, or t-shirts and jeans, and had the kind of light, straight figure which inclined her to look disciplined or childlike accordingly. She considered Fred, whom she could not imagine in a pair of jeans: 'Did you sleep in your shirt and tie?'

He nodded. 'And my waistcoat.'

'You used to do that when you were at school.'

'Sleep in my uniform? It saved time.'

'What for? You didn't do anything then except sleep or work. Same now, really.'

Fred had a job in the City, something so new to his family that nobody understood what he did or asked him to explain. He dressed with elaborate formality so as to convince himself that he was in costume. To him, making money was a game; he enjoyed the rules but did not show much interest in the result. He understood money well enough to know that when it accumulated it insisted upon change, something Fred was not good at and resisted. He never spoke about how much he lost or made, just as he did not acknowledge that the house in Khyber Road was quite different to the flats his colleagues were buying near the common and the park.

Fred followed Juliet into her room where she turned on a small heater and began to select clothes from the neat stacks of black, white and grey on her metal shelves.

'Shut the door if you're staying,' she said. 'It's freezing.'

Fred had been a child who acted the part of a grown-up. Now he was a grown-up acting the part of a grown-up. He was the same height as Juliet, but did not have her coherence. With his red-and-white looks, fizziness and wild hair, he might strike you as badly wired whereas Juliet *was* wire.

He hopped from side to side. 'I meant to say, to tell you, to warn you, the thing is –'

'Could you stop jiggling about while you speak? It's very annoying.' Juliet had taken off her trousers and jacket, and was climbing into woolly tights, jeans, a vest, flannel shirt and jersey.

'The thing is Caroline, a girl from work, tonight.'

'You invited someone here?'

'Not as such. Someone's birthday party. She asked me to be her *escort*. She's picking me up at seven.'

'If you're her escort, you ought to be picking her up.'

'Really?' He flushed and looked so worried that Juliet assured him it didn't matter, and they went downstairs to light a fire.

In winter, they moved around the house like this, in a huddle, rushing from one source of heat to the next. The house was volubly falling apart. The bare stairs sagged and creaked. Few of the windows opened and some didn't shut; all rattled. Ill-fitting doors created odd drafts and pockets of mustiness. There was a spurting growth of mould in the bathroom and the walls had begun to shed their plaster.

'So where is this birthday party?' Juliet asked.

'In a bar on Lavender Hill.'

'And you're going in your suit?'

'It's what I wear.'

'Perhaps a t-shirt? Or at least not a tie. You ought to show that you can differentiate.'

There was a firm knock on the front door. Fred leapt up and rushed into the hall but then started backing away towards the stairs. 'Please, I better, like you said, change, could you just . . .' He was gone.

Juliet brought Caroline through to the living room and shut the door.

'It's a very interesting colour,' the girl tried out, looking around. Her voice was airless and emphatic. She perched on the edge of the sofa, smiling and wincing and trying to avoid the broken springs asserting themselves beneath the worn cover.

'The sofa? Our brother Carlo, he's training to be a pathologist, says it's the exact tone of an exsanguinated corpse. You can tell from the seams that it was once bright pink. In full health, so to speak. So yes, it is interesting.'

'Exsanguinated?'

'Bled to death.'

Caroline looked so sincerely horrified that Juliet briefly felt guilty. She watched the girl push back the padded velvet band that hovered over her flat hair. Her upholstered jacket creased across her stomach and rustled as she shifted from side to side. She's like a badly wrapped present, thought Juliet, and leaned over to shovel more coal onto the fire.

'I meant the room. This . . . brown.' Caroline leant back, trying to relax, remembered the springs and lurched forward. Her skirt caught and there was a tear of perhaps half an inch on her left hip.

Juliet explained: 'Allie, the speedfreak who lives in the attic, painted it this colour because he thought it would help him sleep. We hate it, but our lives are a lot easier.'

Caroline looked mildly thrilled. 'In the attic?'

'Not now. He's in hospital.'

'Oh dear, an overdose?'

'No. Blood poisoning. He gashed his leg and then he encouraged it.'

'Oh dear.'

'Don't feel sorry for him; they have central heating in hospital.'

There was a pause before Caroline hit on a new subject. 'I knew someone who knew someone who slept in a room with a coal fire. He died of carbon monoxide poisoning.'

'That old wives' tale? Well, just to make sure, we've nailed polythene over the windows to keep out the cold, so the place is absolutely airless,' snapped Juliet. Where was Fred?

Caroline rose. 'I'm sorry to have imposed myself on you like this. You must be wanting to get on with your evening. I could wait for Fred outside –'

Juliet stood up to stop her going. She had to admit that Caroline was rather impressive after all. 'It's nice to meet you, and very kind of you to come and collect the boy and hugely impressive that you found us. Khyber Road isn't in the *A to Z*, so we're entirely off the map.'

Caroline looked as if she could find anyone anywhere. 'I live nearby, actually.' Not in the tower blocks, nor on the estate, but on the other side of Clapham Junction.

'I live with people from work – Jane and Graham. We're married.'

'You're married?'

'Me? No, no, did I say me? No, no, I'm not married, *they* are. Graham and Jane. No. Them. Graham and Jane.'

Caroline's face was scarlet, as if the fire she was staring into had suddenly produced some actual heat. Juliet watched her fiddle with the tear in her skirt, and wondered.

Fred appeared, wearing some old trousers and an untucked shirt, and they set off awkwardly into the night. Juliet wished them well but she was not hopeful. It must take a lot to make someone like Caroline blush, she thought, and she was right. Later, after Fred had walked Caroline home and Jane had taken her sleeping pill, Graham would creep into the box room they rented to Caroline for most of their mortgage payment, and it would be his finger that would find the hole in the tartan taffeta, and enlarge it.

When Barbara came back with a bottle of wine and saw Jacob sitting on the sofa as he always did, half kneeling and almost curled, she had to stop herself saying, 'You look as if you never left', or 'Make yourself at home, why don't you?' What pleased Jacob was knowing silence, so Barbara looked briefly struck and then got on with pouring them both a drink. Even though two people could have sat between them, she felt the shock of being close to him again. It had been three weeks since he moved out, if it could be called that.

'What is it like then, your room?'

'It has all I need – a table, a bed.'

'I know, Jakes. A table, a bed, a scrap of cashmere, a drop of cognac . . .'

'Oh come on, don't be so leaden.' Jacob's mouth tightened at the corners as if someone had turned two screws. No one else teased him or called him by anything other than his full name.

'Where do you wash?'

'In the sink.'

'I hope Tania hasn't made the mistake of laying on hot water.' She lit a cigarette. 'You must be in heaven.' Barbara still found her husband so interesting that she leaned back in order to scrutinise him more thoroughly. She knew what he was made of, parts that did not belong together and which ought not to fit: a bulky, almost square forehead, a cleft chin, a mouth unbalanced by the comparative slightness of the lower lip, a long thin nose with flared nostrils, heavy brows, and wide pale eyes that scattered light. Although he looked still, even disengaged, Jacob was continuously in the throes of process and adjustment, at a chemical level barely discernible to the eye. From moment to moment, he was a different creature.

Now, without moving or speaking, Jacob stopped being a man laying claim to a home and became nervous and rigid, a boy. To stop herself feeling sorry for him, wanting to do something for him, Barbara got up and went to run a bath.

'Come on, Jakes.'

He would not look at her but let her raise him to his feet and steer him into the bathroom. As she reached round him to close the door, he leant back against it, pulling her towards him. They were about the same height and their bodies were the same mixture of angles and curves.

With Jacob pinned to the door, Barbara caught sight of herself in the mirror that ran along one wall, floor to ceiling. She looked clumsy, aggressive and unwelcome. 'Christ, I feel like a man,' she said and took a step backwards.

Jacob caught her arms with his fingertips. He turned his head away and slumped a little. Poor Jacob. Barbara pressed a hand against his jeans and felt a flick of attention. She knelt down, unbuttoned his flies and took the whole of his soft cock into her mouth. For the few moments in which nothing happened, Barbara felt the purest and most generous tenderness. She would have taken his body into her mouth entire, if she could.

Jacob made the small sound he made when he came, undressed and slipped into the water. Barbara stood in the middle of the stone floor and hitched her skirt up to her thighs before deciding to announce that she needed to pee, only she chose to say 'piss', 'I really must piss', and did so noisily, keeping her eyes fixed on his as she talked: 'I love the light in here, how it's so sort of steely and marine. Do you remember what you said when we first had it done? How it was like being in a bathysphere.' She stood up and took off her clothes, at first angrily and then coquettishly. She had been undressing in front of Jacob for twenty years and wanted him to realise what that meant, and to want still to watch.

13

Naked, she hesitated. 'They were right about all those scatter spots giving it a salty atmosphere. Absolutely right. It's my favourite room.' Then she put one foot on the edge of the bath, her groin towards his face.

He made no space for her. 'I know.'

'It's yours, too, isn't it? Your favourite room,' she continued, climbing in to crouch at his feet.

'Don't you think,' Jacob was saying as he stood up so abruptly that the water rocked, collided with itself and washed over the side, 'that you overdid it? Just a bit?'

He got dressed, still wet, and had his hand on the front door when she jumped out of the water and ran naked through the flat to stand behind him.

He waited, blank and tolerant, as she fought to control her voice: 'You wanted it . . . as much as . . . I did . . . more . . . so . . . don't . . . don't . . . make me feel . . . all this is . . . just . . .'

Jacob had buttoned his shirt wrongly and left it half untucked, not because he was in a hurry but because this was what he did. About five years earlier, Barbara had stopped finding it charming but she had never done what she did now, which was to reach out and tidy him up.

'You're forty-three, not seventeen.'

In his smallest, most exhausted voice: 'May I go now?'

Juliet wrapped herself up in an eiderdown, turned on the television and drank whisky from a teacup, as if that made it good for her. Nothing worked. The room did not become anything more than its four brown walls, its grey windows and warped door; it did nothing to hold her. Damp sat in the icy air and the air sat in her lungs so that what circulated in her body was a kind of slush, neither forming nor melting, grubby, soggy and chill. She wondered why a stranger's voice could affect her so much.

The pain began, as it often did, when her thoughts ran out. The first twinge at the base of her spine repeated itself and then unfurled, pushed and gripped. I'm not in agony, she thought, it's not like earache or toothache or being burned, but the pain travelled and accumulated until it possessed her. More than that, it occupied her so fully that she felt thrown out of herself.

She decided to prepare for bed and clutching the eiderdown around her shoulders, moved into the kitchen where she boiled the kettle and filled two hot-water bottles. These she carried upstairs. Then she fetched a can of paraffin and filled the two heaters that stood in the hallway upstairs, heaving one into her room and the other into the bathroom. After trimming and adjusting their wicks, she persuaded both to stay alight. Downstairs again, she coaxed the boiler into action, filled her cup with more whisky, and then went up and ran a bath.

She undressed in a cloud and lay back in water as hot as she could stand, knowing that it would soon cool and that the steam would condense and drip down the walls to feed the mildew, which she would then be able to see, like her poor pink body, far too clearly. The bitter paraffin fumes stung her eyes and mouth, but the smell was a sign that something beyond this bath was giving off heat.

Wrapped in a towel which would never quite dry, Juliet scuttled to her room and turned on a tiny fan heater. She had the largest bedroom, the one with two windows, at the front. It was painted matt duck-egg blue and she kept the navy slatted blinds down, preferring striated light to a view of towerblocks and corrugated iron. Her clothes were arranged on a rail and folded on shelves and in boxes. Her desk, chair and lamp were army surplus, metal-framed and painted grey. She allowed herself one postcard at a time. Her floor was painted dark green and covered in a rug that had belonged to her grandmother. Since childhood, she had loved its lack of traceable pattern.

She surrounded the rug with dullness in order to see it more clearly. She thought about things like this a lot and had impressed Tania at her interview with her ideas about framing space and the importance of absence in display. The truth had been that she liked the empty gallery so much that she knew she would never like anything brought into it. Her PhD, which she planned to finish the following year, was titled 'Framed Departure: the Empty Metaphor in Post-Iconoclastic Netherlandish Art'.

She got dressed in vest, socks, pyjamas and jersey, and was in bed reading when Fred knocked on her door. Pleased to see him, she moved over and he climbed under the covers, claimed one of the hot-water bottles and lit a joint. Allie had grown cannabis in his attic room, punching holes in the roof above each plant to let in light. His crop had been so successful that the cupboard under the stairs was crammed with large plants hung upside-down to dry. No one had been sure when they would be ready but over the winter they had turned into something like dried seaweed and had a striking effect.

'How was it?' she asked.

Fred was too full of delight at his evening with Caroline to want to talk. He shrugged and shook his head, giggled and sighed and smiled so hard that Juliet laughed for the pleasure of something as absolute as his happiness. She was still laughing as she tried to get up, so at first Fred didn't notice that she couldn't straighten and when he did, he waited.

When she could speak again, Juliet said, 'I keep meaning to see someone about this, but then it goes away. It's as if someone's turning a switch off and on. And it's not just

16

my back any more. There's so much blood and it's full of –'

'No!' Fred covered his ears.

Fred's room was at the back of the house where he slept in the brass bed he had had since growing out of his cot. He had painted his walls red, thinking this would make the room warmer. His shirts, pounded in a bathful of suds and inadequately rinsed and ironed, were arranged on hangers suspended from picture hooks hammered badly into the wall. His two suits were squashed up on the back of the door while his shoes and ties, underwear and waistcoats were scattered about.

Juliet came to wake Fred at six-thirty. He had to be at his desk within the hour. She stroked his cheek. 'Every time I come in here,' she said, 'I think you've just exploded.'

TWO

Juliet continued to listen through the office wall. Jacob Dart might have been sitting beside her, including her; she had no choice.

'Hullo, Sally.'

Juliet had guessed by now that Sally was Jacob Dart's sister. He talked to her in the kind of shorthand that siblings use, swore a lot and laughed more from his belly. She imagined him sliding down in his chair as if he were at home and it was just after dinner, and he and this sister (they also talked about a Monica – 'Bloody Monica', 'You know what Monica's like') were drunk and up for a late night of banter.

'Hullo, Sally.'

He said 'Hullo' in the old-fashioned way, with an audible 'u' rather than an 'e'. Juliet tried it out when answering her own telephone: 'Hullo. The opening? Yes, she'll be delighted. You're not sure? Fine. I don't suppose she'll notice whether you're there or not. Yes, I can spell it.'

'Right . . . right . . . right . . .' with each repetition, the word grew smaller. 'Which hospital? Are you there now? I'll be, it's alright, I'll be right there. It's OK Sally, I'm on my on my my way.'

Juliet realised that he was crying. He cried for a long time, as if letting go of something that once it began to unravel would go on and on. What came to mind was a story Fred had written as a child about a magician who was cursed and went to hell, where, 'leaking small tears and tidy sobs', he had to spend eternity pulling a scarf from his sleeve.

She couldn't go and knock on his door. They had not yet met and what would she say? Then his door opened and shut. Juliet looked at her watch and saying loudly, 'Time to go home!', put on her coat and stepped outside.

As she cycled into the alley, she glimpsed a figure in a pale coat and a dark hat passing under a lamp, and hurried to catch up. She turned into the street so fast that she found herself overtaking him and had to keep going so that he wouldn't suspect. Guessing that he was heading for the main road, Juliet sped on and hid round a corner. How could he not spot her immediately? He continued past with a loose stride that made him seem more like a farmer walking his fields than someone hurrying across a city to a hospital. She liked this walk; it made her think of him as a generous man.

The road was a one-way system which gathered up everything heading west and forced it east for a while, around the bend where Jacob vaulted over the railing and danced across four lanes. He hopped over a crash barrier and crossed through the traffic on the other side, where drivers accelerated, relieved to be once more heading the right way. Juliet cycled round and was just in time to see Jacob slip back onto the pavement through a gap where the railings had been wrenched out of place. He continued, half running now, lightly, lightly, disappearing as the road squeezed under the first of the railway bridges which fused here so thickly that they created long tunnels of blackened brickwork and squalid tiles, under-powered striplights and dummy speed cameras, encrusted girders, pallid chickweed, lush moss, pigeons and power cables, all faltering on and on.

'Can I help you?' The man patrolling the hospital fore-court was wearing a vaguely military uniform and carrying a walkie-talkie.

'I'm visiting,' Jacob whispered.

'What's that?'

Jacob shrugged and the man decided that the best way out of this was to pretend that he had heard.

'Know the way?'

'No,' Jacob admitted, then turned and walked off.

'Which ward then?' the man called after Jacob, who loped up one of the ramps marked 'Ambulance Only' and then came down the other side.

'Which ward then?' the man repeated, more challengingly.

'How should I know?' Jacob murmured, heading for the steps that led to the even-numbered floors.

'What you say, mate?'

Jacob came strolling back down the stairs and headed for the opposite set. The man bellowed after him: 'Here!'

Jacob stopped and turned very slightly, and the man half sang, half spat: 'Where did you get that hat? Where did you get that hat?' He grinned, expecting Jacob to grin back only he didn't but took the hat off his head and held it out: olive-coloured corduroy with the high cleft crown and a feminine, extravagant brim.

'Have the fucking hat,' he said evenly. The man coughed to disguise the red in his face, and put his hands in his pockets.

Level 3 looked like a section of multi-storey car park

filled with signs that said 'Do Not Park Here'. The patients who had come out to smoke, some in wheelchairs, others toting drips, huddled together on a strip of turf-like matting. They threw their dog-ends into flesh-coloured plastic barrels planted with dwarf conifers. The man in the floppy hat and coat hurried past. He jumped to peer through the dark glass façade, which was designed to be looked through the other way. At one point he even went up to the glass and pressed his hand against it. Eventually he stopped by the smokers, who indicated that the doors were right there, just behind them. He would have to go in now.

Jacob walked past the hospital map and along a corridor until he reached a lift. He walked back to the map and ran his eye down the list as far as 'N': Nye Bevan Ward. The name was in pink and so when Jacob set off again, he followed the line of pink tape on the linoleum floor only then he was following the blue, or the green. Where had the pink line gone?

'There you are!' Sally found him by the emergency stair-case. He had got as far as the right floor and had not been able to go further. 'You must have got lost. She's through here.'

Jacob's sister led him along a row of blue-curtained cubicles, so tightly packed that they billowed inwards under the pressure of neighbouring furniture and visitors. He sidled along the edge of the bed and squeezed himself into a chair just as a toddler visiting her grandmother rolled under the curtain's hem. He edged the child back with his foot and leant over to kiss his mother.

'Hullo there.'

'Hello, love.' She tried to raise a hand to greet her son.

'You sound completely pissed. So you still know who I am, then?'

Monica smiled. The left corner of her mouth had been

yanked down, making that side of her face sadder and younger.

Jacob ran a finger across her cheek as if testing a surface. 'A half smile! You know how they say in novels "She half smiled"? I've never known what that meant before and here it is – a half smile.'

'If I could lift this arm, my boy, I'd give you a clout.'

Jacob took her hand and stroked it.

She could see how tightly wound his mouth was and knew what that meant. 'Don't worry. Not much damage done. Good thing I was staying with Sally when it happened. They say London hospitals are the best.'

Sally leant in from the foot of the bed and patted her mother's leg: 'You're to stay put. If we let you out, you'd only frighten the horses.' She was speaking too loudly, Jacob too much. They would have liked a little distance from which to observe what had happened to their mother and she, too, would have appreciated more space than the cubicle allowed. Jacob and Sally veered and loomed in front of her as parents must appear to a newborn.

Jacob found a tissue and dabbed Monica's lips. 'You're drooling. Must be the smell of that hospital dinner. Now let's run a few checks!' Jacob was going to be bluff and cajoling because this is what would make his mother feel comfortable. He could adapt perfectly when he chose.

'Who's Prime Minister?'

'That bloody woman. She is a woman, isn't she?'

'Clement Atlee! Absolutely right. And who's on the throne?'

'That other bloody woman.'

'Boudicca! Nothing wrong with you at all! And the year?'

'Just another bloody year . . .'

Half an hour later, Jacob and Sally fled. When the lift

22

doors closed, Sally asked, 'Did you understand anything she said?'

Jacob shrugged. 'Not a word, poor old cow. Still, at least something's finally rid her of that dreadful west-country burr.'

Sally screeched, delighted. She did not notice that her brother was shaking.

Jacob walked down to the river and east along the difficult north bank, where he was forced into detours among churches, coffee houses and money houses on streets that jack-knifed or divided, or brought you into alleyways and newly inserted corners, as if to compel you to keep up some kind of attention and pace. He walked tirelessly and lightly, and believed that he could keep moving forever and leave no trace. He hated his mother. When his father died, fifteen-year-old Jacob had caught her looking at him in church in a way he could only describe as triumphant. He hated his father, too, for forcing her to be so *small* and for, in the end and despite everything, belonging to his wife and not to his son.

It was raining hard. Jacob walked on with his coat open and his hat in his hand. His hair grew wet and his face cold and still he walked, wanting to find the dark that ought to come. Further east he reached a certain street where he stopped and waited. Two hours later, Barbara came downstairs and found him. She ran him a bath, took off his wet clothes and left him.

'You can stay if you like,' she said when he re-emerged wearing things he had found in cupboards neither he nor Barbara had emptied. 'In the study, though, not –'

'Thank you.'

Jacob offered to make soup. He found potatoes and kale, chopped them roughly and cooked them briefly with a lot of garlic and chilli. He made Barbara watch him cook and told her when to sit at table. He watched her eat and jumped up to fetch whatever she might need – a napkin, a glass of wine, a tissue for her streaming eyes. She praised him energetically and he cleared everything away, and although Barbara knew that nothing would be properly clean or in its right place, she let him.

That night, they were gentle.

'Will she be alright?' Jacob asked.

Barbara had spoken to Sally, made some calls and done some research. 'Not entirely, but within a month or so she ought to be able to go home, providing there's some local care.'

Jacob had nothing left to do, so he sat down.

'You must be exhausted,' Barbara said. 'What a shock.'

He shrugged, stretched and closed his eyes. 'She's a tough old boot.'

'Yes.'

'And she gave up on me years ago.'

'When did you last see her?'

'I don't know.'

'Was it at Sally's fortieth, in that nasty little restaurant?'

'Suppose so.'

'Not since then?'

'What's the point? She has no interest in me.'

Barbara could have pointed out how avidly Monica tried to follow her son's career and that she only telephoned so rarely because Jacob made her nervous, but she also knew that this was what he did when he thought someone might leave him – insist they had left him already. As for when *he* wanted to leave . . .

'Are you really here?' Barbara asked. It was a serious question but one she knew she would have to answer for herself. 'I don't think I ever believed, in all those years, that you were really here. Or even that you were real.

Because you don't even feel real to yourself, do you? You haunted our life and you haunt yourself.'

'It is,' said Jacob, without opening his eyes, 'a question of style.'

'As serious as that?' said Barbara, with more kindness than you might expect.

The next morning, Juliet woke up and blushed. 'I was spying,' she said to herself, and then to Fred as she hauled him out from under his blankets, 'Do you think I'd make a good spy?'

'No, too bad-tempered.'

'Why can't a spy be bad-tempered?'

'Because people notice you. They notice your temper. But don't worry, it's your charm.'

'Don't you mean part of my charm?'

Fred considered this. 'No.'

THREE

One Saturday afternoon, Fred came home with a large and smelly parcel under his arm. He went upstairs, ran a bath and came back down.

'Are you in for dinner?' he asked Juliet. 'And what's that you're reading?'

'It's about the picture outside the picture if you must know.'

'Aren't your swotting days nearly over? I thought you were about to become the Doctor of Departure.' It was his joke.

'Just trying to keep up.' The book was by someone who taught at Littlefield, the Massachusetts college which had offered her a year's research post.

Fred took the book from her hands and raised her head so that he had her full attention. 'I've invited a couple of people round.'

'Who?'

'Caroline and the others.'

'Others?'

'The ones she lives with, Graham and Jane. They had me to dinner last month. I told you, remember? A mansion flat with those ceilings that have been iced like a wedding cake, balcony windows like barn doors, low-slung chairs with metal bars, candles like tree trunks, good steak.'

'And you want to reciprocate.'

'It's the polite thing to do and anyway, I've bought a salmon; it's in the bath.'

'Isn't it one of those things that has a season?'

They went up to the bathroom where a flabby grey fish lay on its side in an inch of water.

Fred looked nervous. 'It is a salmon, isn't it?'

'I don't know what they look like, not a whole one with its skin on and everything.'

'The man in the market said it was fresh.'

Juliet considered the fish's slack mouth and clotted yellow eye. Its scales looked as if they had been brushed with glue. She thought of all the things she might point out but she was tired and Fred was excited, and so she decided not to.

Caroline, who was the only one to have visited Khyber Road before, took it upon herself to act as interpreter. Juliet wasn't saying much and Fred was in the kitchen.

'Isn't this room an interesting colour!' she declared.

Graham nodded, 'Absolutely,' and leant back against the mantelpiece. He would not sit down. His wife Jane had retreated to a stool and she also nodded, but did not speak.

'It's to help them sleep,' Caroline continued. 'They have this little man who takes drugs and lives in the roof and never sleeps only he likes brown, so . . .'

Graham became interested. 'You live with a junkie?'

'I wouldn't call him that,' said Juliet.

'What would you call him?' asked Caroline. 'I mean what ought one say?'

'It's alright,' said Juliet, 'he's gone back to his

mother's. I won't be effecting any introductions.'

Graham looked disappointed and then bored. In fire-light, his colourless English looks took on the urinous tinge of a weak streetlamp. He was resting a hand on the mantelpiece and from time to time the hand would creep along reaching for something to toy with, an invitation or an ornament, only there was nothing and so the hand would go limp and slide back towards Graham, who would then scratch his head or nose, as if to distract the others from its wanderings. He was accumulating streaks of dust on his face and was trying to stop himself rubbing one ankle against the other, unable to get rid of the notion that fleas had settled in his trouser turn-ups.

'Is the man in the roof an insomniac?' asked Jane. 'I never sleep.'

Juliet had already forgotten that Graham's wife was sitting beside her, almost behind the door. She looked from Caroline to Graham and then back to Jane, and had to stop herself leaning over to push the girl's hair out of her eyes.

'He doesn't trust himself to sleep,' said Juliet, wondering what she meant.

Jane gave a hiccup of a laugh and for a moment lit up as if she understood this perfectly. Caroline reached out her foot and tapped Graham's leg. He nodded and moved across to kneel in front of Jane, who squeaked and drew away. Juliet was fascinated.

'Jules!' Fred bellowed from the kitchen. She picked up the bottle of wine and carried it through.

'Shut the door.'

The room was full of steam but Juliet, who did not cook much herself, trusted her brother knew what he was doing. The hot tap was on full blast and the kettle was being kept at a boil. Fred was dancing between the two, trying to waft steam towards the fish which was draped bumpily across two roasting tins straddling the two front gas rings of the stove.

'It wouldn't fit in the oven so I had a great idea. Poach the bastard. Only it got a bit dried out.'

'How will you tell when it's done? You can't see a thing in here.'

'By feel. Now, can you give them another drink? They brought something rather nice with them.'

'I put that away.'

'And there's a bowl of Ma's olives to pass round and a plate of that ham she sent down. On the windowsill.'

'Fred.'

'What? The olives, come on, Jules!'

'Don't call me Jules.'

'What?'

When he had decided that the fish was ready, Fred opened the kitchen window and back door. The walls were slick with condensation and their variegated surface of plaster, flock, graffiti and brick was exuding a smell of leftovers. Juliet returned to the kitchen with the plates of olives and ham, almost untouched.

'Graham chewed a corner of ham and then spat it into his hand and rolled it along the mantelpiece. I think he must have pocketed it in the end. Then we had the "I didn't know your mother was Italian, how romantic, all that fiery blood" conversation. I said "Don't you mean all that fiery breath?" at which your Caroline produced a packet of mints and offered them round.' Juliet did not tell him that Jane had been vacantly scratching at her cheek with an olive pit until Graham took it from her.

Fred put his hands on his sister's shoulders. They were both smaller and darker than their three red-headed siblings, and were referred to in the family as the Little Ones, even though Carlo came in between. Carlo was the size of the two of them put together.

29

Fred was shaking, not trembling but pulsing. 'Please.'

'The fish looks . . . tremendous. What are we having with it?'

'Parsley.'

'You can't just . . . I mean, we can't eat in here. Let's take the table in there.'

They slung the pots and pans onto the floor, separated the top of the table from the legs and carried the pieces through, angling them round doorways and along the narrow hall. The three guests stood up and offered to help but in the end had to wait pinned against the fireplace, their legs reddening while Fred and Juliet banged the table back together, collected up chairs, found a sheet to serve as a tablecloth, lit candles and brought in the salmon, which had broken into several pieces but was so liberally covered with parsley that no one could tell. Fred, brandishing a cake slice and a grapefruit knife, made a great show of carving it.

No one ate very much, Juliet least of all. She drank quickly and said little.

Caroline observed this and suddenly asked, 'Are you not well?'

'One ought not . . .' whittered Graham. 'Not at table, it's not quite . . .'

'Are you?'

Juliet's eyes filled with tears. 'Since you ask –'

'Now look what you've gone and done,' said Graham, moving his chair away from Caroline's. 'Do you know what they called her at school?'

'Don't,' said Jane.

'Blunderer. Blunderer Broad-Jones. Good old Blunderer!'

Fred, who had been helping Jane to more wine, slammed the bottle he was holding down on the table. 'Shut the fuck up you fucking creep and get the fuck out of my house.'

Graham went purple. 'Stand up and say that!'

'I am standing up,' faltered Fred, and everyone laughed except Graham, who hadn't got the joke and so could only conclude that they were laughing at him.

When they had calmed down, Fred said quite amiably, 'I meant it though. Out of my house, creep.' Graham made a show of not doing what Fred asked until Jane and Caroline led him away, thanking Fred loudly and repeatedly in the hope that he couldn't hear what Graham was muttering about slums and drugs and darkies waiting to rob them on the way home.

'Off to bed with you!' said Fred to Juliet who was still sitting at the table. 'I'll clear up.'

'I need a hot-water bottle.'

'I'll bring you one, and a cup of tea.'

When he knocked on her door, Juliet was lying in bed smoking a joint.

'Is that good for you?'

'Very.'

She offered it to him, which he took as an invitation to sit down beside her.

'What are we going to do with all that salmon?' he asked.

'I don't know, smoke it?'

Fred exhaled as slowly as possible. 'Really? Do you think it would have any effect?'

Juliet opened the door to her office to find Tania kneeling on her desk, pressed against the wall. Juliet laughed and said, 'You can hear every word, can't you?', making Tania start and turn. She was holding a tape measure.

'I'm sorry?'

'I mean . . . Shelves?'

Tania unnerved Juliet with the proficiency of her

warmth. The younger woman could not bring herself to trust it. It did not help that her boss looked a bit like her mother. They had the same heavy, waved hair that was fading dramatically, and which they knotted into a chignon that kept itself in place.

So Juliet, the naughty daughter, chattered all the way to the new DIY warehouse on the Old Kent Road, promised she knew what she was doing and ran up and down aisles collecting everything she could think of which would block out the wall and his voice. Chipboard, brackets, rawl plugs, screws, batting, primer, undercoat, matt white gloss, large and small brushes, and a new drill. She had a drill at home but Fred had broken it trying to engrave his and Caroline's initials into a vaguely heart-shaped piece of slate. Tania insisted on buying a face mask and gloves for Juliet, as well as an apron because the teenagers and pensioners who worked in the store all wore one. Juliet said thank you but intended to put it straight in the bin.

'We should warn Jacob that there'll be some noise,' said Tania as she drove them back to the gallery.

'Jacob?' Juliet could not admit that she knew who he was.

'I'm so sorry, have I not introduced you yet? I've been rather caught up. Jacob Dart.'

'Jacob Dart?'

'You know, who wrote *Foucault's Egg*.'

'Oh.' Someone had given Juliet a copy and for a while she had meant to read it. Somehow, she had forgotten the name of the person who wrote it.

'He needed a place to work, at least that's what he said.'

Juliet kept quiet so as to encourage her to go on.

'Barbara and I have known each other for years. I know them both, which is why I offered Jacob the room. How was I to know he'd use it as a bolt-hole?'

Tania swung her venerable French car off the main road, and nudged and bumped her way through the back-streets to the gallery. When a fender scraped against a wall, Juliet made a sound of dismay but Tania did not flinch.

'I'll take you round to meet him.'

'No!' Juliet was too emphatic.

Tania smiled, to show that she found this reticence charming. 'He won't bite.'

'No, it's just that I'd prefer . . .' Prefer what? 'I'd prefer to introduce myself.'

Tania chose to appear as if she understood.

Juliet knew what she was doing. She had selected the bit, a masonry bit, according to the size of the rawl plugs. All it needed now was decisiveness and heft, and then she would have the shelves up and so full of files and books that she need never hear him again. She placed the tip of the bit against a pencil mark (one of three) and leant into the drill as she pressed its control switch fully down. The bit ground and then burst through the plasterboard too easily, right up to its neck.

'Jesus Christ.' Juliet yanked the drill back but it caught and swung round, enlarging the hole. She turned it off and put her eye to the wall. 'Fuck.' She could see light on the other side. 'God. Fuck. Christ.'

Juliet could not stand her first meeting with him to be in order to give an apology so she wrote a note, 'Sorry. Wall crap. Will fill', rolled it tightly and prodded it through the hole. After ten minutes or so, a note came back. 'Don't worry and don't fill. What did you mean "Dog muck nice"?' God. Fuck. Christ. It made her laugh out loud and she dashed off a reply: 'Why don't you listen? I said "Rugs pack lice."'

This continued for a week.

'Why so rude on the phone?'

'Because I prefer it stewed on the bone.'

'Too many "Why me?"s, too many "Thank you"s.'

'I must be more careful. Can you really catch diseases from bankers?'

On the day of the opening, he sent a note which said 'Your singing gave me a fright,' and before she knew what she was doing, she had written back, 'What do you mean not coming tonight?' God. Fuck. Christ. She screwed up her reply and threw it into the bin, looked at it for a while, then screwed it up some more and pushed it down to the bottom.

FOUR

Juliet decided that most of the women at the opening were variations on Tania. Like her, they had vague features defined by bright lipstick and characterful glasses, and wore detailed clothes in strong muted colours such as mustard and plum. Their shoes were ill-fitting and overly eccentric. There were others who wore black and grey, and did not use their hands when they talked. They varied from slender to statuesque but always along straight lines – like Juliet.

She shoved her way into one knot of people after another, elbowing and grumbling and thrusting out a tray of drinks, and was hovering crossly by a group who had not noticed her when she nudged someone's back with her tray so that he turned and the group parted and she came face to face with the person they had been listening to. This woman was taller, fairer, heavier and maybe ten years older than Juliet, who instantly thought of her as someone to be admired.

The woman kept talking as she took a drink. Her hair was a blend of silver, ash and sand, and her clothes were an equally technical combination of kingfisher and cobalt blue. She wore jade leather boots and a cashmere shawl in the babiest of blues round her shoulders. Her eyes were dolly blue and her face had an expensive liquid finish. Her voice was avid and cool. She did not look at Juliet or say thank you, nor did she pay any attention to her audience but peered beyond them. Just as Juliet turned away, the woman craned forward and seemed to grow and to soften, and then her over-stretched smile collapsed into a small 'o'.

'Oh,' said Barbara as she realised that the person at whom Jacob was directing the full force of a smile she had not seen for years was not as she had thought for a moment herself, but someone standing between them. The plain thing handing round the drinks. Boyish, cropped and scrubbed, with the virtue in Jacob's eyes of not being one of the grown-ups. 'Oh.'

Juliet, who had seen none of this, was looking for another group to interrupt when a hand landed on her shoulder and a mouth brushed her ear. 'You are so rude.'

Juliet put the tray down on the floor and reached up to embrace her brother. 'Have a drink, Carlo. Thank you so much for coming. Fred's buggered off to some banker's do. Have six.'

'I'll have two. A green and a blue?'

'Good choice. The pink's dreadful.'

'Come outside for a smoke.' Juliet grabbed the hem of Carlo's jacket and leaving the tray on the floor, led him towards the back door.

'Do you have to stick around all night?' he asked.

'I'm not going to.'

'The Natural Fringe are playing at The Glory Hole. We could walk over and give them a bit of an audience.'

'Double family duty for you tonight then.'

They were about to go back inside to get more drinks when a man approached and asked for a light.

'Sure.' Carlo pulled out a box of matches and began

to strike one after the other into the man's cupped hand. They would not stay alight. 'Sorry.'

The man shrugged and dropped his cigarette. 'Never mind.' He did not walk on but stood there, smiling at Juliet.

'Hello,' said Juliet.

'Hullo,' he replied. 'Hullo, you.'

Even after Juliet had explained to Carlo about the wall, and how they had to listen to each other all day but had never before met (not mentioning the notes), and Carlo had laughed and introduced himself ('The big little brother!'), and everyone had run out of things to say, Jacob made no move to leave them.

'What do you think of the show?' he asked.

Juliet had spent days helping to hang works and lay out installations. There had been nothing that she would choose to touch or enter.

'It's a shipping office,' she said. 'I should be recording cargoes not collating mailing lists.'

'Same thing,' Jacob countered softly.

'No it isn't, it's more like –'

'We really ought to be getting over the river,' said Carlo, offering an apologetic nod to Jacob.

'We have to go and support . . . someone we know, who . . . sings a bit,' Juliet explained.

'Sounds great.' Jacob was nodding at everything she said. He kept nodding until Juliet found herself nodding back, which he appeared to take as an invitation.

Carlo began to walk towards the main road and Juliet wanted to follow him but was unable to turn away from Jacob, who was still nodding, smiling, staring.

She stepped backwards, 'It was nice to meet you at last,' and then tripped and stumbled, which meant that he could catch her elbow, steady and steer her.

Carlo looked resigned when Juliet appeared with Jacob,

who had only just let go of her arm. She could not think of anything to say because the situation seemed so momentous, but also hilarious. Jacob raised his arm to hail a taxi and then dropped it again because Carlo spotted a bus, which took them as far as Waterloo.

Crossing the bridge, they passed a girl huddled against the wall in a sleeping bag, who reached out and tugged at Jacob's coat.

'Got any change,' she sneered. The styrofoam cup in front of her contained a few coppers.

Jacob muttered 'Sorry,' without looking at her and did not slow down. Carlo appeared not to notice whereas Juliet paused, dug into her pocket and passed the girl some change. Jacob looked back, hesitated, patted his own pockets and walked on. He reached the next beggar first, a man who cradled a can of beer inside his leather jacket and did not look up but belched as Jacob dropped several coins in front of him without being asked. Juliet looked cross, even more so when the young man asked her if she had any change.

'I only give to women,' she announced and strode past.

Going down the steps on the north side, they passed another beggar who was buried in his sleeping bag with one hand protruding, keeping a grip on his cup. Carlo threw something in, saying primly, 'And I only give to sleeping bags!'

Juliet guffawed and took Carlo's arm, while Jacob hung back as if repelled by the force of her laughter, but he continued to follow the brother and sister through the streets and into Soho, where a weedy neon sign above some basement steps pointed the way down to The Glory Hole.

The more he drank, the more Carlo swelled out of his chair. He leaned comfortably against his sister. 'If he wants to keep buying the drinks, let him. Just be a good girl and give him a nice time later on.'

'He's married.'

'He doesn't look married. He doesn't even look grown up.'

Jacob was making his way towards them, holding three plastic glasses of colourless lager. A withered slice of lime clung to the rim of each.

Carlo whispered, 'Do you think he keeps that hat on in bed?'

Juliet smacked his arm. 'It's only a hat.'

'Oh no it's not,' he said, nodding at Jacob who was trying to squeeze the drinks onto the full table, 'it's corduroy.'

'So,' said Jacob, 'what's this band called?'

'The Natural Fringe,' Carlo replied.

'Interesting, it suggests −'

'They're named after a haircut.'

Jacob appeared about to laugh.

Juliet explained: 'Our friend, the singer − her mother used to cut her hair when she was a child and she had a thing against neatness. You should see the photos. The poor girl looked like a juvenile psychiatric patient.'

'She was one, wasn't she, after she walked on water?' pondered Carlo.

Jacob turned away, not listening.

The DJ began to play some bebop. Carlo stood and hauled Juliet up after him. She shook her head and turned back to Jacob, who was tapping his foot and clicking his fingers in a limp, exaggeratedly offbeat manner. What could she say to him? She followed Carlo.

The Glory Hole had been a jazz club, a discotheque and a punk venue, and in these indecisive times was something of each. Carlo pushed his way onto the kidney-shaped dancefloor. He grabbed his sister, reeled her in and then set off in a tight circle. Used to this, Juliet gave in and kept her balance as best she could, determined not to let Jacob's presence embarrass her; only it did, terribly.

The lights went down and a saxophonist began to play a few notes, then paused and played a few more. He played rushing trills and deep swoops, as if sticking to the edges of whatever piece of music he might have been playing. Eventually, a pianist joined him and their instruments fell into a dialogue in which nothing accumulated or added up. This kind of music annoyed Jacob as things do when they reflect your own nature.

A woman made her way out from behind a curtain to stand between them. She was small and pale, and wore a long black dress that fell from her white collarbone to her white ankles. On her feet were a pair of apricot satin high-heeled sandals, which looked too big. Her mouth was red and her wide weak eyes were outlined in black. Her dark hair was pinned back in a knot. She started to sing: *The cold begins to tell, outside a long long while* . . . and the piano and saxophone fell into place behind her.

Jacob was more interested in the band once the girl had joined them, even though she pushed the words out of shape as much as the musicians did the tune. She looked frail and disturbing, and her voice was so clear that her singing seemed to move meaning out of the way, leaving the air full of unanchored feeling. What song was it anyway? People stopped trying to work it out. They liked her voice; the details didn't matter.

The band finished, the audience began to clap, and the woman stepped forward and froze. She raised a hand as if about to reach out, only her palm flattened and her gesture became a sign, 'Stop'. Then she was gone. There were one or two whoops and whistles, and a call for an encore, but the applause quickly faded. At this moment,

Carlo and Juliet got to their feet and began to chant 'Mary George! Mary George!' and the rest of the crowd, encouraged or amused, joined in: 'Mary George! Mary George!'

A taxi pulled up in the sidestreet next to the Shipping Office and a woman in a fluffy blue coat and noisy heels got out. She marched round to the back of the gallery and banged on Jacob's door. She rattled the handle and gave the door a kick, but Jacob was not there. He was at The Glory Hole, standing behind Juliet, his mouth inches from the back of her neck and his finger tracing, without touching, the shape of her large flat ears and the pattern on her nape where her cropped hair revealed its curl.

Barbara Dart had gone to the Shipping Office in the middle of the night to take Jacob his post. Every envelope had been opened and some had been scribbled on. Barbara had no doubt about her right and need, a practical one, to know what was going on.

As she expected, the padlock on his door was not quite in place. When she first met him, he had carried a knapsack full of books, cigarettes, fruit and beer, overloaded and loosely buckled, and whatever escaped had been left where it fell. She laid the post on his bed and began to flick through his papers: half an essay on Bob Dylan and the flâneur, the beginnings of a letter to his mother, an old-fashioned porn magazine, a list of what looked like payments and debts, a gift catalogue and other circulars to which Jacob paid so little attention that he did not even throw them out. Barbara opened every cupboard, box and drawer in Jacob's room, not looking for anything in particular and finding nothing she wanted.

The night Barbara realised that Jacob was not coming back, at least not for now, she had poured the contents of his study into binbags and left them here on his

41

doorstep. Now they were just inside the room, squashed and split and leaking a mixture of intimacies with which she was rawly familiar. Jacob asserted his independence by leaving his secrets around, and Barbara had spent years coming across things beginning with the notes from other girls while they had been living together at university – heated, high-minded exchanges he insisted were necessary and harmless. Even back then, in his twenties, he had kept copies of everything he wrote to other people and here they were. There were letters to people he wanted to sleep with or wanted to be, so finely tuned that you might think him calculating and manipulative. To Barbara he was none of these things, just frightened, driven and beyond himself. 'You understand me,' he liked to say and she liked to believe she did.

Juliet and Carlo, with Jacob close behind, emerged from The Glory Hole into the heightened air of a cold still night. They shivered and toughened, and Juliet wondered that she could feel so distinct. Carlo whispered something to her and said goodnight. Jacob offered to put her on a bus.

Juliet savoured these after-hour streets with their residue of drama and secrets; it was like being on stage just after a play had ended. She walked carefully beside Jacob, who led her left and right and into dead ends which turned out to be alleyways connecting places Juliet recognised but had not known to be within reach of one another.

A heavy, anonymous door swung open and a giant in evening dress hauled in a cordon of purple rope knotted onto silver plastic bollards. Further, a dug-up pavement herded them into a cratered hallway next to a board on which two hands held out a pair of perfectly circular breasts. They negotiated the pungent, leaking binbags outside a restaurant and the heap of empty crates propped against the shuttered windows of a delicatessen. Jacob noted the charm of the boarded-up front of a fishmonger's, which Juliet thought sad. He complained about the hard-lit, alarmed and bolted entrances of photographic agencies and film companies, and said nothing about the side-doors lined with cards and intercoms. A café, little more than a counter, served coffee to a couple wearing city suits who could not stop kissing. A pair of teenagers in pumped-up jackets and low jeans swaggered past looking flushed and lost, and Juliet watched them go with the feeling that they were carrying on something she had left off. She did not listen to their music or take their drugs, and was about to remark on this to Jacob when she realised that she could probably say the same about him, too.

A tall, finely painted woman brushed against Jacob (deliberately! Juliet could tell) and dropped an elbow-length glove, which he leapt to retrieve. The woman said an elaborate thank-you in a crooning baritone and sailed on as if it were a hundred years ago, a time when ladies wore gloves and their dropping one meant something. Three men, arms linked, walked past with luxurious slow-ness, their skin wet and their breath feathering the air. A police car idled by.

Juliet and Jacob continued on, past the all-night cinema where Carlo was fighting sleep in the back row, strug-gling to follow the plot of a subtitled Russian film in which a telephone kept ringing. He was there because he had a crush on the projectionist, who was also a masseur, and whose card was on the noticeboard in the cinema foyer. Jonathan Mehta. Carlo tried to concentrate on the film. No one picked up the telephone.

A woman came in and pushed past him without saying 'Excuse me'. Her bag knocked against his knees, but she didn't apologise. She sat down beside him and stuck out her elbows, letting her fluffy coat spill against his arm. When her body started shaking, he turned to join in her laughter only to see that she was crying. Although she swung her head so that her slithery blonde hair covered her eyes, Carlo had seen her face, its feathering surface and the dark runnels under her eyes, and he apologised, 'Sorry', and standing up said 'Excuse me', as he left.

Jacob, who had had something to say about every other building they passed, stopped talking, giving Juliet the chance to wonder: 'So what is it you do . . . in your room?'

'I write.'

'What?'

'I write.'

'No, I meant *what* do you write?'

'You are endearingly emphatic. I write on art and architecture, and about the cultural life of the city.'

'Should I have heard of you?'

'Yes.'

Juliet snorted. 'Well I have, sort of. That is I've got *Foucault's Egg*, but I haven't read it. I forgot it was by you.'

'You didn't know me.'

'Actually, I didn't read it because I thought I *did* know you, at least your type.'

'And what is my type?'

'You use words like "quiddity" and "ineffable" more than you ought. Your prose is awash with parentheses and you usually throw in some casual Latin and slangy French, oh and an anecdote about Goethe's socks which makes it sound as if you washed them yourself when you haven't even actually read him . . .'

She stopped and looked at his face. He was staring at

the ground with a tight smile that she took to signal amusement, especially when he said, with such dryness, 'Do go on.'

'You use cricketing terms, and refer to your "wireless". At parties, you look ostentatiously blank if anyone refers to a television personality, but you sometimes throw in a reference to something terrifically in-touch like hip-hop or acid house.'

'But who am I?' His smiling face revealed nothing.

'I only said I know your type,' Juliet continued unabashed, 'not *you*.'

'And do you have a type?' he asked, still showing no sign of annoyance.

'Inevitably. Do you know it?'

'I think so.'

'Can you sum it up? Like I did?'

'Is that what that was? The summary of a type? Well, well.'

Juliet stumbled, feeling that the path beneath her feet was nothing more than ice and that at any moment she would plunge through and drown in her own embarrassment. 'I'm sorry, I didn't mean, it's just that there's so much of all that.'

'All what?'

'So much *charm*, and it works. I read that kind of stuff and I *am* charmed but I'm not satisfied. I don't feel I've been given anything to grapple with, to grasp. It's so mobile and non-committal. It wants to come across as modest when it's not even shy, just unwilling.'

'Unwilling?'

'Unwilling to really truly absolutely say something.'

'Really truly absolutely?'

'I know I sound like a five-year-old; anyone who speaks with any emphasis these days does.'

'I admire your energy,' said Jacob, taking her arm.

'You think I'm a child.'

He didn't deny it.

They walked on in silence, which made her nervous so she tried again. 'I'm sure your book's not particularly dull but the title does put me off. Yet another so-and-so's something-or-other.'

'It refers to the pendulum.'

'What have pendulums got to do with eggs?'

'Foucault's pendulum stays in the arc of its swing while the world moves round it.'

'I know that.'

'I'm sure you do. However, if other forces exert pressure, they disturb the pendulum's swing and instead of tracing an arc, its path becomes elliptical, ovoid, like an egg.'

'I understand the concept, but what does it mean?'

'It doesn't mean anything. It's a record of process, a map of accumulating disturbance.'

'And what's it got to do with the city?'

'How we move and think and meet – everything, really.'

He gave something of a laugh and letting go of Juliet, turned into Green Park where the sky was the green-black-blue of medieval pigment, so rich and strange that some of those who looked up at it wished that everything else, including the stars and even themselves, would disappear.

Jacob was enjoying the silence between them, but Juliet was caught up. 'Do people buy that? God, I bet they do. We love patterns, even anti-patterns, as long as they're graceful.'

'What's an anti-pattern?'

'Fuck knows, I just made it up. And what is your egg? No, don't answer that. I bet I could carry on asking you questions all night and you would always have an answer, and every answer would take us further away.'

'From what?'

'The point. And if you say "Does there have to be one?", I just might puke.'

Jacob looked a little shocked. 'So no more questions?'

'No.'

'Tania told me you've almost finished your thesis.'

'She talked to you about me?'

'No more questions – although I would like to know more if you want to tell me.'

He took her arm again and they walked on to the end of the park while Juliet explained her theory of the empty metaphor and the frame. By the time they had reached Hyde Park Corner, she was exhilarated because no one had ever been so interested or had understood it so well.

He had surprised her and now she surprised herself by saying, 'You're quite patient, really.'

'Yes, I am.'

They were walking unnaturally slowly and for a long moment, nothing was said.

'I'm going away,' Juliet announced in the tone of someone remarking that they had lost a glove. 'In six months time, to America.' Jacob did not react. She went on: 'A visiting professor at the Institute, Merle Dix . . .' Did he recognise the name? She wasn't sure. 'She's going back to Littlefield and has offered me a research post.' Still nothing. 'At the end of August, for a year.'

A bus pulled up as they reached the stop. Juliet stepped forward, then turned back to face Jacob and found herself turning in his arms. To stop herself meeting his kiss, she said the first thing that came to mind: 'My father was a medical student in London in the Fifties and he used to talk of a walk that took in every bridge.'

He lifted his hands, spread his fingers and pressed them to either side of her face. 'Have you done it?'

'No.'

'How long have you lived here?'

'Ten years, nearly.'

'Let's do it then.'

He tipped her head to one side. She felt his teeth electrically sharp on her earlobe, and then her head was tilted forward and his whole open mouth was on the back of her neck.

She stepped back, meaning to say 'You're married', but what she said was 'I'm going away'.

A bell rang, an engine revved and the conductor gave a torn-off shout. Then Juliet was leaning her head against a window watching her jittery reflection, and Jacob had gone.

On the steps of a City banqueting hall, Fred held Jane's hand. Her head lolled on his shoulder as she hiccupped and gurgled. He tried not to look down at her breasts which were shying away from the bodice of her strapless dress. He drew her fun-fur coat more tightly together at her neck. She flinched and Fred trembled.

'Grem,' Jane mumbled. Then more urgently, 'Grem? Grem!'

'Graham's gone to find a cab. Caroline's helping him.'

'Going home are now? Um, we?' She was shivering, so Fred took off his rented dinner jacket and put it round her shoulders, giving her dress a restorative tug as he did so.

From the hall above them came a continuous baying, as if everyone in the room had worn out their voice and could now only make noise. Five hundred young financiers were trying to live up to the stories they had heard.

Their bosses sat at the top table – men in their thirties and forties, veterans of the economy's most volatile years. They were bored with the games and pranks but clever enough to encourage the belief that if money was a tool, it was also a toy.

A group were competing over the most amusing thing to do with the chocolate mousse. A man wiped it across the bottom of a passing waiter, raising a cry of 'Shit-arsed dago!' but the one who provoked the greatest cheer pulled a fifty-pound note from his wallet and used it as a spoon. This caught on as if no one had done it before, and those who had only tens or twenties used several at once. A window opened and a hand threw a spike-heeled sandal into the night. Fred retrieved it and noticed the price label on the sole, £449. He passed it to Jane, 'Look at this.'

'Gord!' she blurted, 'Y fnd m shoe!'

He looked down. 'You're wearing your shoes.'

'Wanted *these* shoe. Thuz a waitin list.'

To Fred, the one in her hand looked identical to the pair on her feet.

'This is somebody else's, and anyway there's only one.'

Jane clutched the shoe to her. 'Sbetter thn nn.'

'Someone will be looking for it.'

Jane held the shoe more tightly.

Feet were pounding the floor and a chant had gone up: 'Off! Off! Off!' but at that moment someone at the top table gave a sign and the lights flicked on, and all the young men in the room straightened themselves out as best they could and began trying to help the nearest woman out of her seat. They trailed out with elaborate courtesy, shaking hands, helping each other into coats, holding open doors and volunteering (like Graham and Caroline) to find cabs. Some would go home and wonder at themselves but being young and excitable and rich, as well as so very tired, none would let this bewilderment harden into anguish. They would sleep and if they couldn't, they had no qualms about pursuing sleep through whatever means they chose.

'Cold a long long while,' Juliet was singing to herself on the almost empty bus as Mary George got out of the saxophone-player's mini-van and climbed five flights of stairs in Block A, North Square of the Hugh Carmodie Trust Estate in Walham Green. Mary had moved there five years ago and was used to its treeless concrete squares. She knew by name the twelve-year-olds who rose out of dark corners to sell bags of powder. She knew the wandering encrusted toddlers, the coddled pitbull terriers, the girls who smoked and shrieked beneath her window, and the boys who careered past in stolen cars refining their handbrake turns. She was on first-name terms with the women who kept their flats spotless and swore at their children, who were brought up in the old-fashioned way. They were free to play outside all day, given duties from an early age and retained respect for their parents. Many of them had aunts, uncles and grandparents living nearby.

Mary let herself into the dark hall, stubbed her toe on a piece of motorbike engine and then bumped into a clothes-horse draped with washing and positioned just inside the living-room door. In the bedroom, she took off her clothes and put on a t-shirt that Tobias had left on top of the laundry bin. She lay down and reached out, her hand meeting first his cropped hair, then the coarse stubble on his cheek and then, beside him, the heat and force of their two-year-old daughter, Bella George Clough.

Mary propped herself up and put her lips against Bella's

head to kiss her, catching the odd smell of biscuit and vinegar that collected in the child's clammy hair. Bella began to wake, her mouth opening and closing with a sticky smack. Her free arm waved and her legs kicked out as if the world had all at once let go of her. Her fists clenched and her first sleepy agitations hardened into a wail, and Mary wondered as she often did if Bella sometimes forgot having been born and was furious to find herself here.

Tobias began to sit up. Mary lifted Bella onto her chest and pushed him back down. He smiled, mumbling Hello, Good night and How did it go, trying to find her to kiss her. Mary kept her hand on his shoulder, saying 'Goodnight, fine, sleep now,' as he subsided back under the quilt. He was working as a despatch rider and had to set off at seven-thirty. Mary settled herself back against the pillows, feeling the child's fist knock against her ribs as she sang to her:

Somewhere over dawn's early light,
it begins, the holding hands,
haunting me to tell,
a long long while outside.

Soon Bella was sleeping again and Mary continued to sit, one hand caught in Tobias's sleeve and the other pressed against the solid back of her daughter. She started to drift off but even this sketchy darkness brought the rushing feeling back, and as her eyes closed her hand shot up and she shouted 'Stop!'

Tobias turned towards her.

'Sorry, did I wake you?' Mary asked, putting her hand on his shoulder. Stop.

He opened his eyes. 'Is something wrong?'

'I don't know why I said it, I'm sorry.'

'Said what?'

'Stop. I shouted "Stop".'

'It was just a dream. You didn't shout anything. I would've heard you.'

Even if the post had not been lying on his camp bed, Jacob would have known that it was Barbara who had broken in. He would say nothing to her. The spilled papers and books were worthless to him now. He would leave them where she had dropped them until the day he gave up the room, and began now by walking over them to collect a notepad, a bottle of whiskey and a packet of Egyptian cigarettes. He wrapped the Mexican blanket from his bed around his shoulders and sat on the step where he smoked and drank, the calm this brought balanced by the stimulus of the cold air. He made notes in writing he would not be able to read, looking up now and then to watch the light enlarging above the river.

Jacob had the air of someone halfway through a door. People thought of him as averted and non-committal and, being Jacob, he enjoyed such misunderstandings. He wondered at the evening, and admired his own insistence. This girl who looked like a boy was still young enough for her gaucheness to be endearing. She had begun to know things about which he knew more. She was more susceptible than she realised and she was in pain, he could see that. She was going away. Jacob knew exactly why Juliet interested him and this did nothing to alter his belief that he was in love.

Juliet sat up in bed. 'Endearingly emphatic! Endearing! Christ. And emphatic. Emphatic! Fuck, fuck. Endearingly emphatic! Fuck . . .'

FIVE

Once Juliet decided that she ought to see a doctor, she began to organise her illness. She made a list. How long had she been having pain? She could not remember when it began, nor could she imagine being free of it, and because it had once been tolerable, she had assumed it still was. It had not occurred to her to worry about the fact that she had to sit down and lift her feet into the air to put on her shoes, or that sometimes she could not breathe well or find words. These things were simply there to be negotiated.

The doctor was a shockingly handsome man of about her age and she was so determined not to be embarrassed, she was a doctor's daughter after all, that when he asked her to undress, she stood up immediately and pulled off her skirt. 'No!' cried the doctor. 'I'll just fetch a . . . someone . . . Please! Go behind the screen and remove your clothes, just your lower half, and lie down. And cover yourself, please, with the blanket.'

He returned with a nurse, who stood by Juliet's head while the handsome young man asked her to raise her knees and then touched her thigh, meaning to move her leg to one side, only he did so too slowly, too gently, and

Juliet blushed and turned her face towards the wall. She felt a chill blob of lubricating jelly and then the doctor started to issue warnings – that this might feel cold or sharp or uncomfortable – and Juliet felt pressure as the speculum was inserted and then opened with that scraping noise that was only the turn of a screw, but which nonetheless frightened her more than the pain caused by his fingers probing parts of her that felt too deep to belong. She had tears running down her face but the only sounds she made were when the doctor asked if this hurt, or this, or this. He was picking over the pieces of glass and stone she had come to imagine were inside her, and he knew exactly where to find them.

Eventually, the doctor peeled off his gloves, washed his hands, went back to his desk and began to type with unexpected efficiency as the nurse handed Juliet some tissue, with which she wiped her eyes. The nurse handed her some more. The doctor typed for a long time.

He asked more questions and Juliet told him in explicit detail about the colour and texture and quantity of the blood, and also about the pain: 'Sometimes it makes me throw up; other times I shit brown water.'

He rubbed his hands together, realised what he was doing and stopped. 'I'm going to refer you.'

'What will they do?'

'Probably a scan and then, if need be, they'll take you in and have a look round.'

'Look round for what?'

'Anything a scan might not pick up. They'll probably go in through the belly button so you won't have to worry about a scar.'

'When will this be done?'

'The current waiting time is five to six months.'

'But I'm going away.'

'You're, what, twenty-eight? You've got plenty of time.

Reschedule if you have to. Meanwhile, I'll give you something for the pain.' He had stroked this woman's thigh. He wanted her out of his surgery as quickly as possible.

When Juliet arrived at the gallery that afternoon, there was a note from Tania asking her to pick up some contracts from an insurance company whose offices were near Chancery Lane, in that uncertain area where banks and newspapers hovered close to what had for centuries been their home. There were many parts of London that Juliet did not know and this was one of them. She had found her routes, her places and her perspectives, and it was not in her nature to wander. She hated getting lost and was cross to find that she had, emerging from the Tube station confused by a choice of exits. Still phased by the handsome doctor's touch and the residual pain from his examination, she followed other pedestrians as they made their way between traffic cones and scaffolding, realised she was heading in the wrong direction, turned a corner and found herself at the back of Smithfields meat market, which had already closed for the day. The tall doors looked as if they hadn't been opened for years but splashes and clots, theatrically scarlet, persisted in the sluiced gutters and among the cobbles. She could not see a way past the market, nor was it going to let her in, so she turned back to the station.

As Juliet approached the company's offices at last, she was thrown to the ground. She had heard a profound boom and a large hand, an enormous hand, had pushed her. She lifted her head and looked back. There was no one, nothing behind her, but she had felt the force of something heavy and close, as if a building had collapsed at her shoulder or a skip full of earth had been dropped at her heels. She pulled herself up onto her feet with the sensation of having to peel an electrified swarm of something off the ground and pull it into shape. It was as if this sound, which travelled so unnaturally through her body, had separated every cell.

Around her, the noise of the city was changing. The dragging tension of grid-locked traffic broke up as drivers pounded their horns, wrenched steering wheels and scraped their tyres in a bid to inch their way out. There were footsteps, someone running, cries and shouts, sirens, odd silences. A man she couldn't see almost singing it: 'A bomb! A bomb!'

In ten years, Juliet had absorbed the insecurity of the city. She did not avoid declared targets or the scenes of past explosions but was after all not much interested in Christmas shopping in the West End or royal tournaments or Lord Mayor's shows; nor did she spend time in embassies, barracks and department stores, but she never passed them without being aware. She took note of emergency exits when in crowded or official places, and she acknowledged the briefcase left on the Tube or the van parked outside a bank. She listened.

With some effort, Juliet began to walk. She was trying to get home but while she thought she was heading west, she was making her way south towards the river, confused by the sirens that bounced off tall buildings and made it seem as if a fire engine or ambulance were hurtling towards her round every corner. She had not been close by and had seen nothing but could not seem to get away from it either. Later, she would see in a newspaper the office block with its blown-out windows holding their broken blinds like handkerchiefs. A bomb. She did not recognise anything.

Jacob had not been going to open the door but was made curious by the silence of whoever it was and the way they kept rattling the handle. He had been listening to the radio and had heard the news. Juliet looked alright, just a bit stiff. Then she held up her scraped hands. He led her to an armchair and noticed, as she sat down, that her knees were bleeding. He wrapped her in a blanket, fetched a cup of warm water and pulled off his t-shirt, which he used as a cloth as, tenderly and minutely, he cleaned her cuts. He gave her whiskey by the teaspoon, and then sweet tea. They each recognised the rituals of shock and enjoyed them. He laid her down on the army cot and when she turned away, placed a hand on the small of her back and said, 'Breathe'. The pain disappeared instantly. Jacob sat beside her all night, one hand pressing her head to the pillow.

Juliet woke at six, whimpering and saying that she wanted to go home. She was worried about Fred. Jacob soothed her and called a cab. He held her hand all the way to Khyber Road and when they arrived, helped her out and knocked on the door.

It was thrown open by a tall woman with a wicked face and splendid red curly hair. She nodded at Jacob, hugged Juliet and propelled her through to the kitchen where Carlo and Fred were waiting.

Fred threw himself on Juliet and burst into tears. 'I thought you too!'

Juliet was embarrassed. 'What is this? I'm sorry if I had you all worried. I couldn't get back. This is Jacob.' He was standing beside her. 'You've met Carlo, this is Fred and my sister, Clara.'

The woman nodded again but did not speak. No one spoke. Juliet was bewildered. 'Christ, Fred, I should have rung. I was close to it, I fell down and then I walked. I fell asleep.' His greater distress made her feel strong and, her voice restored, she said firmly, 'We're safe. We're all safe now.'

Fred raised his head. She watched his mouth. He was saying 'Tobias'.

'Tobias? The bomb?' Something deep in the earth reached up and pulled all her substance downwards.

Fred gave a peculiar laugh, as if this were a novel idea, a connection he would never have made himself, and shook his head.

Juliet fell into a chair. 'Thank god for that. I think I'm going to be sick.'

Clara knelt by Juliet, holding her bruised hands too tightly. 'After the bomb, there was another alert. Tobias was on his motorbike, going through the Hyde Park underpass just as they cordoned off the road ahead. The traffic in the tunnel backed up. He came round the corner into the back of a car. Too fast.'

'We don't know that!' shouted Fred.

Juliet drew herself in. Carlo put his arms round Fred. Jacob stood in the doorway, watching.

Eventually Clara got up. 'I'll make some tea. Would you like a cup, um, Jacob?' she asked and Jacob shrugged, a gesture that in such absolute circumstances enraged Fred.

'Who the fuck are you?' he snarled, like something small and cornered.

'Leave him alone,' said Carlo half-heartedly.

Clara was standing at the sink under the window with her back to them and her extraordinary hair with its several reds seemed to float in the light. When she turned, Jacob found her face no longer witchlike. It was stunningly ugly.

Jacob crossed the room and began to take cups down from a shelf and pass them to Clara as if he had been doing such things for years.

'Make yourself at home,' said Fred.

'Oh for god's sake,' snapped Juliet.

'Well what's he doing here anyway? No one should be here now except us.'

'He looked after me,' admitted Juliet. 'All night.'

'While we thought you were dead. You should have come home. I would have looked after you.'

'I couldn't get home.'

Everyone in the room, except Jacob, was crying while they tried to be doing something else, even if it was just looking at the floor.

Fred saw Jacob glance at his watch. 'Don't let us bore you,' he sneered and then, formally, making a point of the presence of this stranger, 'Where are our mother and father?'

'They're with Mary,' said Carlo, taking hold of his brother again.

'They should be here with us.'

'Alright Fred,' said Clara. Jacob could see she was holding herself extremely carefully. 'For today you can say whatever you like. And I'm warning you, the rest of us can say whatever we like too.'

Fred looked at Jacob. 'I bet he says whatever he likes all the time,' which made Jacob smile and seeing this, Clara smiled too and murmured an apology as Carlo grabbed Fred and took him out through the kitchen door into the yard. Jacob kissed the top of Juliet's head and stroked her cheek as he nodded to Clara, and left.

Although this was not the hospital where he worked, Carlo knew where to go. He found the back stairs down to the basement corridor, at the end of which lay the unmarked doors. He had pulled on a white coat over his clothes, as if it might help.

He was coming through the doors when the woman who ran the mortuary found him. She smiled and, nodding towards the row of fridges, said, 'Lost someone?'

'Yes,' said Carlo, 'I have.'

She looked kind and amused. 'You'll get used to it. Anyway, you should be too busy to care.'

'I'm sorry?'

She looked at him more carefully. 'There's always one who won't let go. Regardless of how many more you lose, and there'll be plenty, believe me.'

'Yes.' Carlo stared at the ground.

'So have you got something to say to them?'

'Who?'

'Your patient. I can let you have a quick look, if you don't make a habit of following them down here.'

Carlo shook his head and the woman said, 'In that case, you ought to get back to work,' but Carlo went on shaking his head until the words rolled into place: 'I have come to identify my brother.'

When he looked up, a different woman was standing in front of him. Someone had ironed her face and her hands were no longer in her pockets but clasped in front of her chest. She said something about being so sorry and if only and what was she thinking of, but Carlo wasn't listening.

She led him into a hushed and painted world where she stopped outside a door and Carlo knew that she was about to ask whether he wanted to go into the room or look through the window.

He pre-empted her: 'Please, leave me to it.'

She jumped back and Carlo realised how sensitised people become around the relatives of the newly dead. Of course. Anything. Absolutely.

Carlo had been shown the Chapel of Rest in his hospital, with its abstract stained glass, modest arrangements of plastic flowers and pastel cubes of tissues. He knew its protocols, but had spent little time on that side of the fridges. He had not yet met a relative. Now he was a relative and had to go through this door.

It could have been any room, any kind of waiting room, without a body in it. A waxed blind hung in strips across the frosted window, and the chairs, floor and walls were of colours so neutralised that it would have been beyond Carlo to describe them. The room admitted just a trace of noise and daylight, and was decorated with collages representing three of the four seasons and a copper sculpture which, at the flick of a switch, became a waterfall.

There was the body, like a subject waiting to be restored to a picture. Carlo looked, looked round, looked back, looked away and the collages and waterfall were there for him to rest his eyes on. All he could think of were the stories – of the people who fainted, threw up, wet themselves; of those who howled and those who were furious; of the fights that broke out. Some stayed for five minutes, others for hours and if certain rites were to be observed, they could be there for days. People prayed, sang, whispered and raved but most were quiet and still, and some were dreadfully embarrassed.

The nurses would have wiped some of the blood from Tobias's body, but they would not have been allowed to wash him properly. A death like this had to be treated carefully, the details preserved until they had been recorded. Carlo pulled the bedclothes back. Why did it surprise him that Tobias was naked? When had he last seen him naked? His body must have been stripped in A&E, which meant that he would have been alive when they brought him in. How alive? Had he heard and felt things still?

Carlo laid a hand on his brother's arm and wondered what he was touching. (On their introductory tour, another student had grabbed his hand and plunged it into a body bag. 'See? Just like cold chicken.') Tobias's head had been aligned and propped up, but Carlo knew that his neck was broken. He made himself take note.

Evidence of extensive lacerations around the eyes. Had he seen what was coming? The air splintering and rushing towards him and then himself rushing, to collide with the abruptly unmoving world. Had he screamed? Carlo noted his brother's snapped wrists, crushed pelvis, smashed legs and unrecognisable foot. He knew that despite all this damage, it was what had happened inside that had killed him.

The next day, Tobias's post-mortem would be performed. The fridge would be opened from the other side, and his body would be unzipped from its bag and laid upon a porcelain table. There would be a cradle for his head and a block would be placed in the small of his back to arch his spine. Beside the table would be a steel tray containing scalpels, knives, pincers and an electrical circular saw.

Let whoever is going to do this be loving, Carlo prayed as he sat beside his brother, holding his broken hand. This body was loved. Love this body.

Will you make the first cut behind the right or the left ear? Think about it, and don't think about anything other than what you are doing as you draw the blade down one side of the throat and then the other. And if you're not alone, don't make conversation; don't speak as you open this body down to the groin.

Part my brother's flesh with tenderness and crack each rib in a swift and certain style. When you lift out his bowels, wash them softly, and as you reach for the heart, the liver, kidneys and lungs, think how precious this man was, how full. As you examine and weigh each organ, I hope you see that these are unlike any other you may have beheld. As you note each compaction, inflammation, haemorrhage and perforation, contemplate my brother's pain but also acknowledge that these were once the good strong parts of someone.

When you arc your blade over the head, loosing the scalp, you might want to kiss my brother's lips as his face folds itself away. Do not do this. Your touch must not disturb.

Is it your habit to tap the skull with a knife? If it is fractured it will sound dull, like a cracked plate but don't think of a cracked plate, or an egg, or of anything other than this as yet human head, and as you saw into the skull, do so with confidence and artistry, remembering to tilt the curve down towards each ear so that when the crown is returned, it fits neatly.

Lift up my brother's brain as if you were about to lift the whole of him to safety, adjusting your stance to the weight, which will always surprise. Take your time in locating the dark pools among all the pale containment and make sure that you know what each of them means.

And when you have finished, put a finger on my brother's throat, here, as I am now, to know for certain that he is dead.

Tobias died because the traffic stopped because there might have been another bomb. Perhaps also because, and Carlo wasn't ready to consider this, he had been driving too fast. This was likely. He crossed the city all day according to his map of shortcuts and rat runs, skimming pavements and jostling his way between lanes of traffic. Had he been happy? Tobias had trained for six of the seven years it took to qualify as an architect. He had been supposed to build things, not fetch and carry, but he got stuck looking after Mary and the child. Carlo did not like to think of Tobias as losing momentum so much as being taken up by love.

The dead struck Carlo not as absent but as removed.

Now he would begin to understand what they did to what they were removed from.

In the days that followed, the Clough family dispersed and waited. Fred and Juliet spent as much time as they could at work, where Fred was surrounded by noise and Juliet by silence. Carlo made arrangements, and Clara went back to her husband and children in the country. Five miles away, in a large and empty house, her parents tried to help one another move through the days but each found that their pain became trapped in the other's. At night, they lay and waited for morning. On the fourth night, Francesca Clough rose and left her husband's bed for ever.

Juliet's friends tried to surround her, but she felt that just as their circle formed, she slipped outside it. Her feelings were of such a size that everyone she spoke to or passed in the street had to stay where they were, miles away. Tania tried a few times to send her home, and then settled for bringing her cups of tea and slices of cake. Juliet stared at the wall.

Hour by hour, the truth of her brother's death accumulated. She did not think about that other pain, or kissing a married man, or going to America; and then she did and forgot about Tobias with such entirety that when she remembered she had to begin again at the first shock.

She didn't know that she had moved or made any sound until the door opened and Jacob was there, holding her and saying 'You can stop now,' and she did stop and asked, 'Stop what?' and he said, 'Banging on the wall. You were banging so hard, I thought you'd bring what's left of it down.'

*　　*　　*

Just outside the village of Allnorthover, Carlo turned into a gravel drive and pulled up outside a large, shabby grey-stone house. Jacob looked out of the window and then at Juliet who asked, 'What is it, what are you thinking?', which made Carlo frown. He did not like the fact that Jacob had come with Juliet, nor that she would not let go of his hand.

An hour of inching their way north through the city and an hour of signs and fields, more like fields of signs thought Jacob, a chain of mini-roundabouts, and a brief wind through a wood. Primroses, ice and mud.

Jacob answered Juliet's question: 'It's barely outside London. Hardly the country at all.'

'And here it is,' said Carlo as he watched Jacob helping Juliet out of the car, 'Hardly a home at all', and Jacob laughed so warmly that Carlo felt pleased, which then made him cross.

Fred, who had chosen to come up by train, was in the kitchen perched on a particularly ugly chair that Jacob noticed was held together by string.

Francesca Clough turned from a sink piled high with dirty dishes and held out a soapy red hand to Jacob, who pursued her attention in her eyes, as dark and unreadable as Juliet's, and sunk in brown hollows within planetary yellow rings. Her strong skin was still smooth but had lost its light and was shadowed by the mass of wiry hair, black spliced with grey and white. The bones of Francesca's face were rising up as the flesh receded.

'What did you think of Ma?' Juliet asked later.
'That she looks like a ghost of you.'
'And Clara? Did you like Clara?'

*   *   *

65

Clara, he had thought full of light. She strode into the kitchen with a baby on her arm, buttoning the front of her dress. Her twins, who looked four or five, followed her as closely as courtiers as she plonked the baby on Juliet's lap and shook Jacob's hand while reaching up with her other arm to tidy her hair. His eyes flicked from her smooth copper shoulder to the damp shock of orange in her raised armpit to the tight bodice with its two patches of milky wetness. He stared frankly at her hair. That evening, as they sat smoking in the garden, Jacob asked her about her painting, which he managed to suggest he knew by reputation and not just through Juliet. Clara had scoffed at every good thing he said but did not move away, even though he was sitting powerfully close to her.

Juliet's father was known fondly in the village as Dr Kill Off. He was a dignified man with a face that naturally looked full of grief, so that the change brought about in him by his son's death was not generally noticed. At the funeral, he had spoken in a voice so cracked and agonised that it was the sound that people remembered rather than what he said.

Juliet and Fred walked into the church behind Mary, who was wearing the black dress in which she sang. Her parents had come – her mother, Stella, from Hay-on-Wye where she ran a chain of antique shops and her father, the architect Matthew George, from New York. Carlo carried Bella, who gave sudden shouts throughout the service and hit out with her fat fists at anyone who leant over and suggested that they take the child outside. Mary shook her head as she stared at the coffin. She could not believe that Tobias, with all his strength and capacity, could fit inside it.

She was whispering something.

'What was that?' Carlo murmured, but she didn't reply. It had sounded like 'Stop'.

After the funeral, the entire village, it seemed to Jacob, came back to the house for tea. He stayed by the French windows which gave onto the garden, smiling at whoever passed. An aunt approached. She had Juliet by the hand and took one of his and looked for a moment as if she were about to demand some sort of vow. Her mutterings of hope and approval panicked Juliet, who was not ready to admit that in these last few days something had begun.

In the evening, there was a dinner of odds and ends: a salad of dandelion leaves that Francesca had pulled out of the lawn, luncheon meat that looked like something freshly skinned, slices of cold fatty lamb, white sliced bread, an enormous cheese that had gone glassy with age, cake left over from the tea and a blancmange rabbit. This last was placed in front of Fred who decapitated it and auctioned off the head.

The children were in bed and so these were the children, and as such they recovered themselves and talked all at once in a condensed coded language punctuated by the same unattractive laugh. Juliet reduced it to a snort and Fred to a horse-like snicker, Clara trumpeted and Carlo rumbled. Fred made Clara a crown of dandelion leaves and flicked spoonfuls of blancmange. Mary sat next to Clara's husband Stefan and they talked to one another. Jacob tried to catch the eye of Francesca, who ate slowly while staring past his right shoulder. He also tried to talk to the doctor, who was interjecting in his children's banter but did not seem to listen and could not be heard.

Later, when the parents had disappeared, Jacob went into the kitchen to get a glass of water. The dirty pans were still on the stove but someone had moved each plate, bowl, spoon, knife and fork onto the chair of the person who had used it. The table was clear and had been wiped clean. He went to find Juliet.

'I was about to wash up, only half of it's been sort of arranged . . .'

'You mean on our chairs?'

'Yes.'

'It's Ma's rule. She tried to get us to help but we just argued, so she said the least we could do was to wash up our own things and when we forgot, she put them on our chairs.'

'And what if you still didn't clear them?'

'They would still be there in the morning.'

'But why does she still do it now?'

Juliet looked confused.

After Jacob had washed up, he found the family slumped in front of a television in a small room at the back of the house. Clara, Juliet, Carlo and Fred were squashed together on a sofa, their arms and legs trailed round and over one another. Mary sat on the floor at their feet and Stefan was asleep in an armchair. When Jacob said goodnight, only Mary replied.

How odd the Cloughs looked, drained by the television's light. Their outlines were so harsh. Fred was too delicate, epicene even, and Carlo venal. Clara in profile was a hook-nosed witch and Juliet was, well, plain. Then they all threw back their heads and laughed at something Jacob couldn't see, and he watched their shadows bobbing on the far wall – infantile, hilarious, monstrous.

SIX

One Sunday morning in April, Jacob arrived at Khyber Road.

'Why does he just turn up like this?' Fred hissed to Juliet in the kitchen. 'You must have given him the number by now.'

'What for?' retorted Juliet, who admired Jacob's lack of manners. 'Would you tidy up? Bake a cake?'

'No, I've got more important things to do and anyway, if I knew he was coming, I'd leave.' He took an ostentatious breath, 'He's not right.'

'How would you know? You've hardly spoken to him.'

'He doesn't look right.'

Jacob did look wrong: too tall for the low-ceilinged room, too clean for its murky walls, too well-made for the failing sofa. He was wearing an indigo shirt, half unbuttoned and untucked. One sleeve was rolled up over a fine-boned golden forearm.

Apollo, thought Juliet as she came back in with a bottle of wine and two glasses. Fucking Apollo. He did take up a lot of space.

*   *   *

'How's Federico?' Jacob asked, taking Juliet's hand and leading her up the stairs to her room. He stood by the open window, a concentration of blue and gold against the fading blue and gold sky.

'Still in love with that girl Caroline, who works on the same floor. She rents a room from this dreadful couple and I think she's sleeping with the man.'

'That sounds,' Jacob began, pulling Juliet down on top of him as he lay back, 'like a tedious story.'

Juliet did not like to talk about Jacob. She wouldn't have known what to say. He disappeared from the gallery and appeared at Khyber Road, and they would lie like this and he would kiss and stroke her, not where she might expect him to but on her calves, ribs, cheekbones and wrists. It was as if they were starting obliquely, with Jacob approaching her from the steepest possible angle so that she couldn't see him until he was absolutely there.

His attention turned her in on herself. She hadn't noticed how inert she had become when she was with him or that their conversation consisted of Jacob's questions and her answers. She made the assumptions about his quietness that people usually made, and thought of his interest in her as a pleasing but not particularly useful thing. She did not know what she felt, and anyway she was tired. Two months had passed since Tobias's death and Juliet was not sleeping well. Her pain had not got worse but she could bear it less, her physical pain that is, for Juliet acknowledged no other. There would be a moment when the small of her back burst into flame, and then the glass and stone in her would rise, and her voice and breath were sucked down into the fire. She took the painkillers as the doctor had instructed, and more when she needed them.

*   *   *

70

As Fred plucked each petal from the rose, he stopped himself saying 'She loves me, she loves me not.' Whether or not someone loved you was not the point of loving them. He laid the petals out and selected a dozen of the largest and roundest. Parchment, the recipe said. Parchment.

As Jacob unbuttoned Juliet's shirt, there was a knock at the door and Fred's tremulous voice called: 'Jules?'

She pulled the shirt together and stood up. 'Juliet. What is it?'

Fred asked as casually as he could: 'Have we got any parchment?'

'What?'

'Parchment.'

'Parchment?'

Jacob reached for his cigarettes.

'Why?'

'Cooking.'

'You mean greaseproof paper?'

'No, parchment.'

'Oh, for god's sake go and talk to him properly!' One of Jacob's other voices – vicious and shrill. The fire in Juliet's belly leapt through her skin and she had a sense of herself drawing back, as if violently recovering her edges. She buttoned her shirt and went downstairs with Fred, where she spent a long time looking through drawers until she found an old manila envelope which she opened and flattened, assuring Fred that it would do perfectly well as parchment.

When Juliet came back up, Jacob was standing naked by her shelves. He was confident, imperfect, and made nothing of his beauty. He flicked through one book after another. 'Who is G. Clough?' he asked, holding up an annotated edition of *Hamlet*.

'I am.'

'G.?'

'I was christened Giulietta. No one could spell or pronounce it.'

Jacob had remembered something and was reaching for another book: 'Oh yes, I found this.' He brandished the title page of a broken-backed copy of *The Catcher in the Rye*. 'Another incarnation?'

'Don't . . .'

In curlicued script, 'Juliette C.' The dot over the 'i' was a circle.

'Your French period? Left Bank?'

Juliet grabbed the book. 'Just think yourself lucky that I didn't draw smiley faces.' She pushed him towards the bed. 'Or hearts.'

He snatched the book back as she unbuttoned her shirt once more. 'And somewhere you will have written "irony" in the margin. Oh yes, page sixty-five . . .'

In the kitchen, Fred balanced a small saucepan containing a broken-up bar of dark chocolate inside a nest of chopsticks and skewers suspended over a larger pan of boiling water. Every time the teaspoon he was stirring it with got too hot to hold, he chucked it onto the floor and reached for another. Six teaspoons later, the chocolate had melted. He moved the pan onto the table and rushed off to the bathroom to fetch Juliet's tweezers.

He held up a petal with the tweezers and dipped it into the chocolate. It disappeared. He tried again and the second petal stayed in his grip but wilted to a stringy blob. It wouldn't work. He went and got his back-up rose out of the sink and shoved it in, head first, stirring it round in the chocolate as if loading a brush. This he laid on the parchment and put in the fridge without looking too closely.

*   *   *

Jacob was running a finger up and down Juliet's spine. 'Giulietta! Juliette! Juliet!' he recited, the first in theatrical Italian, the second in pouting French and the third as dully as he could. Then in an imitation of Fred's plaintiveness, 'Jules! Jules! What an ugly diminutive.' He was a poor mimic and sounded like a boy trying to amuse and impress other boys.

'You can be really quite unpleasant,' she said and meant it, but did not feel it.

She lay on her front and Jacob pressed himself down onto her back and then was inside her. The shock of pleasure was so strong that she lifted herself up to encourage him to push deeper. Jacob tilted his body to one side and as he pushed again – once, slow – he touched the centre of her pain so exactly that she cried out. She waited for Jacob to move, but he didn't. He took his weight off her but stayed where he was, a containing pressure. He laid his head next to hers, one hand on her shoulder.

When the pain passed, Juliet shifted onto one side and began to speak. No one could have listened to her more carefully than Jacob did then, his head against hers. Juliet told him about the glass and stones and fire, and then, when he showed no sign of distaste, the blood and vomit and brown water. With these details he began to stroke her breasts, belly and thighs so lightly that her body, used to retreating at the first sign of pain, had to travel back towards him in order to make sense of his touch.

'You aren't going anywhere,' he murmured and then moved her onto her front once more, and ran the tip of his tongue down her spine and on and on, flooding the pain with pleasure, nothing more than the tip of his tongue, even as she parted her legs again and raised herself again and craved him.

Juliet woke to find Jacob lying dressed beside her. His stare was so forceful that she was unable to meet it and because he stared so much of the time, she hardly saw him. When she tried to describe him to herself, she found she couldn't. What did she know about him? That he had a wife, a sister and a mother.

'How is your mother?'

'My mother is nothing to do with us.' He pulled back the sheet and ran his hand over her shoulder, waist and hip. 'You are ideally angular,' he said in a voice that thickened with desire and then lightened again. 'What you have to understand is that no one is anything to do with us.'

When Fred came downstairs he found Jacob in the kitchen, making a pot of tea.

'Good morning,' Fred conceded and was annoyed that Jacob didn't offer him some tea although he would have been just as annoyed if he had. 'Where's Juliet?'

'Sleeping, I hope.'

'You hope?'

'Her pain was particularly bad last night.'

'Her pain . . . oh, her pain. And what do you know about her pain?'

'That she needs to see a doctor.'

'She's done that. She's got pills.'

'Then she needs to see a good one.'

'And are you a good doctor?'

This was important, so Jacob made himself reply.

Fred expected not to hear what Jacob said, which is perhaps why he didn't. 'You're always whispering like that, as if the world's one big private joke!'

Jacob had no idea what to do with other men's anger. He tried to smile.

Fred continued: 'How long have you known about Juliet's pain?'

Jacob shrugged.

74

'Exactly. You barely know her and you certainly don't understand her condition. She's always been like this. She sees a doctor and she takes pills. Today she's bad and tomorrow she'll be better, especially if you leave her alone.'

'She's not herself.'

Fred smiled. 'We none of us are. How can we be? We lost our brother, remember?'

What Jacob had been about to say was as cruel as it was true, but there was something about this boy – a need not to know – that stopped him.

That day, Juliet began to cry. It started as she cycled to work. At first she thought it was because the pain in her back was so tiring, even though she had taken the pills; the pills, too, were tiring. She arrived at the gallery and wiped her eyes, sat at her desk and wept some more. The more she cried, the angrier she felt and by the end of the day, after she had struggled through several phone calls and made a number of mistakes in writing letters and organising files, she decided she had to talk to someone. Not one of her friends, because that would take the thing out into the world and she wasn't yet ready for that.

Carlo drove from the hospital to collect Juliet from the gallery, persuading her to leave her bicycle there. As soon as she saw him, Juliet started to cry once more. He took her to an old and charmless trattoria in Holborn, where everything tasted the same and of nothing so much as yellow and red. They drank fizzing wine and warm tap water, and Juliet crumbled breadsticks as she sobbed and tried to explain.

'I can't concentrate.'

'Why not?'

'I never know what's about to happen any more.'

'No one does, most of the time.'

'That's just one of your mortuary lines.'

'I don't live my life according to the dead.'

'Of course you do, we all do. Look at us now. The only thing we know for certain about the future is that Tobias will go on being dead and we'll go on rattling about, trying to take up the space he left behind him until the next one of us dies and leaves even more room.'

'Space is filled.'

'That depends on how you define it.'

'So it's Tobias?'

'No. Is that wrong? I don't think it is. I know what happened to him. It's me that's making me so cross.'

'You're cross? I thought you were sad.'

'Oh no. I'm furious.'

'Why?'

It took Juliet some effort to look up and when she did, her eyes blinked, her mouth wobbled and her forehead contorted.

Carlo had never seen her so unclear. He asked her again, 'Why are you so cross?'

'Because I feel so much and I don't know what I feel.'

'It never ceases to surprise me,' said Barbara as she kicked the car door shut, 'that you grew up in a bungalow.' She pressed her key fob and the car gave an obedient yelp.

Jacob had not spoken since they set off from London. He had refused to answer Barbara's questions about his plans, about his room and about Juliet. He walked up the mossy path kicking a little at the squat succulent plants along its edge, and waited for Barbara to ring the bell. Through the wired glass they could make out Monica inching her way towards them, propelling her walking frame through the pile of the carpet. She was repeating a long croak: 'Coming! Coming!'

Barbara set down two large shopping bags on the step. Jacob took her hand and held it tightly. They waited.

As Monica inched towards them, Barbara took charge. 'Couldn't we just go in the back? Or get a key? I know she's scared that if she can't answer her own front door, we'll put her away but –'

'You talked to my sister?' It was something Sally had reported to him, too.

'Why do you have to bring Blue Eyes!' Monica was shouting as she neared the door. 'Still got you on a lead, has she? You thought you'd given her the slip but oh no, here you are at her heel. I'm surprised she deigns to come down here at all – never used to. Hello Blue Eyes. See? I'm not dead yet.' Her voice sawed and mewed.

Barbara knelt down to the letterbox to call, 'Hullo, darling. Here we are!'

The Shipping Gallery Spring Show was to feature four young artists known as Collective Urge. They lived and worked in two flats at the top of one of the tower blocks near Juliet's house in Khyber Road. A week before the show opened, the council had declared the block unsafe due to leaking asbestos, and the collective were refusing to move, claiming that it was a ploy to empty the building so that it could be sold off for development. Tania was delighted.

Juliet came through with a phone message. 'Someone from the collective just rang.'

'Who?'

'I don't know. They don't seem to use names.'

'Of course. Well?'

'They want to add something to The Lounge.' This was a replica of the collective's living room, in which one of the group was going to sit watching a television screen showing another of the artists back at the tower block who would be simultaneously watching the one in the gallery.

'Of course. What do they want to add?'

'Asbestos.' Juliet watched Tania's face as she computed the implications of this. Juliet had come to admire her employer's shrewdness and the ways in which she conserved herself.

'This is one for the Arts Council and I'm having lunch with the new Chief Executive today. Oh –'

'I'm sorry?'

'It's just that it's Barbara, you see, Barbara Dart.'

Juliet blushed. 'I don't want to put you in a difficult position,' she began. It seemed the proper thing to say, but Tania looked amused.

Juliet felt nervous. 'I don't know what she knows, if she knows, not that it's a secret or anything, I mean after all they are separated . . . for months now . . . and it's not as if he left her for –'

Tania patted her arm. 'How would I know?'

At that moment, Barbara marched into the gallery swinging a large shopping bag Juliet recognised as being from a shop she read about in magazines. Barbara swooped on Tania, kissed her and held open the bag. 'Look what I found for Monica!' She pulled out a tartan blanket in antique shades of blue and brown.

'It's beautiful,' said Tania. 'Who's Monica?'

Juliet was unable to move. Barbara didn't acknowledge her but spoke as if on stage in front of her. 'Jakes's mother. She had a stroke but is soldiering on. Her memory's shot. She can only really cope with people she knows so we're trying to keep her at home. We go every Sunday.' A glance at Juliet.

'I see.' Tania reached out an arm to Juliet and, without

78

intending to, pushed her away. 'My assistant, Juliet Clough.'

'Yes.' Barbara busied herself putting the blanket back in the bag. 'Never mind.'

Juliet could hear Jacob in his room. There was a note poking out of the hole in the wall but she did not retrieve it. She found three reasons not to come back to the gallery that afternoon. She would collect catalogue proofs, return slides and call in on the security firm who were to install the close-circuit television cameras for The Lounge. Perhaps she would pick up some asbestos and deliver it to the Arts Council. Perhaps she would walk in and slam it down on the desk and say 'Fund that, bitch.' Then again, the Art Council subsidised her job. Bitch.

SEVEN

Mary still sang the one song, but each week differently. The band were always surprised and liked the challenge of following her lead. Some people came back again and again, and knowledgeably compared details of one version with another. She became more confident and sang less, and in these pauses stared into the crowd and felt herself rushing towards and through it. The rest of the time Tobias, his absence, was in front of everything. Stop.

'It's not as if she has to sing,' Clara said. 'She needs to get more work at that bookshop, if anything. I'm sure her nursery would be happy to have more of Bella.'

'But she's had such an awful time and Bella must be exhausting,' put in Carlo. 'You of all people ought to know what that's like.'

'So why don't you ever babysit?'

'Clara, you could always lend her your Mrs Clark,' put in Juliet.

'I'm happy to help, of course,' said Fred, 'but what if something important came up?'

'I suppose she ought to find a proper babysitter,' said Juliet. 'Just in case.'

'But they wouldn't be family,' objected Carlo. 'It's only ever been family.'

Clara said it: 'And it's always been free.'

Juliet babysat more often than the others, but preferred not to be left with Bella while she was awake. She was fond of the child but loathed the tedium of play. Fred could pretend to be a zoo full of animals, wind the musical box and sing twenty verses, the same verse, of The Grand Old Duke of York. Juliet grew terse and bored.

One night Mary was tucking up Bella. 'Don't be sad about Daddy. I can be sad for us both.'

Bella rolled over, turning her back.

'What is it?' Juliet asked as Mary returned to the living room, shaking her head.

'What I can't stand,' she said, 'is that Bella's too young to grasp what's happened but one day she will and then she'll have to go through it all again.'

'She seems to be doing very well.'

'Exactly. She's protected for now by not being able to know.'

'To be honest,' said Juliet, 'I don't know how much I've grasped it either.'

'If she'd been younger, she wouldn't remember him at all.'

'We don't know that for sure.'

'But she's almost three years old. She'll remember just enough to have an idea of him.'

'You'll remember him for her, teach her about him.'

'I've thought about that,' said Mary. 'Why make it worse?'

'Because he's her father! You have a duty . . . to his memory . . .'

Mary was surprised to see Juliet so upset. She remembered how self-possessed she had seemed at fourteen. Mary had turned up at the Clough house too early for a dinner party to which she hadn't been invited – a seventeen-year-old tripping over her mother's shoes and clutching a bottle of homemade elderberry wine. Tobias had been mending something on the lawn. She hadn't met Juliet till later. Clara had been frightening enough.

Juliet meant to say something to Mary about finding a babysitter. This time though, she didn't mind because Jacob, whom she had left in her bed at Khyber Road, was coming to keep her company.

He turned up at ten-thirty, annoyed because the Hugh Carmodie Trust Estate had little in the way of signs or lighting, and he had gone up and down two sets of stairs before finding the right place.

'Did you get some work done?' Juliet asked.

'So so. The house is bloody cold, you know. As far as Khyber Road's concerned it's forever midwinter. I found that little fan heater under your bed but even that on full blast for hours barely took the chill off.'

'That thing? It eats money.'

'Didn't Wally fix the meter?'

'Allie. He tried to but said it just kept going faster and faster, although that might have been the speed.'

'Poor old Wally.'

'You should work in your room, at the Shipping Office.'

'How can I? It's full of stuff. Tania says the lease needs renewing and am I going to stay, as if I should know that. She's always sniffing around, looking for things to report.' This was another voice – so energetically complaining that Juliet feared it might go on all night.

'To Barbara you mean? Tania said they were old friends.'

Jacob laughed. 'Not exactly. Bar used to find Tania a complete chore but now she wants to be friends and so they are friends; she does it so well that Tania will feel as beholden to her as to a lifelong chum. I've never known anyone so *assiduously* connected.' This pleased Juliet, more so when he added, 'Not like you.'

'I don't know anyone worth connecting with, do I?'

As if this were a serious matter, 'No, you don't, do you.'

'She turned up at the gallery. How was I to know? How was I to know that she's in charge of everything now?' Why did she sound as if she were apologising?

Jacob put his arm round her. 'I don't understand.'

'Arts Council. Tania. Your mother's blanket.'

'My mother's what?'

Why was it so hard to ask? 'Do you, do you, when you go to see your mother, does she?'

'Oh, that,' he laughed. 'You mean do I get a lift with Barbara? Of course I do.'

'Why?'

'You know I don't drive, not in this country, and the trains are terrible. There are never any cabs at the station. How else would I get there?'

'But why does she go?'

'God knows. She used to find any excuse not to.'

'But you're separated. Doesn't your mother know?'

'I'm sure she does.'

His fingers were in her hair; she tried to concentrate. 'You haven't told her that you and Barbara have separated?'

'She's had a stroke remember? And I do loathe the word "separated".'

'She's your mother, not Barbara's! Most people would

think it peculiar, visiting her every weekend with your ex-wife.'

'She's still my wife. And what's this "most people"? Surely you don't care about most people . . . My mother's not going to last much longer, you know, and if I didn't go with Bar, I wouldn't be able to see her.'

'I can drive. I could hire a car and take you.'

Jacob laughed. 'That's very sweet of you but . . . no need.'

At eleven-thirty, they were struggling to watch a film. Whichever way Juliet bent the wire coat-hanger that served as an aerial, she could not get rid of the angry bars that leapt across the screen. Mary's neighbours came home, rattling her front door as they slammed theirs. Juliet and Jacob listened to them discuss whether to have another drink or a cup of tea and what to watch.

'Do they have to shout?' Jacob asked, his face puckering.

'They're not. It's just the walls.'

'It sounds as if they're in here with us. Perhaps I should put the kettle on for them.'

The brass clock belonging to the elderly couple above chimed on the quarter hour. 'It's like living under Big Ben,' said Jacob, covering his ears.

'Turn it up!' the man next door demanded and the room filled with jumpy orchestral music. When Jacob went to fetch another beer from the fridge, he heard someone run a tap, cough richly and spit. He came back doing up his coat.

'Are you cold?' worried Juliet. 'I could light the gas fire.'

Jacob had grown-up in front of a gas fire. 'I hate gas fires, don't you? Student bedsits and old people's bungalows.'

A child was crying and Juliet suddenly realised, 'It's Bella!'

This amused Jacob so much that he lifted Juliet into the air and slid her slowly down again, pressed against his body.

'I'd better go and see.'

But Jacob was kissing her and his hands were everywhere – in her hair, on her breasts, up and down her spine. How could anyone have so many hands? She struggled free.

Although Bella had gone back to sleep, Juliet knelt beside her and held her head so that the child would not hear what was coming through the wall, a man screaming: 'You don't make the fucking rules! There are no rules, you stupid bitch! Get it?'

In the living room, the gas fire was on and Jacob had gone.

When Mary had been waiting for Bella to be born, she walked each day in Brompton Cemetery. Bella, who would grow to be almost as tall as her father, was already out of proportion to her mother. 'Posterior oblique', she was unable to get her head down into Mary's pelvis where it would butt against her cervix and prompt labour to begin. She pushed Mary's stomach up under her lungs, drummed her feet against Mary's ribs, pinched Mary's bladder and rounded out her long back against her mother's strained spine. From time to time, Mary's heart, forced to work hard, fell out of rhythm, lagging behind and then rushing to catch up, and Mary would panic because she thought she must be about to die, and then she would want to die rather than endure this until Tobias, stronger than everything, surrounded her.

The cemetery was the only open space nearby. It lay

between the squares of South Kensington and Stamford Bridge football ground. Stamford Bridge's east stand cast a long shadow over the graves and when Chelsea were playing at home, the roars and chants of the crowd bounced off the cemetery's opposite wall and drifted back towards the stadium confusing those who were not familiar with this acoustic and making them wonder which direction they were heading in after all.

The central avenue of the cemetery was lined with colonnades. Below these lay the vaults of Victorian entrepreneurs, the new rich who had gentrified the city west of Kensington and to whom it had not occurred that there might come a time (so soon!) when there would not be enough family members to fill these shelves.

This symmetry gave way, as it did all over the city, to a disjunctive hotch-potch of developments. Plain stones told the stories of artists, inventors and theosophists. Broken columns and angels, fortified sepulchres and the truncated epics of the Crimean and Boer wars were interspersed with Polish and Russian Orthodox crosses with their graceful cyrillics. Indestructible granite with gold-painted lettering overshadowed crumbling green stumps and the wooden crosses stuck with plastic letters that Mary took to be temporary markers until she realised that most had been there for twenty years or more.

Mary liked to pursue her worst imaginings and made her way to the corner of the cemetery where there were more cherubs than angels, and where the crosses were tiny and set close together. She imagined her child as small as this grave or that, calculated ages and considered possible causes.

A week before Bella arrived, London experienced what came to be called a hurricane. Tobias slept through it as he slept through everything. Mary listened to the bang and crash and roar, so marooned in her pregnancy and lulled by hormones, that she simply observed to herself that the world might be ending.

The next day, Mary went to the cemetery. She chose the side paths that led to the more overgrown and interesting parts, and along which men strolled, slowly and deliberately, in hope of meeting other men. Mary tried not to notice how two strangers eyed one another and chose their turnings so that their paths might cross and cross again. The atmosphere, even on this damp late autumn afternoon, was erotic and tense. Beautiful men sat on tombs and were so still that, in the dusk, they might be taken for angels. Mary walked among them feeling not unlike an angel herself – elevated and sexless and free.

Several trees in the cemetery had been blown down the night before and in falling had so disturbed the earth that lids slid from tombs and graves were ruptured. Mary peered, but not too closely.

She looked up and realised that the light had gone, just like that. The men withdrew into whispers and shadows. Mary gathered herself – I am invisible, untouchable – and set off for the gates only to bump into Carlo. She giggled and he gave a small scream.

'Mary George! Shouldn't you be at home knitting bootees instead of here counting bones?'

'I think I saw some . . .'

'God, don't. Me too.'

'Part of your studies?'

'Shall we head for the gate?' He took her arm.

'Careful,' Mary shook herself free. 'Think of your reputation.'

Carlo took her arm again, and Mary realised that he was unnerved. When they got close enough to the Fulham Road to see streetlights, they looked behind them and realised how dark the cemetery had become and hurried on to the gates, which were locked. Each month in winter, the cemetery's closing time moved an hour earlier and that day, it had changed to five o'clock. Carlo and Mary pressed themselves against the railings. The rush-hour traffic was intent on itself and the few who hurried by on foot did not pass close enough to see or hear them. Carlo stepped back and looked up. The railings were fifteen feet high and topped with gilded spikes. He looked at Mary, spherical in her winter coat, and shook his head.

'Let's walk to the other end. The gate's right on the road there so we'll be able to get help.' The more worried Carlo became, the more Mary felt in charge. It was a new feeling. Tobias would have scoffed at the open graves, and would have marched her through to the other gate. Carlo clutched her hand as she pulled him back into the dark. The central avenue had retained a little light and as their eyes adjusted, it began to seem once more like dusk rather than darkness. They passed an uprooted chestnut tree and a ruptured tomb.

'Stop,' said Mary, 'I want to see.'

'I've seen enough dead bodies, thank you.' Carlo backed away. 'When are you due exactly?'

'Last Thursday.' She was clambering over fallen branches. 'Ow!'

'Christ, what was that? Did your waters just break?'

Mary laughed. 'Don't panic. What sort of doctor are you?'

'A doctor of people who lie neatly on tables not scattered about the place rotting and then, at the slightest excuse, it was after all just a strong wind, climbing out of their graves.'

Mary returned to the path and they set off again. 'There were quite a few misbehaving people here this afternoon . . .' She said it to keep him distracted.

'Nosy cow.'

'Can't help it. All those young gods lounging about on tombs.'

'While the old gods, the ex-gods, or those of us who never made god in the first place shuffle about looking desperate . . .'

'All those tiny paths crossing –'

'– and diverging.'

'It's like a village-hall disco. You know, people sizing each other up for the slow dance.'

'Oh please! The village-hall disco where the queer gets lured out the back? That village-hall disco?'

Mary had forgotten that. She had woken up in Tobias's arms at the age of seventeen and had not raised her head or looked about her since.

It had become properly dark now and while they continued to hold hands, they could not see each other's faces.

'Carlo?'

'Yes?'

'Being at the hospital all day, all that illness, cutting up bodies, does it make you want it?'

'Yes,' he said, 'Yes. And you?'

For a moment, Mary didn't understand the question.

'I mean . . . do you want it?'

She had lived with Tobias for ten years. She was pregnant. Did she want it? Did she want it with Tobias?

'I'm so, um, absorbed . . .'

As they approached a side-gate held open by a frowning policeman, someone stepped onto the path in front of them and smiled at Carlo.

'He can absorb me any time,' Carlo murmured, taking them back into the lit world without embarrassment.

Since Tobias's death, Mary had brought Bella to the cemetery most days, hoping that she might get the idea of death, just pick it up and so not need to have it explained. She introduced her to the marble figures and pointed out carved garlands, plastic flowers in vases set in varnished gravel, and wilted posies in jam jars. Mary directed her to smell cow parsley and elderflower, and lifted her up to see the lion, eroded and benign, who lay stretched across the top of the tallest tomb in the cemetery. Bella disappeared behind it and then came running back out shouting 'Dad!'

'What is it?' Mary asked. A shadow, a rustle, a flicker.

'Lift me up! Lift me!' Bella shouted and as Mary did so, she stretched to pat the lion's nose. 'Daddy!'

Mary settled herself on the grass beneath the lion with Bella in her lap. 'Daddy!' Bella said from time to time contentedly, and, as if they were having a conversation about him, Mary would answer 'Dad?' or 'Daddy . . .' or 'Daddy!' Why not?

'Daddy?'

'Juliet?' She was the only one who had called him that, and not for years.

'Daddy?'

'What is it, darling?'

'You sound tired.'

'You phone in the middle of the night to tell me I sound tired?'

'The thing is, *I'm* tired. That's what I want to talk to you about.'

'What do you mean?'

'I get . . . very tired.' And she felt it then, too tired for words.

'That's not surprising, with your job and everything. And it'll take us all some time to get used to things.'

'Yes.'

'So don't worry. Go to sleep.'

'Daddy, I can't sleep. Not when I'm like this. The pain.'

'What pain?' His voice was gathering its professional energy.

'You know how I always had a bit of pain, every month . . .'

'Yes. Anti-inflammatories, hot baths, exercise, regular meals and *rest*.'

'It's got really bad and there are –'

'Have you seen your doctor?'

'Yes.'

'What did he suggest?'

She gave him the list of pills. '. . . And they're going to have a look inside. A scan, I think, and then something else maybe.'

'I'm sure you're fine and it sounds as if they're taking all the right steps. Be patient, darling. Once they know what's going on, they'll be able to put you right.'

'But it's not just the pain, I –'

'I know. It's the same for all of us.'

'But –'

'Be a good girl and don't mention this to your mother.'

'I –'

'Goodnight, darling.'

'Goodnight.'

EIGHT

Five miles west of the village of Allnorthover, the countryside briefly altered its expression and became beautiful. Hedgerows marshalled impressively and the pattern of the fields suggested history rather than expedience. There were single oaks, inky copses, and enough of a rise and fall for shadow to animate the landscape. In the middle of this fine view, an avenue of cedars led to a honey-coloured, intricate, magical, crumbling house. It had been bought by Stefan Brucke seven years earlier, when he had fallen in love with Clara Clough's painted skies, and had found and married her.

With the birth of her third child, Clara had begun to work more intently. The harder it was to do so, the more ambitious she became, believing that only something that insisted upon absolute concentration could wrench her beyond the guilt of not listening out for or thinking about her children. So the small-scale studies of land and sky for which she had become known, as far as she was known, had grown into what one critic had described as 'monumental abstractions of shifting light'. She worked in the old library, matching the scale of her canvases to its high ceiling, and the harshness of her palette to its northern light. The East End gallery that had offered her a joint show only had room for two works. One morning she received a letter saying that they had both been bought by the Arts Council for its own collection.

Stefan was concerned. 'It's a bit *corporate*, don't you think?'

'It's money, validation. Anyway, you're corporate.'

He worked for his family's bank and spent half of each week in Geneva.

'They'll just stick them in an office somewhere.' Stefan was removing marmalade from his daughter Mabel's hair while she tried to pick his nose. Her twin, Sidney, was cutting his toast into tiny triangles, each of which he chewed for a long time.

'If they can fit those works into an office, it's going to have to be a big one, somewhere important. It can't hurt. Anyway, the Chief Executive, Barbara Dart, has asked me to lunch.'

'In town?'

'Well, she's hardly going to trek out here, is she? And I could visit Mary, lend a hand with Bella.' She halved an apple and gave one piece to Mabel, then peeled the other half and cut it into triangles for Sidney.

'Who's Barbara Dart?'

'Comes from the City side of things, arts sponsorship.'

'Any relation to Juliet's Dart?'

'His ex, I think.'

Clara could always find a reason to go to London and now she had several: lunch with Barbara Dart, visiting Mary, and trying to sort things out between Juliet and Fred, who were having some kind of argument.

She drove down the avenue of cedars and along the green lanes. It was a hot, close afternoon in late May.

The fields were burgeoning and toxic, and the air sagged. Clara breathed more easily once she was on the train.

Barbara had suggested a new Spanish restaurant, flattering Clara by assuming she knew where it was. She found it eventually and was led towards a woman who rose delightedly to shake her hand. They were the same height and made of the same stuff, and sat down in unison.

Barbara ordered two glasses of white manzanilla – a toast to the fact that they liked one another immediately. She told Clara that she had first seen her paintings ten years earlier at a student show, and how much she had liked them; that she had followed her career since and had been delighted to acquire those two works for the Arts Council collection. She spoke of Clara's work with such attention to detail that what she said did not sound like flattery but the most connoisseurial expression of respect.

Clara found that she had ordered wind-dried sausage and pebbly beans, a slick of tomatoes and a heap of fiery potatoes. It all tasted rough and delicious, and the sherry was followed by a pale green wine that sang on her tongue. She talked and Barbara led her.

'Have you ever thought about getting a studio in town?'

'I have one at home.'

'That must make it hard.'

'Hard?' Everyone else said how beautiful the old library was, how lucky she was.

'To concentrate.'

Clara found herself telling this stranger exactly how hard it was, and not only that but '. . . I didn't know before what it felt like when someone died, how it leaves everything so clean, I mean the details fall away.'

'Yes,' said Barbara, 'I understand.'

'So now things are more clear. I have to work . . . properly. I mean, do you know what my life is like?'

94

'I can imagine.'

'From the minute I wake up there are breakfasts, school bags, lunches, Stefan's shirts, suitcases, dentists, doctors, meals and noise, and when everyone's gone there are all those crumbling walls and rotting windows and leaking roofs and outside the door acres of stuff that keeps on dying and growing, and I swim up through it all and if I'm lucky I get to break the surface and take a breath. I work in snatches. I get it done but I don't get better. I don't have time to learn.'

Barbara echoed, underlined and agreed, and then held out her gift: 'A space has come up in the Quondam Building. I'm on the board and wondered –'

'The Quondam Building?' The first purpose-built artists' studios in London, sixty years old and famous for their light.

They drank tiny cups of coffee and agreed that it was perfectly plausible for Clara to spend a few days each week in London. It would be good for her. The children were alluded to only vaguely, which Clara told herself was out of delicacy as Barbara had none.

That evening Clara arrived at Khyber Road feeling bilious and tense. What had she been offered? What had she agreed to?

Fred opened the door. 'You never call,' he said. 'You just turn up.'

'Is that a complaint?' Clara asked, feeling the tightness with which he hugged her and knowing that it was not.

'No, I love it. Someone still just knocks on the door, and they come all the way from the suburbs to do it.' He wrinkled his nose. 'You've been boozing.'

'I had lunch, a business lunch; and I do not live in the suburbs.'

'You will soon.'

She pushed past him and went into the kitchen. 'Would you like a cup of tea, Federico?'

'Oh!' he said like an amazed guest. 'That would be lovely.'

They sat at the kitchen table and eventually Clara said, 'You're upset.'

He spoke to the table. 'We all are, aren't we?'

'That's Dad's line. You know what I mean.'

Fred flung up his hands and sighed, 'She's really going.'

'Caroline? Going where?'

'Not Caroline, Jules. After everything that's happened, she's still going to America.'

'Yes I am,' said Juliet coming in crossly. She was wearing a shirt which Clara recognised as having once belonged to Tobias. 'May I stay to discuss myself?'

'Shouldn't you be at work still?'

'I had to go and see someone about my visa.'

Fred gave an indignant snort and the three lapsed into silence. Clara was thinking how like Tobias Juliet was – Tobias as a child.

She wanted to be encouraging. 'Littlefield College is a very good place.'

Fred rolled his eyes. 'I know. Juliet keeps telling me, but what I don't understand is the point of going there to do something you can do here. And it's not just about you, Jules. It will upset everything.'

'For me, alright? It will be a good place for me!' Juliet shouted wearily.

This argument had clearly been going on for days.

Fred continued: 'And what about me?'

'Stay here, or go anywhere you like. We're grown-ups now, we can do what we like.'

'No,' said Fred. 'It's because we're grown-ups that we can't.'

Clara intervened. 'Why do you think Juliet ought not go?'

Fred looked round the room and then, as if he had lit on something, 'Bella.' He could just as easily have said Door or Dishcloth.

'I'm not Bella's mother,' said Juliet.

'No, you're her aunt and her father, your brother, is dead. Mary needs our help.'

'So you help her.'

'I will,' Fred sniffed, 'I do.'

'When did you last babysit?'

'I thought we decided not to, to encourage her to get someone proper . . .'

'You mean you didn't want to be pinned down.'

'The babysitting is a separate issue, a practical one,' said Clara. 'The point is we're not going to make each other feel better but we can give each other less to worry about by taking care of ourselves.'

'But you don't take care of yourself. You have Stefan and Mrs Clark and all those little men . . .' said Fred.

'It will be good for you, Juliet. It'll do you good to get away.'

'From me, you mean?' Fred's voice was exhausting.

'No, from –' Clara stopped herself.

Juliet understood and an idea arose, provoked by child-hood and sisterhood – a complication of wanting to surpass, to subsume and to be. 'Jacob,' she said, enjoying his name, 'might be coming with me.'

Clara left the next day. She had tickets for a matinee performance of *Salome* and Mary was going with her. It was the first time they had done something without children for years. Clara caught a train to Waterloo. In the city, she tended not to let the crowd impinge on her vision, and so did not notice anything unusual about the people gathering in the station, what they were carrying or how they were dressed.

'Clara!' Mary was struggling to reach her. 'We can't go to the theatre, not now.'

'Why not?'

'It's the rally. I completely forgot.'

'Oh, right. I remember hearing something about it.'

'We have to go.'

'Really? Can't we just go later? We spent years marching and shouting. Can't we have this one day off?'

Mary hesitated. It was true that they had marched a lot, and was tax really a matter of life and death like apartheid or neo-nazism or the Bomb?

The play ticked by. Clara concentrated on Salome's anger – punishing a man for his resistance, punishing herself for her desire. She was trapped by it, just as others were trapped by their reaction to her body, even him.

Mary could not stand the way these actors spoke and moved. To her, it did not suggest tension at all, just going through the motions while hanging on to your dignity. Desire was not like that. She grew bored, and became aware of noises outside, a surge of running and . . . horses? As the play continued stiffly on, she listened harder – whistles, clatter and roars. She was sure they would leave the theatre that sunny afternoon to find the city ablaze and under martial law, and could not understand how the rest of the audience could remain so absorbed by this preposterous drama. Nor could she persuade herself to act. She wanted to say something, to Clara at least, but stayed quietly in her seat.

The actors hurried through their curtain calls and a man in evening dress appeared onstage: 'Ladies and Gentleman, I regret to inform you that due to a civil disturbance, Charing Cross Road has been closed off by the police. Please would you all follow me through to the exit at the rear of the theatre.'

Clara was amused as they picked their way through the backstage clutter and out into a rubble-filled lot. 'It's as if we're the Romanovs, being led off to be shot.'

'We deserve to be,' said Mary. 'We should have been out there.'

'Now we are.' Clara found an alley which led through to Charing Cross Road. 'Come on!' They could not resist.

The police had forced the protesters back down to Cambridge Circus, where Mary and Clara found themselves looking over the heads of the crowd at two grey police horses – massive and empty-eyed – which suddenly galloped towards them, forcing people to fall over one another in their hurry to get out of the way. Who knew what such creatures were capable of?

Mary was rooted to the spot, the horses coming straight towards her, when Clara grabbed her hand: 'Run!' They ran. A sidestreet brought them to Long Acre where the world was ordinary again until they passed a burst window, its jagged glass holding the metal bin that had been hurled at it. A couple came round the corner with a child in a push-chair, still shopping, followed by half a dozen riot police moving at a calm trot. Mary and Clara took a number of shortcuts westwards but every time met a police line and were turned back.

Mary thought of Bella, somewhere on the other side of that line, and felt sick. 'I have to get home. Now!'

Clara took charge. 'We need to head south, cross the river and then we can come back over later.'

They did this, walking the other way until the police line petered out and they could cross at Southwark and make their way west along the south bank of the river.

'Are you alright?' Clara asked. She felt protective of Mary, as always.

'I thought this didn't happen any more. We had so much of it and then everyone seemed to just give up and stay at home.'

'That bloody woman wore us down.'

'Or we wore ourselves out.'

'Doing what? We never did that much – just the odd rally or march.'

Mary frowned. 'Maybe there's less to us than we think.'

'Mary George, you are never less clear than when you are being serious.'

They walked on and their journey became one of those unexpected crossings of the city in which it falls open and you marvel at how quickly you get from one place to another, how remarkable it all is, and how remarkable you feel. By the time Clara and Mary reached Victoria Station, they had worked their way down to something of their teenage selves. Each had recovered a sense of authenticity and wakefulness which had not been felt for so long that they had forgotten it never lasted.

NINE

Fred had given the matter of Juliet's surprise leaving party a great deal of thought. Her friends, for instance. Who were her friends? The only ones he was sure of were her college gang and they all scared him to death. Sara was an Ethiopian princess who had just qualified as an architect, Ritsu already lectured at the Institute where they had studied and Hannelore had taken a second masters degree in philosophy. They were all striking, and Sara was beautiful. Why couldn't Juliet have ordinary friends, girls like those in Allnorthover? She had refused to have anything to do with them and spent years alone (although there might have been a boy at some point, Fred couldn't be sure) before this international trio of goddesses had come along. Sara and Hannelore were tall but Fred rather liked that, the way they towered over him and smiled down. Caroline was taller than him, too.

He rang Ritsu at the Institute and asked her who else to invite, adding glumly that he supposed he ought to ask the Dart.

'The what?' asked Ritsu.

'The who. You know, Jacob. Jacob Dart.'

'Jacob?'

'Juliet's . . . you know . . .'

'Her what?'

'You mean you don't know?'

'Evidently not. Jacob Dart? Any relation to Barbara Dart at the Arts Council?'

'I don't know. Who's she? Do you think I ought to invite her as well?'

Carlo arrived first with Mary and Bella, who was put into Fred's bed. It was seven o'clock on an August evening. Bella lay down, closed her eyes for a few minutes and then sat up. Mary took a dark blanket from Juliet's room and hung it over the window. 'It's called Black Out,' she explained. 'Same as Lights Out only more so.' She laid her daughter back down, hoping that this new kind of darkness would interest Bella sufficiently to let it have its effect.

The plan was that Tania would take Juliet for a farewell drink and then offer to drive her home at eight. She was flying out to America the next day. Mary had brought along Tobias's pliers, screwdrivers and soldering iron, and set about getting Juliet's stereo to work. It was a system that the Clough children had inherited from an uncle who liked to be up-to-the-minute and who had died young – waist-high speakers and monolithic slabs of dusty black plastic covered in knobs and dials, and connected by a tangle of fat cracked cables.

That afternoon Fred had remembered that there ought to be food and dashed into a deli to buy a ham, a cheese and a large jar of small silver onions which he'd liked the look of. The goddesses arrived with champagne and travel-size, elaborately wrapped presents. Allie, who was out of hospital, had donated a large bag of his homegrown grass and was sociably rolling joints at the kitchen table.

Just before eight, a car was heard approaching.

'That'll be Tania and Juliet! Come on everybody, hide!' Fred ushered them into the kitchen and then crept up to the front door and crouched behind it, waiting for the knock. There were footsteps, and then more footsteps, too many footsteps and someone, a man, saying: 'We really ought to have beaten you to it!'

Juliet's voice: 'I'm sorry?'

'Pritt,' the man said. 'Graham Pritt. We came to dinner back in the spring.'

'Hello!' A woman's voice. Fred leaned hard back against the wall. It wasn't Graham's wife Jane, but Caroline! He had issued only a casual invitation and had never thought that they, let alone she, would come.

Before he could recover himself, Juliet had opened the door and was letting them in while saying something about packing and an early start and 'Fred? What the hell are you doing behind the door? There are people here to see you. And I need to get on.'

'Fred! How lovely to see you,' said Tania. She stepped aside and waited for further instructions.

Juliet went straight to the stairs, turning only to say, 'Yes, well, thanks for the lift Tania, the drink and all that. I'll, um, be in touch . . . And nice to see you again, and you . . .'

They all noticed that she looked tired and none of them could think what to say to stop her continuing up the stairs. When they heard her door close, and a lock being turned, Fred remembered the people in the kitchen.

'Christ,' he said, shaking his head. 'What now?' The gaggle in the hall looked back at him, politely expectant, and he realised that Caroline was here, in his house, and that he was in charge. 'Into the kitchen with everyone else,' he said. 'I'll get her down. She'll be delighted.'

By the time Fred had persuaded Juliet to come

downstairs, she was irritated and the guests were bored. He made her go in first and she kicked open the door, turned on the light and stared at her siblings and friends, who, convinced that the time would never come, stared back. Fred was determined on his moment and so raised his arms like the conductor of a recalcitrant school choir, but then lost his nerve: 'SUR-prise?' The guests, too, were caught out. 'Surprise!' someone barked, 'Surprise!' another grumbled, then a yelp, a hoot, a whisper: 'Surprise!' 'Surprise!' 'Surprise!'

Clara refused to look at her watch. She was enjoying this too much: being in town without children, not lugging a portfolio around and not leaking breast milk, but drinking gin and tonic in a backstreet pub near Clapham Junction with a man who was evidently pleased to have bumped into her and who seemed to be in no hurry either. She studied him as he waited at the bar, not leaning forward, not raising a note or waving a hand, just standing two or three people back, smiling perseveringly at a pretty young woman who, once she saw him, served him right away. The woman's face had lit up at the sight of this charming man; he would, Clara knew, have held her gaze for a little too long.

'That man,' Fred had observed, 'is quiet in a loud way.'

As Jacob paid, he dipped his head and looked up humbly, so grateful that the woman would take his money, so astonished to be given change. As she put the drinks down on the counter, one slopped and spilled and he rifled urgently through his pockets and brought out a handkerchief, his hands flapping as he insisted on mopping it up himself, unaware that the woman had found a cloth and would far rather have done it herself. That was her job. Couldn't he see that he was being embarrassing?

There it was, the flaw in Jacob, the thing that made

his charm real and his artifice redeemable. He was not, after all, in control. The woman, for a moment so animated and alert, had withdrawn her interest as his attention lost shape; just like that – too much. Confused, disdainful, she dropped the cloth on the bar and turned her back. Clara noticed that Jacob left his handkerchief beside it.

Graham was leaning against the mantelpiece, just as he had the last time he visited Khyber Road, only now it was because otherwise he would not be able to stand up. There had been the champagne and some surprisingly good wine, and a lot of grass which he had smoked in order to encourage Caroline, who said that she had heard it was an aphrodisiac. She was sitting next to the other brother, the fat one, whose arm rested along the sofa behind her back and who was pretending not to look at her breasts under her slippery shirt. The fat brother was waving his other hairy hand in the air and whatever he was saying was making her laugh.

'How's the wife?' It was Fred.

'The what?'

'Jane – your wife?' Fred persisted, standing annoyingly in front of Caroline.

Graham's mind swerved around an awkward thought.

At that moment, Caroline rose up behind Fred and asked where the bathroom was. He took her arm and led her upstairs.

Graham slumped beside Carlo on the sofa. 'She's asleep,' he said. 'Upped her dose since she got the boot at work.' His eyes thudded shut and his head jolted onto Carlo's shoulder.

Tania gave up trying to get upstairs to say goodbye to Juliet. It would have been awkward anyway as Fred was sitting on the stairs with that big girl more or less on his knee. They didn't appear to be kissing. His eyes were closed and her face was buried in his neck. There was a wet patch on her nasty short skirt. Were they, despite the loud music, asleep? Tania went back to the doorway and smiled efficiently round the room before leaving.

On the doorstep, she met Clara and Jacob. They were flushed, as if about to melt into the mucky sunset behind them.

'Bad idea!' Tania laughed and they looked caught out. What was that grass, some kind of truth drug? 'I mean the party. Juliet went straight back up to her room and hasn't been down since. Still, now you're here, Jacob . . .' She stopped as if struck by something terrible, opened her mouth and shut it again, pushed past them, turned the corner and vomited into her handbag.

Jacob and Clara stood in the hallway. Eventually, Clara gestured towards the stairs in a manner she knew would annoy him: 'Off you trot.'

He put his hand on the small of her back. 'I don't think so.'

Graham came to and climbed back up the mantelpiece. He was clutching at it and trying to pass off his swaying as dancing. If only he could get his body to move back-wards and forwards, because that seemed to be the way people danced these days, or at least these people. They had their arms up in the air and were doing twiddly things with their fingers. The fat brother was touching the ceiling and those three lovely women had formed a ring and were stroking him. Graham looked down at the pale girl who had been crouched over the stereo all evening. She kept searching through boxes of records and tapes, pulling something out, putting it back. It was only music, for god's sake, and not very good music at that. It kept getting stuck, repeating itself, all stop and start. She did look dull.

Someone shouted 'Go on!' and the tall black woman, the really beautiful one, wrapped an arm round Graham and pulled him towards the ring. 'Someone wants to dance with you,' she said and tugged him forward. His feet wouldn't adjust and tripped over themselves so that he staggered towards the Japanese woman with the shaved head (or was she Chinese or Taiwanese? Some sort of -nese), who stepped aside and then he was falling, falling down the body of the one with the long blonde hair, past her long golden neck, bouncing off her powerful shoulder, catching briefly on the point of her breast and then sliding all the way down the taut line of her black dress, on past a mile of fuzzy brown leg, on and on to the surprising length of her shoe.

Mary looked round for a different tape, something that would calm everyone down while Carlo and Clara helped the idiot in the tight ironed jeans onto the sofa. They propped him up and Clara undid a couple of the buttons on his pink shirt because its high collar was pinching his spotty throat.

Graham did not dare open his eyes. Was one of those goddesses actually undressing him? The smell of her skin was unexpected – tobacco and gin, and then milk, sweat and the tang of something deeper. 'Try to breathe,' she said and her voice was not charmingly accented as he had imagined, but tough and dry. He opened his eyes and it was not a goddess at all but the older sister, whose breasts he had tried not to stare at. Her face had seemed striking in a handsome way, what with all that hair but up close, shaded and enlarged, it became that of a 'Witch'. Had he really said it? 'Take your hands off me, you fucking witch,' all the time with a smile on his face because he was drunk and stoned and melted on the outside while in his heart, he felt one clear thing: how much he hated women like this.

'Witch!' He said it again and couldn't stop laughing even though people were pulling at him and he was out on the street where the pavement ought to have been only there wasn't one, not even a kerb, and he sat down anyway, or fell because where were his bones and god did it smell bad, worse than her, the witch, the bitch, but he didn't get up until someone threw a bucket of water over him, after which he remembered a bit more and wondered what he was doing in this slum and made his way home, for once not getting lost in the half-made streets of the estate and for once not on the lookout for black men with knives and for once looking so shabby and relaxed that those who passed him, carrying knives or not, smiled and some even said goodnight.

Graham tottered under the railway bridge, stopping to greet a tramp he passed every day and never usually spoke to: 'Weren't we at school together?' to which the man replied, 'Actually, yes. I was a friend of your brother Simon's.' He continued across the main road, waving cheerily after the car that nearly knocked him down, 'Do I know you?' and off behind the burger bars and charity shops into the solid streets of mansion blocks. No dog shit here; just signs telling people to clear it up. Graham concentrated on getting from one lamp post to the next and read each sign he came to: Neighbourhood Watch, a lost cat called Timon, a choral society, plans for a conversion, a petition for CCTV, a petition against CCTV, a holistic gardener, a local celebrity giving a poetry reading (his own poems) in a library, an advert for a private security firm.

On the fourth floor, behind deep walls and double-glazed windows, Jane sat among cushions and waited. She did not sleep as much as they thought. Graham had insisted on going along to protect Caroline from desperate little Fred Clough. Why had Caroline wanted to go in the first place? Jane hadn't.

She was pleased that Graham came home alone. He reeked of dogshit and vomit and curry, perhaps the goat curry they sold in that tiny shop by the station, where he called the owner by his first name but got it wrong. Graham liked to take his friends there after a night in the pub, daring them to eat goat and insisting that they would not be able to take the heat. He would eat leftover spicy orange patties for breakfast and then fart all day in front of the television.

Graham slid down the wall, looked up at his wife and asked her if he had a brother called Simon. For once, Jane thought of the right thing to do at the right moment. She guided Graham into Caroline's room and put him to bed.

Barbara Dart returned to Jacob's room. She hadn't seen him for over a week and he hadn't answered his telephone, which she knew did not necessarily mean that he was not there. Sometimes Jacob chose not to answer the telephone for days. Still, she was unnerved, more so when she found the room empty and more or less unlocked again. Where was Jacob? With the girl, perhaps, which did not matter because she knew from Tania that the girl was going to America. Poor Jacob, the girl had been going away all along; she had never meant it. Barbara scanned the room and saw that the things she had gone through last time were still strewn about. Then she noticed something stuck on the wall, no, in the wall – a rolled up note. She read it and took it.

*   *   *

Fred had woken long before Caroline but had stayed put, mostly because he had lost all feeling in his right leg, the one she had been sitting on. He didn't care if he never felt anything again. All he had to do was move his head slightly and his lips could touch her cheek. He could smell and taste her. Fred knew that most people would not find Caroline beautiful. Her forehead gave way too steeply to a chin already cushioned by a creamy fold. Her teeth had the quelled look that English teeth take on once they have been vigorously straightened, as if her smile had retreated. Her eyebrows were excitingly heavy but her eyes were pale. He could never decide on their exact colour. Her hair also eluded colour. It had been strained into shape and had now flopped.

What really excited Fred, what really moved him, was Caroline's skin. It was so lively. One winter morning she had arrived at work and he had thought her face looked remarkably liquid and clarified, magnified, as if behind glass, so that when she asked him why he was staring at her, he said 'You look like a frozen pond', which was exactly right but all wrong because everyone laughed.

When Caroline stirred, he raised her to her feet and limped stiffly along to his room, forgetting that Bella was in his bed. He scooped the snoring child up with one arm while letting Caroline gently down with the other. Then he settled Bella in a heap of clothes and left them both to rest.

The goddesses were squeezed together on the sofa, eyes shut. No one could keep still on that thing usually, let alone go to sleep. Fred lay down at their feet.

Up in the attic, Allie, who smoked the stuff all day and still didn't sleep, was sharing a joint with Mary. She would have liked to have danced with Carlo but Juliet's friends were so scary that she chose instead to climb the ladder and finding Allie there, asked if she could sit for a while and get some air. It was dark, like the club, and she couldn't see anyone, not even Allie who had crouched in

110

a corner as he always did because 'they' were out there watching and would be coming to get him. Mary sang:

> *. . . dawn's early . . .*
> *haunting me . . .*
> *where will you be . . .*
> *cold . . .*

The door to Juliet's room opened and Carlo came out onto the landing, where he stopped to listen. He stopped again in the hallway because he could see that in the kitchen Jacob was making coffee in a pot on the stove, and Clara sat at the table slicing ham and cheese. They were silent, apart and turned away from one another, but something was clear. If they had felt the need to make conversation, Carlo would not have worried.

'What're you doing?' Fred bumped up against him, rubbing his eyes.

'Observing,' replied Carlo.

'What?'

'The Dart. I mean, who wears black these days? Especially all black . . .'

'Undertakers. Referees. Shadows.'

'Didn't you enter a fancy-dress competition once as a shadow?'

'No.'

'I'm sure you did. That first summer we were in Allnorthover, when Ma bribed us to go along to their fête. My god it was medieval – some modern version of the ducking stool . . .'

'That was Julie Lacey in a polka-dot bikini. Boys were paying to knock her off a ledge and into a pool.'

'How would you remember? You were only eight.'

'Come on, it was Julie Lacey in a polka-dot bikini. It was talked about for years.'

'That and Tom the Drowner.'

'Was that the same year? Christ.'

They both looked up towards the attic where Mary had stopped singing.

'And it wasn't a shadow,' said Fred. 'It was a puddle. Nobody bloody well got it, but it was brilliant. A puddle.'

Everyone woke up at the same moment and was hungry, even Bella, whom Caroline brought down and held on her knee and fed. When Bella punched Caroline on the arm and Mary jumped to apologise, Caroline smiled and punched Bella back.

They heard Juliet go into the bathroom.

'We need to check the time of her flight,' said Carlo.

'Whose flight?' asked Caroline.

'Jacob, don't you think it might be a good idea if –' Carlo faltered.

Jacob was leaning against the open back door. 'I will wait for her,' he said.

'Wait for her to come downstairs or wait for her to come back from America?' Fred could not stop himself.

'Yes.'

'Which?' He always managed to do it, the bastard, somehow he always got right under Fred's skin. 'Down or back?'

Jacob shrugged and Fred would have hit him if Caroline had not interrupted: 'Oh! I thought you were *her* husband!'

For once, Jacob looked surprised. 'I'm sorry?'

Caroline gestured towards Clara: 'Her husband.'

'No,' he said eventually.

'Oh,' said Caroline. 'Sorry, um, whatever your name is.'

'Clara, my name is Clara.'

'But you do have a wife, don't you?' Later, Fred would

blame it on Allie's grass. 'Although funnily enough, she's not either of my sisters, is she?'

'Yes.'

'No she isn't!'

'No.'

'Don't play your games! Even when Tobias was killed, you were playing your fucking games. You think you're so *exempt!*'

Two or three people in the room had grasped what had been said and waited for Jacob to explain. In the end, it was Sara who spoke and her tone was that of a goddess leaning over the earth to disentangle a couple of fishermen's nets. 'Yes, he has a wife. No, it is not either sister.'

'So who is your wife then?' Caroline demanded.

Jacob said nothing. Hannelore, Ritsu and Sara passed food and poured coffee. Juliet had not discussed Jacob with them, so they assumed that he could not be that important. They carried on pouring and passing as Jacob, without a hint of capitulation, went upstairs.

Clara stood up and yawned. 'Only Juliet would contrive a situation as drearily complicated as this. Carlo, can I go back to your place to get some sleep? It must be getting on for six o'clock and I've got a meeting with someone about a commission.'

Caroline looked up. 'A commission? How *fantastic!*'

Clara ignored her. 'Keys, Carlo? I'll call a cab. Anyone else going east?'

Mary took Bella back to bed, Clara gave up trying to explain to the taxi firm how to find Khyber Road, and set off with Hannelore, Ritsu and Sara to meet the cab. Carlo went into the living room, shut the door, picked up the phone, dialled Jonathan Mehta's number and put it down again. This left Fred and Caroline alone.

When were they ever alone? There was usually someone else there – Graham, say, or someone to deal with, like

113

Jacob. Terrified, Fred bolted for the back door and taking a deep breath, suggested that Caroline might like to get some fresh air 'while it lasts', and she came to stand beside him and looked up with him beyond the concrete yard, past the dilapidated roofs, above the high windows of the fenced-off primary school and the higher windows of the tower blocks. Up there, jet trails persisted, solidly white, as if it really did take a considerable effort to move through the air and a long time for the sky to recover.

TEN

Juliet continued to pack and unpack until she had worked up the courage to ask a direct question: 'Should I be leaving you?'

Jacob could tell what this was costing her, but his fear had its own momentum. He tried. He opened his arms and drew her to him and she tried to believe that this was answer enough. And even though for Jacob the feeling of falling away from her slowed and he felt that after all things might be alright, he could not stand to bring his dream of their romance and its unspokenness down to the level of her question.

No one heard Jacob come downstairs and leave, so when Carlo went up to knock on Juliet's door he was surprised to find her alone.

'Is Fred very cross?' she asked.

'He's spent half the night with Caroline on his knee and right now he's walking her home. I don't think he'll be cross.'

'Then he's not here to say goodbye?'

'You didn't even attend your own leaving party. Why

should anyone stick around to say goodbye?'

'I didn't mean not to want a party. It was just that I had a lot to do and seeing all those parts of my life in one room, well it was . . .'

'You're a secretive little bugger, aren't you? I thought all that not sharing was a boy thing.' He hugged her in passing. 'I'll take your bags down to the car. Now go and give Mary and Bella a kiss.'

'I can't face anyone.'

'They're asleep, they won't notice.'

Juliet crept into Fred's room and brushed her lips against their cheeks so lightly, that even if they had been awake they might not have noticed. As it was, Bella's dream adjusted to this touch and the lion from the cemetery reached down and skimmed her face with his paw. She formed a fist and punched, catching Juliet in the eye.

At the airport, Carlo sidled into a cubicle to use a phone. It was no bigger, and no more private, than a segment of a playground roundabout.

'Ma, it's me. I thought you'd want to know she got off safely . . . Sorry, did I wake you? . . . Good, it's just you sound . . . She'll be back for Christmas . . . Me? I'm fine. It's you I worry about . . .'

Carlo hung up and rang Jonathan Mehta, whose number he now knew by heart.

As the plane swung west over car parks and golf courses, civic lakes, roundabouts, sewage works, dual carriageways, the drab tessellations of processing plants and light industry and a surprising amount of green, Juliet liked to think she had flown over Khyber Road and that they were all just as she had left them and would stay that way till she came back: Mary and Bella tucked up, Fred and Caroline hand in hand, Allie crouched under the roof, Hannelore, Ritsu and Sara poised to surround her, Jacob on the stairs, perhaps, Clara circling and Carlo keeping watch.

Juliet rewrote the previous night, starting with the moment when everyone had shouted 'Surprise!', when she had had a premonition of horrible muddle, of them all adrift and crashing into one another. In this revised version, she thought of something clever and funny to say, and did not notice the two who were missing; nor did she hear them under her window when they had turned up later, together.

As Jane sat in a department-store coffee shop composing a note to Graham, he caught Caroline coming out of the bathroom and pulled away her towel. 'One last fuck,' he said, grabbing at her nipples. 'One last fuck, you dirty stop-out. I think old Jane is beginning to get the idea, so let's make it a good one.' He pressed the palm of his right hand hard against her groin and rubbed in a brisk circle. His other hand kneaded her buttocks and she winced as he tried to push a finger with a ragged nail between them.

'I want to fuck you up the, er, the –' Alone, Graham had said this line many times, till he came in his fist having let the dry skin of his hand chafe against his cock because that was how he imagined it must feel, to do it to someone *there*.

'I want to fuck you up the ass,' he said aloud at last, pushing her along the corridor into her bedroom and back into the sour air of the night before.

Caroline sat down on the bed and asked, 'Do you know how?'

Graham, proudly wriggling out of his trousers, was so

surprised by this response that he lifted one leg having forgotten that he had just lifted the other, and fell to the floor. 'Fuck, fuck . . .'

'And can you say "arse", please, because "ass" doesn't sound dirty enough.'

With that, it became exciting again because this was what Graham liked best about Caroline, that she was so frank and efficient, and how what they did had nothing to do with anything else, nothing at all.

As he stood up, Caroline rolled onto all fours. Graham stared at her buttocks, and between them at darkness and dark hair. He trembled. 'Shouldn't I use some . . . something?'

She was rocking herself back towards him. 'Baby oil, butter, whatever.'

He stepped back. 'You mean you really will?'

Caroline sat back and looked at his frightened penis. She never wanted to see it again.

When the plane was halfway through the arc of its journey, and the map on the screen showed it blinking over the ocean and near neither Greenland nor Labrador, Juliet began to panic. I don't like places I can't get out of. She wanted to sleep but her eyes felt so dry that it hurt to close them. Whiskey, wine, coffee and half a glass of luke-warm water. Her body itched and her back throbbed, and even though she knew it was because she had been sitting in this cramped seat for several hours, she thought this was the beginning of the bad pain because she had forgotten that there could be any other kind. She took some pills, just in case.

Later she rewrote the night once more, but this time had everything live up to her fears. Caroline would ditch Fred and go off with her sleepy friend's husband, the one she was screwing anyway. Fred would write poems. Their mother would never speak again and their father would drive into a tree. Tania would have long lunches with Barbara Dart, who would charm her into being malicious about Juliet. Carlo would get beaten up by the skinheads on the estate. Clara, having met Jacob on the doorstep, would keep him there.

Too easy. Jacob would fall in love with Sara, who would agonise and then succumb because Juliet wasn't there to be faced. She would return to London next year and have to confront them at parties. People she knew from the Institute would invite them to dinner. More. Sara would be taken to see Jacob's mother, who would dandle her grandchild on her knee. Sara would design galleries for foreign cities and Jacob would write the seminal cultural text for the turn of the century. No one would remember Juliet Clough, teaching somewhere or other. She curled up in her seat and buried her head. There would be an exhibition of Sara's award-winning models at Tania's gallery. Barbara Dart would fund it.

Pain pried apart feelings so compacted that Juliet had only ever been aware of them as a mass in which she could not discern good from bad, or being hurt from being loved. Her world had come loose, which felt like a good thing when she was with Jacob and a bad thing when she thought about Tobias.

Not wanting, for now, things to become clear, she moved to confuse them once more. There they all were, only Sara was not with Jacob. It was Clara he stood next to, over a coffin. Tears came to Juliet's eyes at last. Clara with yet another golden baby in her arms and Jacob beside her. Juliet's thoughts swam towards a dream in which she opened the coffin and saw herself and knew that the plane had crashed, and then she was asleep and the relief of crying gave way to the stab of changing pressure as the plane sidled down through the clouds to land in the middle of an American day.

Carlo lay naked on his front beneath a tall window veiled in calico as Jonathan Mehta warmed oil between his hands and then ran them over Carlo's back before checking and releasing each vertebra of his spine.

'Ow!'

'Sorry. Too strong? I'll start with your shoulders instead, where you said you had that knot.'

'Ow!'

'Sorry.'

Carlo winced as Jonathan's fingers meddled and jabbed. Jonathan Mehta. He was naked in the presence of Jonathan Mehta and Jonathan Mehta was massaging his back. A hand swooped from the nape of his neck to his tailbone, nudging briskly at the towel that covered his bottom. Something deep in Carlo leapt towards that touch and then the fingers began to pinch his collarbone, setting off needling bursts of pain. He concentrated on trying not to cry out.

'. . . Yes, contemporary dance,' Jonathan was saying. 'But not any more.'

'Really?' Carlo tried to remember how they had got on to contemporary dance.

'Injury.'

'Really? What?' He couldn't resist: 'I'm a doctor.'

'Really? I dropped someone.'

'Oh. I thought you were the one with the injury.'

'I was. I am. He fell on me. I dropped him . . . on myself.' At this Jonathan lifted his hands away and Carlo was shocked by the loss of contact.

When he had dressed and paid ('How did you find me?' 'Your card. On the noticeboard. At the cinema.' 'Oh, the cinema.'), Carlo went home to take some painkillers. He lay in a confusion of bliss and discomfort, deciding in the end that Jonathan Mehta's clumsiness made him more possible than Carlo had thought, which had been, for months now, not possible at all.

Jonathan closed the door, lay down on the couch and breathed. Carlo Clough. At school he might have been Charlie Clough; at university, Carl. Still more or less young – mid-twenties? – but a doctor and grown-up enough to return to his full name. He had taken off his clothes and stood there frankly until Jonathan said 'Lie down, please', taking in the padded shoulders and chest, the firm cushions on the belly and hips, and how this man carried his fat like ceremonial armour and was perhaps proud of it, and anyway ought to be because the overall effect was seductive.

Jacob could not have picked a better time to turn up on his wife's doorstep. She was delighted that he had arrived while she had some adventurous music playing and photographs of artworks scattered across the fleecy rug that lay between her two sofas. She did not explain and he did not ask which, these days, she found reassuring. In this spirit, she produced two cold bottles of Mexican lager.

'Do you have any limes?'

She had limes.

He followed her into the kitchen and pulled some salad leaves from a bowl.

'What's this, red chicory?'

'From that little man on Green Lanes. The Greek with the daughter you couldn't take your eyes off.'

'Yes,' said Jacob, licking his lips, 'I remember.' It was understood between them that Jacob was allowed to savour beautiful women; he made a point of it. They could be sixteen or sixty but if they provoked a response, Jacob let them know. Alert and subtle in most things, in this he was overt. He patted his hair and licked his lips (as Clara, right now licking her lips in front of the bathroom mirror, remembered), and most of all he stared and when the woman in question became aware of this lovely man making himself so clear, she became more animated, better lit.

It would have been enough for Barbara for Jacob to acknowledge this, but he would not allow it. She was imagining it all. Patting his hair and licking his lips? How vulgar. Yes of course he noticed beautiful women, but especially old women, and Barbara was crass to think that this appreciation was sexual. 'You do tend to forget, Bar, quite what an innocent I am.' So this was her compromise – to let him know she knew by sharing the looking.

'I saw her at the pool the other evening. In the showers. She's rather delicious.'

'Yes.' Jacob ran a hand down Barbara's hip.

'High round tits like an odalisque and dark . . . really dark . . .'

Later, when Jacob lay in the hammock on the balcony and Barbara sat ostentatiously on the rail, he said, 'She left me.'

No she didn't, thought Barbara. She's gone to America and anyway, you never formally left *me*. She did not resist as he reached for her hand and pulled her down into the hammock.

'Lie on top of me.'

Barbara did so but Jacob, absorbed back into himself, made no accommodation. She felt the clash of their bones and moved over.

Jacob's hand caught against her breast and squeezed it routinely.

'She left me.' He rarely spoke with such satisfaction.

ELEVEN

From the day on which Juliet arrived in Littlefield, she felt herself to be living under trees. Leaves bristled in each of the nine windows of her cavernous apartment. They looked tough and dull until the sun hit when, as if switched on, they lit up with the lurid purity of emerald and lime. Juliet observed this precisely. There was not much else to do.

The one other woman in her department was the professor who had invited her there, Merle Dix. She was in her forties, and spoke and dressed in a quietly detailed European manner. In London she had had time to talk to Juliet, who had felt so delighted and grateful that she arrived in Littlefield with the expectation that they would become something like best friends, only here Merle was always busy and when they met accelerated past calling out something about meeting for coffee. Juliet was disappointed and when she phoned Carlo imitated Merle's voice – a midwest accent buttoned up on leaving home and stretched in odd places by time spent in London, Berlin and Rome. Carlo told Juliet not to mock and pointed out the odd angles in her own diction. As children, all the Cloughs had tried to fit in more than they would now care to admit.

In those last days of August, the sun slammed down. Everything else appeared strong enough to take it: the leathery leaves, the pumped-up squirrels and wiry chipmunks, the buffed brick, the thickly painted clapboard, the robust young. Light shoved and bounced, and Juliet crept to her office and talked to her students as they sat nursing bottles of water. She sought shade, but it made no difference. She kept her head down in defence against the light, and began to imagine that she had to crouch because of all those branches. In fact, the trees were as ardently managed as anything else that belonged to the town and their branches were kept out of reach.

Am I short? she asked Carlo in her first letter. *I'm not, am I? Only here I feel like Mrs Pepperpot. I said so to someone the other day and they said 'Mrs who?' so I explained that she's a character in a children's story who shrinks and has adventures and they said, 'She does?' which of course I took to be a question and answered in full whereas it was probably a remark, like 'Hi, how are you.' Everyone replies 'Good, how are you', regardless. It's also not a question – more a case of call and response.*

'I've had a letter from Juliet,' Carlo told Fred. He was steadying a ladder while Fred attempted to clear the gutters at Khyber Road.

'How is she?'

'Facetious.'

Fred was standing on tiptoe, brandishing a ladle. 'It's no good, I'd better get the remote.'

'The remote?'

'It's by the TV. Would you fetch it?'

Carlo went off and shouted 'I can't find it!' He returned with a snooker cue. 'I thought this might be more useful.'

Fred took the cue. 'That is the remote.' He angled one

end into the gutter and began to flick wads of rotten leaves into the air.

The night before, Fred had been woken by gurgles and drips, and had called up to the attic, 'Allie, the house is leaking!' before remembering that Allie had moved back in with his parents. 'Tarpaulin!' Fred exclaimed, rushing round the house looking for anything that might pass. He came across a cycling cape, cut it into large squares, found a hammer and some nails, and made his way up to the attic.

Proud and exhausted, he had gone back to bed but the dripping continued. He rang Carlo, who had just got home and who was too tired to explain what a gutter was, so offered to come round in the morning.

Carlo continued: 'Can't imagine what she's like as a teacher.'

'She's teaching? I thought it was just research.'

'No. Graduate students teach some of the basic courses to the undergraduates.'

'What's she teaching then?'

'Painting by numbers, dot-to-dot, that kind of thing.'

'Oh,' said Fred. 'Is that postmodern?'

If I close my eyes, wrote Juliet, *it could be a desert, the air feels so solidly burning and dry. And the light is vicious. It thrusts everything at you and everything is huge and most of it is trees.* There were trees everywhere in London too, except in places like Khyber Road, but they did not encroach. They had character and were interestingly out of step with their surroundings. They told you what a place used to be or what it hoped to become. *And my students surround me after class like an anxious forest, looming and leaning and asking me to repeat myself.*

* * *

'She seems to think her students are trees.' Carlo had pulled out the letter to read the rest to Fred. More rain was falling and they had gone inside. 'I bet she talks to them as if they were. I bet they hate her. Patronising little so-and-so.'

'They hate us all there these days, don't they?' Fred asked.

'It's a generational thing,' explained Carlo. 'You see it in medicine, too. The older ones loved us and wanted to be us and then hated us because they weren't, while the current lot think they can be us better than we can while hating us at the same time.'

'Now that really is postmodern,' Fred announced confidently and then slumped white on the sofa and began to sob.

To give himself a chance to work out how to approach this, Carlo offered to make some tea. In the kitchen, nothing was obviously wrong but once Carlo saw one thing, he kept noticing more. The fridge contained a number of empty cartons and wrappers. The crockery looked as if it had not been disturbed for some time. There was a layer of un-use on everything – a kind of dust that seemed less natural than dirt. Carlo went upstairs. Fred's room could not be entered and his swirl of mess had enlarged until it became fixed, immovable. In Juliet's room, Carlo found Fred's pyjamas on the bed and his suit on the back of the door.

Fred was still on the sofa, rocking and sobbing. Carlo sat down and threw an arm around his shoulders. Fred looked too thin, too hectic, but he always had been and so no one noticed when he became more so.

'Steady on. She's only been gone two weeks.'

'No,' Fred whimpered, 'not her.'

Of course, thought Carlo. 'We all miss her.' He had meant to say 'him', 'We all miss him', only his words had lingered on his first and more manageable thought.

'No.'

'And him,' Carlo found it hard to say, 'we miss him, too.'

There it was. Were they about to admit to each other that since Tobias's death the texture of life had become uncontrollably variable, stretching and crumbling, their feelings too? That everything had lost shape and now whatever shape there was kept changing?

Fred looked up, bewildered. 'Who?'

'Tobias.'

'Tobias. No. Yes, I mean but –'

Whatever else there was, Carlo didn't want to know. He knew enough. 'Are you eating?'

'At work.'

'You don't have breakfast? Or cook when you get home?'

'Do you know what it's like to put one plate on a table?'

'I do it every day. Why don't you eat?'

'I don't have time for breakfast and I'm too tired when I get home.'

'But you used to. You were always knocking up offerings for what's her name.'

'Caroline.' Fred's voice was firm but his eyes filled once more with tears.

'Oh dear,' said Carlo, clamping Fred to his side. 'Things not going well?'

'Caroline Broad-Jones is marrying Oliver Twerp next Saturday. After their honeymoon, they are flying out to Hong Kong, where Oliver works for some bank.'

'You're making it up.'

'No, it's perfectly true.'

'Broad-Jones and Twerp?'

'Well, not Twerp. It's Thorp actually, but if you give it an English spin . . .'

'Hong Kong?'

'Yes.'

'And what happened with that jerk Graham then, the one with the wife?'

'Graham? Nothing. He was just her landlord.'

'Right . . . So Juliet is in America, Caroline is going to Hong Kong –'

'When everything should stay as it was, it was all fine, and now, just because Tobias is dead . . .'

There was a silence before Carlo said, 'He is, isn't he,' and then there was no Caroline or Jonathan Mehta, there was no one else at all because Carlo and Fred were alone and here was a brother, the only person who knew what it was like for a brother to lose a brother.

At the Quondam Building, Barbara led Clara up the stairs and then handed her the key and stood back. The room was smaller, darker and colder than the library at home, but Clara was delighted. She could feel, or liked to imagine she could feel, the hum of contemplation and industry as all around her other artists set about their work while the ghosts of those first artists, from sixty years ago, looked on.

They went out for a drink to celebrate and talked a little about themselves. There was no mention of Juliet, and Jacob's name came up only as they were parting, when Barbara made an extraordinary and irresistible request.

Juliet wanted to submit to America as a foreign country, which it had turned out to be. She was having trouble making herself understood. Syntax, inflection and connotation refused to translate, and there was something about the cleanliness of the American sentence, no matter how grandly constructed, which made her feel over-elaborate. There was a cleanliness to the landscape as well, which she found refreshing. There were no ruins; nothing looked old (or at least no more than picturesque) and everything looked simple. *It is,* she wrote in the notebook in which she was supposed to be gathering research material, *as if my different geography and history give me a different sense of space and time. It's not just my metaphysics that are different, but my physics, too.* It was all rather demanding, which Juliet decided to enjoy as something bound to turn out to have been good for her.

She enjoyed staying in her room and imagining America, and allowed her idea of the grandeur that lay beyond the trees to dignify her loneliness. She acquired the luxurious kind of anxiety that blossoms when there is enough money and time not to get on with things. She worried about the trees, and about her purpose, about her siblings and her parents too, but more as figures on a board than people whose lives shaped her own. If she thought about Jacob, it was of him as a sensation. He was a shiver, a frisson, a prickling of desire; quite overwhelming but no more substantial than that. At this point, she got as much pleasure from her detachment as she did from her susceptibility.

She felt fine until one night when she called home, not Khyber Road but Allnorthover. The telephone rang and rang, and Juliet could not remember a time when there had been no one there to answer.

She acquired an old Ford Mercury, which had neither air conditioning nor windows that opened but which more or less drove itself. She went to see a famous German architect who came to speak in the nearby town of Mount South. Juliet sat in the front row and made notes. Merle

Dix was there with her husband, a pony-tailed theatre critic with a name like a car-part, and when the event was over, they stood by the door and signalled to the German architect while Juliet asked him yet another question. He made his excuses and disappeared. Everyone disappeared and so Juliet drove slowly back to Littlefield and told herself that she had only imagined seeing them – Merle Dix, the car-part (Ratchon?) and the German – laughing and hurrying into a restaurant together. She stopped at a backstreet shop with no name, the only place in Littlefield where you could buy a bottle of wine. It was handed over in a brown paper bag. 'Thank you,' said Juliet, as the man put the bottle on the counter. 'Thank you,' he replied as he took her money. 'Thank you,' she repeated as she took her change, 'Thank you' again as she picked up her bag, and 'Thank you' one last time as she went through the door. The man did not look as if he did not understand so much as if he did not hear. When she pulled up in the drive, she startled a skunk who sprayed the side of the car. 'And thank *you*,' Juliet shouted after it, amazed by the acrid stink and also by how cartoonish the animal had been.

The trees are bad enough, she wrote in another long letter to Carlo, *but they are full of machines, or that's what it sounds like. Punky blue and red birds that sound like dentists' drills. Crickets that rattle away all night, or are they cicadas? What's a cicada? How do you pronounce cicada? Or are they grasshoppers? There are frogs, too, like stuck gears, and what I think is a woodpecker because it sounds as if it is doing exactly that.*

'You need some sleep,' Carlo observed as he turned the page.

And I need some sleep, the letter went on. *It's too quiet and too lonely and they haven't given me that much to do. Love to All. J. PS: After I wrote this, I went out to*

a bar. I've taken up smoking again because here it's consid-
ered such a vice and the only place you can smoke in
public is the sports bar because it's across the town line.
It's noisy and packed but no one takes any notice and
anyway I met an Englishman and got drunk so feel better.
He has small feet and wears snakeskin shoes. Neat and
a bit vicious, I suspect. But a laugh – singular – Ha. A
start, no? Ha. xxx.

'She's getting drunk with strangers,' Carlo said.

'Oh dear,' Fred responded absently, 'I'd better write.'

The English stranger was called Terence Bull and while
Juliet had been walking around Littlefield with her head
down, not noticing anything, he had noticed her.

'May I sit down?' He was a small man with severely
side-parted hair. His cheeks were scraped pink by a cut-
throat razor, which he found aesthetically enticing but did
not handle well. Juliet mistook his redness for shyness.

'You're English!' She had, she thought later, as good as
flung her arms round him. 'God. Sorry. It's just I'm –'

'Bored?' He sat with elaborate awkwardness, drawn
back, legs crossed and thrown to one side, his head tilted
so that the gaze of his small round eyes suggested provo-
cation as much as scrutiny.

'Bloody bored.'

And then she wasn't because that evening, Juliet loved
America – its sincerely helpful waitresses, its plain-
speaking approach to cocktails, its tall plastic beakers of
iced water, its corn chips which tasted white, yellow and
blue, its sloppy tomato salsa, and later, its night, which
was warm and fresh and made her feel that the world
was swarming gently round her.

'Now I see the point of the trees!' Juliet did not know
that she was shouting. 'It's like the circling wagon train!'

Terence winced and a group of students they were passing sniggered. Juliet, oblivious, stopped in the road and fumbled for her point: 'It is! America, it just goes on and on, which is great of course, really great, you can keep moving and all that on the road lark –'

'Cool!' shouted one of the students and Juliet heard this time but did not catch his tone. She walked up to the boy, who looked perturbed. At least now she spoke quietly.

'Fucking cool, actually. The trees are your wagons. With them, or should I say *within* them, you draw your clearing, your circle, your frame.' She was nodding and the boy began to nod too, but Juliet was not convinced. 'You don't know yet. You're too young. In a few years though, you'll need, you'll need your own . . .' The thought that had moved swiftly and brightly through the muzz of cocktails and tobacco, jumped its tracks.

'Trees?' one of the other students suggested. Juliet stared at the pavement. Had they been talking about trees? Terence stepped forward, took her elbow between thumb and forefinger, and steered her away.

The students looked at one another.

'If we don't need our own trees, we must need our own wagons.'

'Drunk bitch. Did you smell her breath?'

'Circle or clearing?'

'Cute, though.'

A week later, the temperature dropped ten degrees overnight. Juliet felt as empty as the air, not least because she now understood that this was not a holiday, which was half about going and half about coming back; this was being away.

She had written three letters to Carlo. Her parents phoned, and her friends sent faxes and postcards. At first she was relieved that no one mentioned Jacob, then she began to think that it was because they did not take her seriously.

'You never ask about Jacob,' she said to Clara, whom she phoned each week.

'Oh. I thought that was all . . .'

'It is. I'm just surprised no one cares.'

'I suppose we thought it wasn't anything much and you were going and didn't say anything yourself, so we just left it.'

'Fine. I've left it too.'

'Good.'

'Good?'

'It wasn't a great idea.'

There was something in Clara's tone, an insistence behind the urging, that prickled Juliet: 'You don't even know him.'

'No, but I –'

'You don't know him. It was just beginning and it might have become something.'

'He's forty-three; he has a wife he still spends a fair bit of time with and they've been married for fifteen years. He got himself sacked from the university and his TV series breached so many rules, it was pulled off air. Not good.'

'How do you know all that?'

'Oh – people.'

'People?'

'I really have to go, Horace is yelling.'

'I wish you hadn't called him that.'

'I only meant that he wasn't a good idea. Now –'

'Not him. Horace. It's a ridiculous name. Your children have such silly names.'

'Why are we talking about my children's names?'

'Because we're not talking about Jacob.'

133

'We just did. Alright, Horrie darling, I'm coming!'

'Not really. I haven't told you anything.'

'That's just what I said.'

'There's a lot you don't know, Clara.'

'I'm sure there is. Are you alright?' This was a real question.

Juliet's throat ached. She was deciding to say something truthful when the line was filled with a child's yells and Clara's muffled apologies because Horace was beside himself and she really had to go.

On the last day of September, Juliet slipped on the steps outside the English Department building and when she got up, her body wouldn't straighten out. Terence took her to a doctor, who recommended an osteopath. Both were paid for by the college's medical insurance scheme.

The doctor took a full history. 'Any previous back problems, Ms Clough?' she asked.

'Not exactly,' replied Juliet. 'I have this, um, *condition*.'

'Condition?'

'Pain, heavy bleeding, that kind of thing.'

The doctor, whose formality appealed to Juliet, prompted her gently but precisely. When she had a complete picture, she asked what investigations Juliet's British doctor had arranged.

'I'm supposed to have a scan and then maybe an operation, just to have a look.'

'When?'

'Oh,' said Juliet. 'Around now. Only I'm not there, am I?' She laughed.

The doctor offered to arrange a scan.

'Can you come in on the fourth?' Two days time.

*   *   *

134

Juliet lay back in the dark and stared at her insides as they floated into view on a screen. There were shadows, clouds, plumes of white and nuggets of black. The woman doing the scan kept freezing the screen and fixing pictures in which Juliet could see nothing of obvious importance. It was all so shifting and vague, one thing obscuring the other, and none of it staying still for long enough to be made sense of.

That evening the telephone rang and when Juliet answered, no one spoke. This had happened four or five times now, and every time she had been on the verge of speaking only she understood that Jacob wanted her not to. The click she heard when he ended the call left her more bereft than his voice might have done, and so she would try to retrieve him through a remembered gesture or phrase. Scenes and conversations left her wondering if her memories were half imagined – they made so little sense.

The one she returned to most often was when he had finally come upstairs that last night at Khyber Road. He had stood in the doorway, staring in his peculiarly active way and using just a corner of his smile. For a moment Juliet thought he might be about to apologise but as she looked at him with the idea of someone unreliable and dangerous, he returned the image of a simple presence offering love. His stillness became injury and endurance as if there were no wife, as if he had always held himself out to her, as if it were she who resisted and refused, an assertion she could not argue with because once, she had meant to.

So she had asked him, straight out: 'Should I be leaving you?'

TWELVE

Merle turned up on Juliet's doorstep with a basket of fruit and a selection of warming pads, ice packs and massage devices. Juliet was managing on whiskey, painkillers and hot-water bottles, and although the osteopath had realigned her neck with one swift click, her muscles were still rigid and her back bruised.

Merle looked around the stark apartment at the neat stacks of books; no pictures, no mirrors.

'If you feel up to it, come to dinner on Saturday. It'll just be us and Terence, quite informal.'

Juliet was amazed.

On her way to the dinner, she stopped at a wholefood supermarket called The Higher Realm for a bottle of wine, thinking that Merle would appreciate something organic. She parked next to a car which had a bumper sticker reading 'Commit random acts of beauty', and scraped it on the way out.

Ratchon, whose name was actually Rogen, served a fine pouilly fumé.

'That steak looks great!' Juliet said determinedly, as Merle put a plate in front of her.

'It's tuna, actually,' said Merle and even though she spoke quite gently, Juliet was stung.

'Do Americans say "actually"?'

Terence intervened: '*Actually*, the only tuna the English eat comes out of tins. Almost everything we eat comes out of tins.'

Juliet did not like this. 'Not in my house.'

'Yes, well . . .' Terence pursed his mouth and his cheeks looked full, as if he had decided to withhold the most delectable piece of information but only so far. Juliet was overwhelmed by a longing for home – not Khyber Road, but the village of Allnorthover.

'Tell us about your family,' Rogen suggested.

'Oh do,' murmured Terence as he topped up her glass.

Juliet thought for a moment. 'My brother . . .' she began.

'Who was in a band called Vermin Death Stack and who rescued the girl who was almost drowned by Ron the loony . . .' recited Terence.

'Tom. No, the other one.'

'The boy who thought he was a puddle?'

'Not really, never mind. The thing is . . .'

Merle sighed, which made Juliet more determined to go on. People loved this story; they always laughed. She was finding it hard not to laugh just at the thought of it.

'When my brother Fred was studying for his A-levels, he used to lie outside on the lawn, revising. There were these students living in the east wing of the house, because the rest of us had left home, and they spent their time devising ways of creeping up on him.'

'The east wing,' Terence mouthed to Merle, as if transmitting a code.

Juliet noticed but ignored him. This was something she liked to remember. 'They frightened the life out of him every afternoon,' she continued, 'usually because he was half asleep, and then one day –'

'Great. Dessert, Rogen?' said Merle, meaning to rescue Juliet.

'No, wait! That's not the story. Wait . . .' Juliet settled back in her chair, swigged her wine and beamed so uncharacteristically at her audience that they submitted.

'One afternoon Fred was lying out there when he heard the French windows open,' – another look passed between Terence and Merle – 'and the crunch-crunch-crunch of someone crossing the gravel path. OK? So he's lying there pretending to be asleep, listening to Radio One on his transistor –'

'Transistor?' queried Rogen.

'Little radio,' Juliet pushed on. 'So there he was, crunch-crunch-crunch, and just as the footsteps got closer, and whoever it was got nearer, Fred shot in the air and roared,' at this point Juliet began a spluttered laughter which made it hard for her to continue, 'he roared "Got you this time, you bastard!" Only . . . it wasn't one of the students, it was our 80-year-old gardener!'

'Gardener,' Terence pointed out.

Juliet slumped. 'Yes, gardener. So?'

'Well, it's all a bit,' he ground out his cigarette, 'middle class.'

'Of course it is. That's *what we are.*'

'Dessert? Rogen?' urged Merle.

'Just a minute, I like this story,' Rogen said. 'And by the way, we are not children. We have some grasp of nuance and irony, also sarcasm, and we do know something of your country.'

'Sorry,' said Terence. 'It's one of the joys of being elsewhere: insisting on type, one's own as well as other people's.'

Rogen fetched dessert and Merle fell into conversation with Terence. Eventually, Juliet took a breath and said, 'I haven't finished the story.' Rogen nodded but neither Merle nor Terence seemed to have heard her.

'You see Fred was so embarrassed,' she began in a quick monotone, 'that he looked round for something to blame his outburst on and there was his radio, so he began, you know, smacking it, the radio, you see, and saying, as if the gardener weren't even there, "You bastard radio! Why can't you stay tuned, you bastard!"' Her voice was getting higher and louder, 'And the gardener, he just, he just, wandered on and began weeding the artichokes or whatever, as if nothing had been said.' Who was she talking to?

'Coffee,' Merle stated as she rose from her chair.

Rogen was smiling at Juliet. 'What an extraordinary family,' he said. His true warmth caught Juliet out and she blurted: 'They are. They really are!' and in order to stop her bursting into tears, Rogen suggested that she tell them about her other brother.

'Tobias?' she wondered.

'Let me help you out,' said Terence, who was feeling a little ashamed. 'Your elder brother, bass player in Vermin Death Stack, despatch rider, architect, baby girl who punches everyone and a girlfriend called Mary who walks on water and who was nearly drowned by the village madman. Didn't she jump through a window or something to escape a fire?'

'Yes.'

'Did I miss anything out?'

'Yes.'

'What? I thought I'd got your family off pat.'

'Perhaps he made a fortune and lost it all,' suggested Rogen.

'No that's Fred,' said Juliet.

'Perhaps he's a brilliant artist with an attic full of paintings, waiting to be discovered,' said Merle, warming up.

'That's Clara,' put in Terence.

They waited.

'There was a bomb. They closed down the east side of the city.'

Rogen shook his head. 'Why don't people just leave?'

Juliet thought about this. 'You think you would, but you wouldn't. In London, if something happens a mile away it doesn't feel close; there's so much in-between and it takes so long to get there.'

'And where would you go?' put in Terence. 'The country is so small, you can never really get away which is why we come here, where you can go on getting away without ever leaving home.'

Bad things must happen in Littlefield, Juliet had decided, only people didn't talk about them. Instead, the gossip was of scandal and tragedy that might have occurred in the next county or in Malibu or Nebraska – places equally firmly outside the town line. Her colleagues spoke of Venice or Cambridge with more familiarity.

'My brother Tobias was out on his motorbike. When there was that bomb.'

'You mean he was killed?' said Terence, too astonished to stop himself.

'Yes.'

'The bomb?' said Merle.

Now she had their full attention: 'Yes.'

Mary George was also thinking about Tobias. It was months since he had been killed and while she felt empty, she did not feel lonely. It was enough that each morning Bella was there, pushing her sticky face against Mary's and muttering endearments. When Mary felt the loss of Tobias it was as an absence of substance and at such times, Bella's emphatic physicality rescued her. The child was there to be washed and dressed, fed and held; she was all the presence, all the contact, Mary needed.

She ate and slept according to Bella; dropped her at nursery, went to the bookshop, collected her and came home again. Other than when she sang, Mary remained within her part of the city, a knot of railways and streets that was neither central nor suburban, and which contained enough to balance its changes. If a corner shop closed down, a supermarket opened. If one road was pedestrianised, a bus lane was built elsewhere. There might not be anywhere left to get your shoes mended but there was a new café, which would pass through several owners and names before closing down again.

For Mary, life on the Hugh Carmodie Trust Estate was an undemanding existence because neither she nor Bella belonged. She felt safe because she knew the people around her, and they would not want to know her better. She thought she understood the fights and the deals, but she was a foreigner and had little idea of the meaning of what she saw or heard said. Once, three young men moved into the flat above and introduced themselves to Mary as students. She passed on this piece of information to her neighbour, who scoffed, 'Students? We heard that. They're police. Look at their shoes.' Mary had scurried back to Tobias, where she could allow herself to be thrilled. Sometimes she and Tobias had a long talk about whether or not to dial 999 and once or twice, they did.

Children who went to Bella's nursery began to knock on the door and ask if she could come out to play. There was usually someone's older sister, of maybe eight or nine, with the group, but even so Mary was fearful. Once, she let them take Bella because she didn't want to appear a snob, but then followed them and the next time, ashamed of having made a decision about her daughter's safety based on what people might think of her, she would refuse.

She knew the other women would think less of her for being indecisive than they would had she just said no.

For now this was alright but soon, it would not be. And something else was wrong, with her, which she tried to solve by taking Bella to Allnorthover. She wanted to speak to Tobias's father.

Mary sat opposite Dr Clough in his study and tried to begin.

'It happens when I go through doorways and sometimes when I turn corners. I know that I'm about to walk into glass and my body stops. It's such a shock. It would be alright, I mean it's just a moment's hesitation but the shock is such a . . . well, such a shock.'

Mary smiled at her own awkwardness, while Dr Clough did not. He leaned back in his narrow chair and regarded his empty desk. Mary looked around. She had been coming to the Clock House for fourteen years and had lived there the first winter after Bella was born when she and Tobias had still been on the housing-trust waiting list, but could not remember having been in this room. Once, her friend Billy had stayed there after a party and the house had been so full that he had slept on the doctor's examining couch and dreamt that he told the doctor all his secrets.

What struck Mary now was how coherent and well-kept this room was compared to the rest of the house. It was small, with one low window draped with mustard velvet curtains. The wallpaper was a fibrous apricot design which gave the impression of an ancient arbour. She was surprised by the antiquated medical instruments: the paediatric scales with their wicker basket, the ceramic and glass pharmaceutical bottles like the ones in which the doctor's wife kept her oil and vinegar in the kitchen, the leather apothecary's case left open to show a selection of squat, mysterious jars. She had not thought of the doctor as a romantic man.

'Walking into glass.' He said it so plainly.

'Not into, through.'

'Through?'

'Through, like the window.'

The doctor looked blank. Was he pretending not to remember? Did she have to say? He looked ill among the warmth and polish of the room. It smelt of pipe tobacco, no, not so rounded, more like ash.

When Mary was seventeen, there had been a fire. She had jumped through a window, landed in snow and had been found by Tobias.

Dr Clough said nothing, which Mary understood to be the way patients were encouraged to speak, so she continued. 'It's not as if I think it's going to smash. It's a feeling of being caught, of being stopped but not like when I did do it because then I ran and jumped and was mid-air when the glass caught me, and the extraordinary thing was that it curved and held me, it billowed, and there was a moment of being still and held . . .'

The doctor looked so steeply down that Mary could not see his face.

'Only it's not like that now. It's not a feeling of being held but of walking smack into glass that will not give. I'm being stopped.'

The doctor leaned back in his chair. The afternoon darkened. Mary was surprised by the sense she was making of herself.

'The problem is that I'm frightened again.' As she said it, she felt it, a fear so pressurised that to allow it would be to permit the end of everything. 'Tobias made me safe and now . . .'

'That wasn't his job.' The doctor's voice was a dry variation on his son's.

'No, of course not, it's just that –'

'You are a grown-up, a mother.'

'Yes, I know, only –'

'We are each of us our own –'

'I didn't mean . . . it's just the glass . . . the shock.'

'Tobias didn't help you jump through the window.'

'No.' He had found her in the snow, and had lain down and held her.

The doctor switched on a desk lamp and leaned forward into the light so that the surface of his face was rendered in extremes. Mary looked. She had never given him much thought.

'I feel alone,' she managed to say, and the doctor smiled a kind of welcome.

Since Caroline had gone to Hong Kong, Fred had volunteered to babysit when Mary sang. She would put Bella to bed, make him supper and then change into her long black dress and apricot-coloured sandals, and set off for The Glory Hole. On this particular night Bella had woken and had just gone back to sleep on Fred's lap. Mary was about to leave when she stopped and sat down beside them.

'I don't know if I can face it,' she said, running her hand up and down Bella's back while looking around the room as if for some excuse to stay. 'I don't feel like singing at all any more.'

'Sing something else, for once,' said Fred in a peculiarly tight voice.

'Like what?' She looked at him and he looked at Bella.

'I don't know anything. You can sing anything.'

That night she looked out from the stage into the dimness of the room and saw Clara Clough.

Foolish things . . .
Foggy dream . . .
all the time . . .
far away . . .

It never seemed to occur to her audience that she could see them, or that she got a strong sense of their collective mood. This was what directed her performance and that night, something got stuck. She started and stopped and looked again.

You said you,
every time you say,
you say you,
but not for . . .

Mary had not recognised Clara at first. She noticed a flow of green velvet, the flossy sparkle of her hair, the presence of angles and curves that commanded the light, defined all the more by the fact that the man sitting beside her was dressed in black.

She and Clara had been friends since the Cloughs moved to Allnorthover. Clara had compelled everyone with her wicked face, her overt body and magical hair. Her impatient loyalty had helped Mary grow up. At seventeen and nineteen, they shared their most adventurous and fragile years, and while no one was surprised when Mary settled down with Tobias, they were amazed that after art school, Clara had returned to the country, married a Swiss banker and had three children. 'It's not what artists are supposed to do,' Mary had wondered but Tobias explained: 'He's taken her to live under the sky she likes to paint best.'

These days, Clara and Mary met only in kitchens or around tables. They used to talk about sex and death; now they talked about food and sleep.

Love too easily,
fall, far away . . .

When Clara and Jacob met at Clapham Junction on their way to Juliet's party, it had been a coincidence, and when a city as big as London throws you up against someone you know, it is too unlikely a possibility to ignore. You may choose to walk past one another, each pretending not to have noticed the other, in which case you will have troubled thoughts for the rest of the day. Or you might make something of it, which they cheerfully did.

The next time they met, Jacob arrived by appointment at Clara's new studio. They talked all afternoon and when it grew dark they continued to talk as they left the building, got in a cab and arrived in Soho looking for something to eat. They found an empty restaurant where they sat at a bleached oak table and ate salads of sour green leaves and semi-dried vegetables, grilled goat's cheese and snappy biscuits burnt with parmesan. It all tasted the same, piquant.

Clara was staying with Carlo, so had no train to catch. It was eleven o'clock and Jacob was suggesting another drink, but where? There was The Glory Hole just round the corner, and it was a Tuesday so Mary would be singing, and to go in there, to choose to be seen by her, would make safe this dangerous night, and so Clara said Yes, why not? She would say goodnight to Jacob soon, and she would see him tomorrow.

Carlo was lying in the bath when the telephone rang. He hurried to answer it:

'Hi!' he sang.

'Hello,' said Fred.

'Oh.'

'Who did you think it was?'

Jonathan Mehta. The man who left this bruise on my throat. The reason why my lips are so swollen and dry, why my groin aches and my cheeks sting.

'Fred, it's one o'clock.'

'I know. The thing is –'

'What?' Carlo managed, faintly. Jonathan had taken him dancing in a place where everything was dazzling and delicious. He had smelt and touched Jonathan's skin. He had watched a bead of sweat trickle down his forehead and had traced its path with his tongue. At midnight, Carlo had said he had to go, he had an early start, and it had been lovely but no, he really had to get some sleep. It had been a perfect evening.

'I don't know what to do!' Fred was whispering.

'What?'

'I can't speak louder, I might wake Bella.'

'Is something wrong with Bella?'

For a moment, the music stopped.

'No, she's fine. The thing is Mary . . .'

'Is she ill?'

'No, the thing is . . .'

Carlo could hear his brother breathing and concentrated.

Fred blurted: 'I think she's in love with me.'

Carlo began to giggle. 'What makes you think that?'

'She touched me.'

This was hilarious. 'Improperly?'

'She ran her hand up and down my thigh.'

Carlo roared and in the midst of his laughter, recalled Jonathan's touch and wondered why we didn't all go round stroking each other's thighs, it felt so good.

Fred struggled on. He needed to make sense of this. 'Bella was asleep on my knee. Mary sat down beside us.

She wouldn't look at me of course, too shy. Except she did say she didn't want to go, to leave me that is, and then she just ran her hand –'

'Up and down your thigh!' boomed Carlo. 'Lucky boy!'

'Lucky?'

'Didn't it feel good?'

'Yes, but –'

'Then what's the problem?'

Fred could not think what the problem was.

THIRTEEN

After the dinner, Merle and Rogen retreated. Rogen was on sabbatical from somewhere in Missouri and in the past six months they had spent more time together than they had in the eight years of their marriage, but Juliet had not asked and did not know, and so felt set aside. Her friendship with Terence Bull had hardened into Wednesday nights at the sports bar, and she found herself wondering who else there might be for her in this place.

She thought of her neighbour, Buckie Buckingham, a semi-retired classics professor. Her apartment sat over the garage adjoining his house. Parked below was a huge old car built on distinctly American lines; it looked like a cross between an ocean liner and a barn. She assumed that the car belonged to Buckie but never saw anyone use it. She rarely saw him – a lanky, flabby man with fat white curls, given to wearing an improperly loose silk dressing-gown – although she heard him singing: arias and *lieder* and what she imagined were songs from his varsity days, full of whoops and slang.

Buckie warbled on as she idled over the *Littlefield Fencepost* in which the week's entire police activity was reported on the back page: mother raccoon and cubs escorted from dumpster back to woods; officer called out to investigate a complaint about the smell of coffee. The only things that suggested the town made any mischief at all were the personal ads – caringly worded requests from married couples in search of a third person. Juliet thought of Merle and Rogen, and then Buckie. She turned the page.

It seemed that Littlefield offered no further possibilities. Everyone who might come close moved firmly past. Juliet was established in her isolation and found the circuit of routine more bearable than talking herself into going out and trying to discover any more society or entertainment. Besides which, the place had come into a kind of life. One day, walking across the common, Juliet noticed that where the morning sun fell on a beech tree, the leaves had turned yellow – precisely so, the yellow cutting a line across the leaves regardless. This interested her and so she looked up and around and noticed, elsewhere, the imprint of light: one curve of a pale broad maple flushed at the tips, a swathe of orange across dark green, the gradual encroachment of red on brown, no, more than that, crimson on bronze. Apricot, peach, citron, rose, olive, cream, chestnut: the colours of the leaves that she brought home demanded such comparisons. Using the names of pigments was cheating, she thought. No burnt sienna, umber or ochre. They had to be things, things from the world she missed; they had to taste of something.

She phoned Carlo: 'I'm collecting dead leaves.' She could hardly hear him.

'People go there in order to do that, but forget leaves, that bloody woman's resigned. The revolution has come!'

'What? Listen. They're like the first photographs. Some of those were of leaves, weren't they? What I mean is they fix the passing light, only here, now, it's all happening in nature and in technicolor.'

150

'I'm sorry?'

'Maybe I'll get a bit of work done after all.'

'What?'

Juliet laughed. She was so far away. She wrote another list of colours and slid it into a file. She pulled out a piece of paper and wrote 'I must not invest.' She remembered something from somewhere: 'Look at the leaf or the wood but never the tree.' Who said that? It was a notion of visual discipline that pleased her more than whatever it might mean.

Jacob rang, as he usually did, late at night. Juliet smiled into the receiver and settled back to weigh the silence when she heard a noise on the line, not a noise, a quiet high cry which formed itself into a voice and said, 'I forgive you.'

Juliet said nothing as the voice went on gathering strength: 'You were not to know, you don't, you can't, I forgive you.' It sounded like an old recording – scripted, over-used and obsolete.

Someone called Juliet from the doctor's office to ask her to come in to discuss the results of her scan but she said that as her back hurt so much, could they please wait. The doctor herself called that afternoon. The next day she showed Juliet some cluttered monochrome images, and tried to explain.

The doctor's view was that she should have the investigative operation: three small incisions, a tiny camera; she could be in and out in a day. They would do nothing more, just find out exactly what was going on. It was what Juliet had wanted for almost a year, since the pain and bleeding had got so much worse, and so she said yes, please, as soon as possible. Everything here happened so quickly, which was good of course. It left her no time to think but that was good, too.

She returned to the hospital for one more conversation and again one morning for what she described to Terence as 'a little camerawork'. He collected her at the end of the day and took her home to bed. Two days later, he took her back to hear the results. This time, they showed her colour photographs. The doctor talked about displacement, cyclical growth, flow and adhesion but all Juliet could see was that everything looked raw yellow, brown and red, twisted and stuck together.

'It looks like an incredible mess,' said Juliet.

'The damage is fairly extensive. It's evidently been developing for some time.'

'What now?'

'We can do a great deal with surgery and lasers these days but I think in your case we should begin with a course of hormones which will suspend your cycle for a while. That way, the growths ought to reduce and we will be able to remove them more easily.'

Terence had to rely on Juliet's rather abstracted explanation: 'It's all to do with displacement. Cells migrating . . . They must burrow or something . . . anyway, they stick to everything else and they grow and bleed like they would normally only they're trapped. I'm full of old blood.'

'You look exhausted. What will they do next?'

'There's more. Other growths, which looked like bubbles and fingers.'

'Can you be a bit more technical?'

'You want names? Do you know, I can't remember.' She was lying, and he let her.

'What will they do?'

152

'Slash and burn, eventually. For now, I have some little white pills which should calm it all down.'

That night, Juliet lay with her hands on her belly and remembered Jacob's touch. At dawn, she got up and realising that she had never known the number for his room at the Shipping Office, she dialled her old office number next door and listened beyond the ringing for someone asleep on the other side of the wall to be woken by this after-hours noise, and to read its signal.

As the last leaves fell and fizzled out, Juliet decided to explore further. She headed out on the main road and then turned off along a dirt track, her headlights sweeping the wreckage of the recent maize harvest, the smashed stalks and husks and in an otherwise bare field, a cluster of pumpkins swelling out of the black earth. A week later the town was lined with jack-o'-lanterns, whose grins were as wide and inscrutable as those of Juliet's colleagues. Overgrown children banged on the door and flatly stated 'Trick or treat'. Juliet gave the first few some dried fruit, which they dropped on the stairs. After a while, she answered the door holding an axe she had found behind the stove and said, 'Go on, my dears. Trick away!'

She was woken at dawn by someone screaming and pulled up the blind to see an owl on a branch a foot or so from her window, surrounded by a mob of crows. It was they who were making the noise. The owl blinked and shook its head as if unable to believe what was happening. Juliet ran outside and shouted at the crows but only succeeded in driving them into another tree, along with the exhausted owl.

'You cruel bastards!' she screamed at the crows. 'You don't even mean it!' and wheeled round to find Merle Dix slipping out of Buckie Buckingham's front door. The old man was behind her, doing up his horrible gown. Juliet turned back to the owl to make sure they knew she was yelling at the birds and not them. 'Get out of here, dimwit, save your stupid self!' Worse and worse. She turned and said as nonchalantly as she could, 'I'm only trying to help.'

This episode did not upset Juliet. The small white pill she took each morning was having magical effects. Her body grew silent and steady; she waited for the pain and the bleeding, and when they did not come, she relaxed. She stopped clenching her jaw, flexing her toes and packing her fingers into fists. She looked at things and made notes, and watched the town of Littlefield continue to happen around her.

Americans have a lot of weather, Juliet wrote to her mother, *but they just move it out the way. All those leaves were blasted with some kind of giant hoover – blown into big piles and then sucked up.* After the leaves were gone, there was darkness and by late November, four feet of snow. *They move the snow too. Ploughs lit up like ships come grinding along, putting back all the streets and drives.*

The snow began one afternoon as Juliet sat at her table drinking tea and fighting sleep. She watched it muffle a cedar tree, by which time the surrounding pines were choked. She felt all the excitement of an English child, to whom there is no such thing as too much snow, until she found that until the plough had been through, she couldn't get anywhere.

Her car was buried, and the surface of the snow thawed and refroze as a layer of ice. To walk was to break glass with every step, so effortful and noisy that Juliet did not want to be seen trying to do it. Every night, more snow fell and every morning the plough came by. She sat in her window and noted how the Americans went about their day, undeterred and properly equipped with snow boots and snow suits, with snow-chains on their tyres, on skis and ski-mobiles. They used sharp spades to cut away slabs of ice from their paths and steps. Everyone cleared the space in front of their house. They knew what was expected of them and how far to go.

There were two more weeks of teaching left. Juliet and Terence drove out of town to see the illuminated Father Christmases, reindeer and madonnas which loomed over small houses that looked as if they were made of cardboard rather than clapboard. Some appeared to have capsized under the joint weight of snow and fairylights.

'So there's life in the place after all,' Juliet said to Terence as they pulled up at the sports bar.

'Oh no, that isn't part of Littlefield proper.'

'So what does a Littlefield Christmas consist of then?'

'God knows, I leave the day after I've finished grading papers.'

'You go home?'

'You thought Littlefield was my home?'

'No, but you never talk about anyone in England.'

'I'm not going there. Leigh's back from six months in Sydney and we're meeting in New York.'

'Leigh?'

Juliet realised that she could not assume what gender this lover might be, and that the idea of Terence as a sexual being surprised her. She had emulated his self-sufficiency and now felt cheated.

In a small dense English wood, Jacob walked ahead of his mother and his wife. He had pushed Monica's wheel-chair along the bumpy path and now that they had turned back towards the car park and the thin pink sun was going down, he let Barbara push instead and hurried on.

Almost immediately, he realised he was an indecent distance ahead and stopped to wait. He watched them catch up: his sharp-edged mother, folded and swathed, and Barbara, always so vivid, always such momentum, skimming the wheelchair over oak roots and clots of dead leaves, pointing and talking and being so insistently present and alive ... They were almost on him now, looming, tugging, and so he swung away, he couldn't help it, at first just in his head and when that didn't work – Juliet, why could he not reach Juliet? – he strode off into the dark light of the afternoon, and his wife and mother watched him go, knowing it was dark and wondering how it was that they could still see him.

Juliet threw her pressed leaves away and sat at her window looking through the branches at the white ground, the white hills and the white clouds in the white sky. While the plough still passed each day, it only skimmed the top layer of slush and sprinkled grit on the compacted ice beneath. There were no more paths or driveways, just contours and outlines filled in with gritty shadows. She was glad of the trees now that she could see through them, glad too of her antique radiators which had woken one morning, hissing and rumbling like elderly snakes emerging from hibernation.

For her students, Thanksgiving seemed to have signalled that work was over for the year. They had returned half-heartedly, making no excuse for not having read the texts she set.

'Let's start at the beginning. There is a central image and there is a frame. Right?'

One of them took the trouble to nod.

'It's like ... it's like this town. If Littlefield disappeared in a puff of smoke –'

'You mean, like, if they nuked us?' The nodding student looked interested.

'Whatever,' said Juliet. 'So, there's no town, but there is a clearing in the forest. The frame remains. The trees.'

'You make frames out of trees, right?'

'This is the conceptual frame, not the literal one,' said one of the bright students, a Hawaiian girl on a rowing scholarship who would contribute more were it not for the fact that even now that the Connecticut River was half-frozen, she had to train at dawn every day. 'It's what happened post-Iconoclasm in the Low Countries – you couldn't paint the Madonna any more, so you painted her flowers.'

Juliet waited for the girl to continue but she had had no breakfast and her fingers were faintly blue.

Juliet took over: 'That's right. The subject has been removed, so the space is there to be filled. The artist invests the framing devices with the meaning of the subject. So instead of the Madonna, we have the first flower paintings.'

'What's that got to do with nuking Littlefield?' someone else said.

In teaching people not much younger than herself, Juliet had become aware of how discouraging she could be. She was trying to develop patience and tact. She thought for a moment and then said, 'If I showed you a picture of all the trees around this town, but with the town removed, what would the trees suggest to you?'

'Picture frames?'

'Yes and no.'

'Yes and no?'

'Do you mean a frame or a framing device?' queried the rower.

'Glue and nails and stuff?'

Juliet lost patience. 'If the frame moves into the centre

157

of the picture then we impose another frame. We insist, in that way, on a clearing, even if we do not, so to speak, chop down the trees. We don't want to see further, we need to have a sense of limitation, for our own safety, instead of boundless implication . . . we need to believe that what we do only travels so far . . . OK, Tommy,' she said to the sleepy boy, 'you know how hard it is to drive in this weather?' He nodded. 'So you have to stay here, only the town has been blanked out by the snow. The town is gone and I, I mean you, are stuck here. How do you feel about that?'

Tommy was flattered to be singled out like this. 'It's totally . . . but you know, what can you do?'

'I kind of like it,' said the quietest girl. 'You have to think hard about if you really want to do something or not, because it's going to be this really big effort, so mostly you don't. It's really quiet and if you do get out there, there's nothing and no one, only sometimes you meet someone you know and that's all of a sudden a big deal. And you can feel the town still happening, even though you can't see it.'

Juliet decided that she liked them after all, so much so that two weeks later, after the last class, she was hurt by their perfunctory farewells. They had three weeks off and were heading home, as was she, only by now she had invested something in them and thought she might miss them, and took a while to remember that they were only nineteen, an age at which it seems natural and effortless to keep up with life.

She was astonished to find that Christmas was a one-day holiday here and that there was no Boxing Day, and began to think of her family traditions with new-found sentiment. 'We still get stockings,' she boasted to Terence.

'Old socks? We always got pillowcases. What can you fit in an old sock?'

'There's a tangerine, a pound and some nuts in the foot, then there has to be chocolate money and after that, anything.'

'Anything quaint or educational. You are twenty-nine, Juliet, and you sound as if it would be a catastrophe if your stocking were not there on Christmas morning.'

Juliet had been drinking White Russians and the combination of sweetness and alcohol was making her tetchy and sentimental. 'What did you get in your pillowcase then?'

'Televisions, that kind of thing. I bet you didn't even have a television.'

'Yes we did, eventually.'

'Black and white?'

'So? We didn't watch it on Christmas Day, though.'

'Especially not the Queen's Speech. You were too busy making egg-nog and singing carols.'

'We did sing carols, it's true. We do. I love carols.'

'That's your last White Russian.'

'Don't you love carols?'

'Come on, I'll walk you home.'

The next morning, Juliet lay in bed feeling sick. She would be back in Littlefield in the New Year and so this trip to London had to be treated as a visit, not a return. Perhaps it was in order to start thinking of Littlefield as home that she decided to have a Christmas drinks party. She would invite whoever was left in town of her colleagues and students. It was the sort of thing her mother did.

What about the following evening? Juliet had never issued any kind of formal invitation and it did not occur to her that people might require notice. Feeling munificent, she designed an invitation and put one in every departmental box. ('Leave your essays in my pigeonhole,' she had instructed her students during the first week. 'Pigeonhole?' 'We'll be discussing that text in a fortnight's time.' 'Fortnight?') She even put an invitation through Buckie Buckingham's letterbox. Recently he had been singing carols: 'Silent Night' in pedantically enunciated German.

The department secretary, the only person to send Juliet a Christmas card, was kind enough to explain that most of her colleagues had packed up and gone the day they finished marking papers. Terence had been offered a lift to New York and so left earlier than planned. Merle and Rogen were visiting friends in Trieste.

Juliet drove to The Higher Realm and bought whatever she could find that approximated the filling of mince pies. In Publix, she bought frozen pastry and cheap red wine, which she planned to mull. She phoned her mother to ask about mull.

By mid-afternoon, she had baked a tray of mince pies which looked convincing enough, and the wine was in a pan with whatever she could find of the fruit and spices her mother recommended. When she returned from her third shopping trip, the garage was empty and, tired of having to dig out her car and then persuade it to start, she drove right in. Buckie must have left town like everyone else, she thought, imagining a faux-baronial pile in the Connecticut countryside, plenty of egg-nog and no television.

Snow began to fall, as it did every afternoon, wiping out all trace of activity – footsteps, paw prints, the tracks of tyres, sledges and skiis. The guidelines drawn by the plough's grit sank and disappeared. Juliet put on a tape of carols that she had seen by the checkout in Publix. She had asked people to come at seven and by six thirty had laid out twenty green plastic cups and red paper napkins, played the tape three times right through and had eaten two mince pies.

She watched (when was she not watching?) the snow flicker and accumulate in the dark, considering the town and what it was to be outside it and at the same time outside yourself, because that was what it felt like not to be in London or with her family – or Jacob. I miss him, she admitted, and then, I miss Jacob even more than I miss Tobias. Or do I miss Jacob because I can't bear to miss Tobias? The two impulses collided with each other, leaving Juliet troubled by a feeling she had begun to interpret as love.

She drank four glasses of the mulled wine, skimming off the powdery scum of ground cinnamon and cloves with a finger. At ten o'clock, a car turned into the drive and skidded up to the house. The beams of its lights were so powerful that she could not see whose it was. She moved away from the window and tried to arrange the place to look as if several guests had just left – crumpling napkins, taking a bite out of several mince pies and swilling wine around the bottoms of half a dozen glasses. There was a loud single rap on the door.

'Buckie!' she yelled as she opened it, intent on not sounding disappointed. He was wearing a powerful looking coat edged in snow. 'You've just missed everyone but never mind. Come on in!' She thrust a glass of wine into one of his hands and a mince pie into the other.

'Your car,' he began, shaking although perhaps not because of the cold.

'My car? You look frozen! Come in, come in.'

He shook his head and stepped back.

'Your car . . .' He knelt and put the glass and pie on her doorstep. He stood and raised his hand, pointing a long juddering finger at Juliet. 'Is in the *garage*.'

'Is it alright?' Juliet didn't understand.

'Move it', Buckie said without expression. No *Please
. . .* , no *Would you mind?*, not even *For Chrissakes move
the goddamn thing!* but 'Move it.' Just about the most
lifeless and graceless thing that Juliet had ever heard.

'Move it?' She heard the rise in her voice and knew
that she was beginning to sound like them, and perhaps
this prompted something.

Buckie pulled himself up further. (He looked sapped
and rigid and something like a tree god, thought Juliet,
another bloody tree.) He pointed at her again. 'I have
seniority in the *garage.*'

There was a pause, during which Juliet ran out of something. 'My brother is dead.'

'Pardon me? Your car?'

'Sure!' she said with a smile. 'I'll just get my axe.'

The raised finger drooped. 'You mean your keys.'

'No,' said Juliet, sounding more herself than she had
in months, 'I mean my axe.'

FOURTEEN

As the train from the airport wandered into Victoria Station, Juliet's impression of London after five months away was of a collapse of light. Her eyes had grown used to the primary-blue skies of Littlefield and the town's clean-cut brightness and shade. It was nine in the morning, midwinter, and the unseen sun was beginning to dilute the grey. At this time of year, the movement between London night and London day was more like a prevarication than any clear shift. Perhaps this was why people tended to look as if they were walking away from rather than towards something. They lived in a city built in a basin, which might encourage them to conduct themselves as if the accountable surface of the world skimmed past overhead.

Juliet's hearing had also retuned itself, to the elastic, shallow, percolating Massachusetts accent. As the bus conductor chided his passengers, 'Moovahlong!', 'Nah standin' on top', 'Chain ja fivah? Yergotter be avin' me awn!', she heard him as an American might, the cockney of the Ealing comedy, his voice somewhere between a cough and a jeer.

The bus swung out of the station and into the one-way

system heading west. An hour later, Juliet arrived at Khyber Road. A rag-and-bone man with a large television on his cart was disappearing round the corner and a woman inched past, barefoot, impervious, her hands reaching out in beseechment. Juliet, accustomed to Littlefield's steadfast courtesy, almost said 'Hi, how are you.'

Walking into the hallway, Juliet experienced a further sense of contraction. In Littlefield she had large rooms, all those windows and solid walls. Khyber Road looked as if it was built of dust held together by damp. She did not remember it being so derelict.

Juliet had been vague about her return and her family, who refused to be provoked, had not tried to pin her down. 'Tuesday-ish,' she had told Fred, who decided that this meant Monday afternoon or Wednesday morning. It turned out to mean Monday morning. Juliet went through to the kitchen. Her first impression was that it looked completely different and then she realised that everything was the same only arranged differently: cups top down and in rows, jars out of place by inches. The jug of cutlery that stood on the windowsill had been put on a high shelf and in the drawer, tea cloths had been folded into rectangles. There were three dirty plates in the sink, traces of butter, crumbs and yoghurt, a bowl and a child's beaker. The kettle was warm and the tiled wall behind it still veiled in condensation. Were they hiding from her? Who were they? Fred hadn't said anything about people coming to stay. In the living room, a rug had been thrown over the sofa, a living pot plant had replaced the dead one and the blind had been left up rather than down.

She found a bag open on her bed. In it, she could see a teddy bear with a head almost empty of stuffing, a heap of cassettes and a glasses case. In Fred's room, she caught the heel of her shoe on something voluminous, slippery

164

and pastel – she didn't want to look too closely. Fred had nailed more plastic over the windows and there was a paraffin heater in each room. Juliet adjusted her breathing, making it level and shallow.

'I need this Christmas, I really do,' Juliet said to Carlo as she filled hot-water bottles. 'This house is never dry or warm, and it's got rather full.'

'You can't mind about Mary and Bella,' said Carlo. He settled himself in an armchair and tucked in a quilt. There was coal in the grate and a thread of white smoke.

'Why not? They were in my room.'

'You don't live here any more.'

'Don't I?'

'They only stay over when Mary's singing. It's no big deal.'

'She's not singing tonight.'

'No but it's the holidays. Are they supposed to sit alone in that flat?'

'Fred doesn't need them. He's got Caroline.'

'Let Fred be happy. He thought he'd never see her again.'

'I've been back for three days and she's been here every night. She's married, which is bad enough but then she goes and tries to make things nice. I found some dried flowers hanging on the kitchen wall yesterday, and a spice rack and a butter dish. The place is a freezing slum and now we've got a butter dish. I can't wait to go home.'

'Back to Littlefield?'

'No, Allnorthover: the pub on Christmas Eve, midnight mass, stockings in the morning, board games in the afternoon, and no fucking butter dish.'

'Not this year.' Carlo looked embarrassed.

'What do you mean? Has Ma gone and got a butter dish?'

'She's going away, on a retreat.'

'On her own? But that's selfish!'

'She's still not allowed a week off?'

'It's not that I mind that much.' Juliet was feeling ridiculously upset. 'It's Christmas and there's Dad and Mary and Bella, they will really need her this year. There's you . . .'

'I'm going away too.'

'You can't.'

'To Thailand with Jonathan Mehta.'

'Who the fuck is Jonathan Mehta?'

Carlo did not respond.

'This is the first Christmas without Tobias, you know.'

His face hardened. 'Yes I know. We all know. So if our mother can't face laying on Christmas, let her escape it and if our father wants to go somewhere where there is no Christmas –'

'No Christmas?'

'He's going to Cairo, to stay with Aunt Virginia. It's been a horrible autumn for everyone. So why shouldn't Mary come and stay, and why shouldn't Fred have Caroline?'

'Because she doesn't mean it. Can't you tell?'

'She makes herself clear and after that it's up to him. Anyway, there's a complication. It appears that little Mary may be making a play for Fred . . .' and Carlo told her the story of the night when Fred babysat and Mary stroked his thigh, only he forgot to mention that Bella had been on Fred's knee, and he may have embellished it a little.

Juliet was struck by something. 'Christmas might not be so dull after all if she and Caroline do battle . . .'

'Caroline's off to her parents' tomorrow.'

'And what about our parents? Have I really got to start worrying about them as well as the rest of you?'

'You mean you don't already?'

Juliet looked away and Carlo studied her. There was something different about her, something and nothing: small changes of shape and texture which might be due to one of those accelerations of age or some other chemical shift, natural and inevitable, or not. He pulled an arm out from under the quilt and pulled her towards him.

'Of course,' he said, 'we might as well argue that because we all lost him, we are the last people to look after one another.' It had just occurred to him: 'We need others.'

'Even so, we are our own trees, aren't we?' mumbled Juliet as she fell asleep because it was only just dawn in Littlefield, 'And once we're gone, there can't be any clearing . . .'

'Talking of trees,' said Carlo, 'I'm going to stick one of the kitchen chairs on this fire.'

On Christmas Eve, Juliet went back to Allnorthover with Fred, Mary and Bella. Clara picked them up at the station. They were already outside on the pavement and, not expecting to see them there, Clara glimpsed them as strangers. They looked like minor characters in a family portrait: Juliet, the crop-headed second son, turning away; Fred, the unlikely late arrival, sporting ringlets and trailing the sleeves and hems of a grown-up's clothes; and Mary bending over the push-chair, her face hidden, her back resisting, who was she in this tableau? By the next evening, when Clara retreated to the roof – furious and shaken – she had decided who Mary was: the chatelaine, the keeper of the fucking keys.

As they drove the three miles between Ingfield and

Allnorthover, Juliet complained. 'Now I know what it's like to live with a decent amount of light. The snow is dazzling, and there it looks like Christmas only no one can really be bothered while here, well look ... No wonder we all ran off to London and began guzzling whatever we could.'

'I live here, remember?' Clara said.

'Your place is different. You always have light.'

Clara looked pleased. 'Yes. My light.'

'It doesn't belong to you –' Juliet began but was stopped by Fred who was sitting in the back and who leaned forward to gather the blaze of Clara's hair in both hands.

'No, it *comes* from you, Clarissima,' he said, twisting a strand through his fingers as he remembered a childhood game, 'and I am going to uncurl your hair and get it.'

'I'm curly too,' said Juliet, surprising the others with her plaintiveness.

Fred ran his free hand over her head.

Clara dropped them off at the Clock House, where they stood uncertainly in the hall as if waiting for something to rush towards them igniting the atmosphere and restoring a world that was its own machine.

'This is the wrong house,' said Fred.

'It's a ghost home,' said Juliet. 'I'm going to make a fire.'

'Looks like Ma left you something to burn,' said Fred, pointing at the piles of typewritten sheets that covered the warped table-tennis table. These were parish-council papers awaiting collation, a task Francesca Clough asked her children to take care of in the ten pages of notes she had left on the kitchen table. These notes also referred to compost, mildew, mouse traps, a leaky tap, boiler pressure, a jammed window and a bucket placed under a hole in the roof.

Bella was asleep in her push-chair, so Mary carried her up – where else? – to Tobias's room. Mary was in the habit of doing things with the Clough family rather than her own. Her parents had left the village years earlier and were either needy or remote, demanding permission to change or reassurance that they hadn't. Mary preferred Tobias's parents; they had always simply been there.

That evening, Juliet burst into tears because Fred laid the table for eight and Mary complained that Bella wouldn't settle with such loud music playing and the television left on with no one watching it and that someone kept turning on all the lights. Juliet realised that she had cooked too much spaghetti and burst into tears again. Neither Fred nor Mary had ever seen her cry so they sat her in a chair by the fire and brought her whiskey. To cheer things up, Fred made another fire in the rarely used fireplace in the hall.

The brother and sister started fights and games, and trailed from room to room as if looking for something when what they were really after was their three, no two siblings. Mary opened the kitchen door and looked out into the night.

'I can't stand it any more,' she called to the others. 'Let's go to the pub.'

'But Mary –' Fred began.

'Why not? It's what we usually do.'

'There's Bella . . .'

'I meant . . . I mean . . . why don't you go? I'll be fine.'

They did not even pretend to hesitate.

Mary went upstairs to tuck Bella up, hurrying past rooms she had never known to be empty. She turned on each light, bringing the absent family into being through whatever caught her eye: a prayerbook and a pomander on a bedside table; the words 'broken knowledge' scrawled on a mirror in nail-polish; a houndstooth-check scarf she had seen worn by the doctor, wrapped round Clara's hair, dangled from Carlo's wrist and knotted round Fred as a sash.

Tobias's room was at the end of the corridor. Mary hurried on but stumbled on something and looking down found a scattering of the nails, screws, nuts and bolts that Tobias carried in his overall pockets. He had always been working on a piece of machinery, always leaving tools around and a trail like this. Perhaps someone had been clearing out his room, and had carried a box along the corridor, from which they had spilt. They had not been there earlier. Maybe Fred or Juliet had moved something.

Mary made herself go on in darkness and was relieved to find that when she crept into the room, lay down and reached out, Tobias was there. He must have come up already. It was his back that met Mary's hand, his hair into which she pressed her face. For a second, she knew and believed it; then it was her and the child alone in the bed, in the room, in the house, on and on alone out into the world and beyond it.

Mary concentrated on the breath of Bella's deep sleep and then left her, shutting the door firmly because, because . . . so as to keep her warm? Apart? To keep Tobias in? These questions came later. She hurried back downstairs to sit by the fire and stared into it, looking for nothing more than a meaningless warmth. Later, she put more wood on the fire in the hall, thinking that Fred and Juliet would look forward to its bright welcome and so would soon come back.

The Clock House was no more solid than any other home. There was a fireplace in every room and although most were boarded up, air flowed from one to the other just as water flowed through its corroded pipes and electricity through the wires in its tired walls. The smoke from the two fires rose and flowed also, or tried to.

Fred and Juliet made their way back admiring the packed sky over their heads. Relieved by their outing, they concentrated on Mary, pouring more whiskey and passing on gossip. No one wanted to move away from the fire or be alone or do anything other than conjure the past. Midnight arrived, then one, then two and they were going round in circles, speculating on the bits of news they had: that Julie Lacey, queen of the youth-club disco, had sold her reproduction antiques business, found god and given her money to the community that had bought the old manor; that her brother Martin had intimidated a couple of Belgian tourists who had gone into The Arms by setting light to his hair; that Mary's friends Billy and June had had a fourth child but June was being kept on in hospital and no one quite knew why; and that Clara was seen on the London train, often, and without her children.

At three o'clock, Fred wished the others Happy Christmas and wondered if he might creep upstairs to put a stocking on Bella's bed. Mary had forgotten Bella. 'No, I'll go. She might need a drink and –' she rushed upstairs, not stopping this time to turn on any lights which was why at first she did not wonder why the corridor seemed misty and could not understand that what was rolling out from around the edges of Tobias's bedroom door was not mist.

It ought not be said that Mary hesitated but before she opened the door, she paused to accept the possibility of what she might find: a choking cloud at the centre of which would be . . . She stepped into a room that did not make sense. There was no fire but the granulated air made everything dim and broken down, and it took all she had to reach Bella, to lift her up and carry her out, where she

171

slipped on something – a nail, a screw? – and more or less fell downstairs, waking Bella with her screaming.

Fred settled Mary and Bella in his parents' room and said goodnight. Juliet went up to Tobias's room, where she sat beneath the open window. The air had cleared, just like that.

When Tobias died, Juliet had been shocked by how absolutely he had left her. He did not even visit her dreams. Since coming home, she had willed him to appear. Not that she expected to see him, but she thought that she would be able to feel him, that she ought to be capable of that.

On Christmas morning in a bungalow in the suburb of Bristol where he grew up, Jacob Dart was trying to tell his mother something. Unable to speak since her first stroke, Monica listened more carefully than she ever had before. Her daughter Sally was there looking after her, but she was very quiet. At night Monica listened to central heating and cats; in the day to cars and doors and footsteps. She recognised her daughter-in-law's urgent clip, and had come to appreciate her weekly visits and her briskly-given lavish gifts. Monica could detect in Barbara's tired bullish features, a sense of duty which had nothing to do with Jacob or love.

'You see, Ma,' Jacob was saying now that Barbara had gone outside for a cigarette. 'There was this girl. There is this girl . . . What was that?'

'Don't,' Monica was trying to say, but what came out of her mouth was a feeble honk. 'I don't want to know, you silly fool. Why can't you just keep it in your trousers?'

'The thing is Barbara doesn't love me. Most nights I

172

have to sleep in my room, this room I have to rent at the back of a gallery. Try to breathe more slowly . . . in . . . out . . .'

Monica strained, and Jacob tried to sit her up but did not know how and losing his balance, yanked his mother half out of bed. Barbara appeared, stepped over him and settled Monica back.

Jacob got to his feet. 'Sorry darling,' he said. Both women looked up. 'I'm pretty useless, aren't I?'

'That's always been your excuse,' said Barbara.

Monica's jaw waggled, her mouth dropped open, her tongue flapped, her eyes watered and she gave a majestic caw.

'I made her cry, Bar,' said Jacob, tears in his eyes.

Barbara, who spent more time with Monica than he did, knew better: 'Don't be silly. She's laughing.'

FIFTEEN

There were three cars parked in the Clock House garage, but neither Fred nor Mary had a licence, and Juliet insisted that now she could only drive in America. Clara came to collect them for lunch, marching into the kitchen shouting, 'Why can't you grow up and stop depending on others to ferry you around!' only the person in the kitchen wasn't Juliet, but Mary.

Fred appeared behind Clara, carrying bottles of champagne and brandy. 'Before we go, we have to have a champagne cocktail. Don't we always have a champagne cocktail before Christmas lunch?'

'You can make them at my place,' said Clara.

'No! We have them here, in this kitchen. Where are the sugar lumps?'

'And we toast the goose, which is at my house. Do come on.'

Clara had set up a table in her studio, the library, because she thought it the grandest room in the house. Two tables huddled together under high windows. Stefan was up a ladder trying to encourage the bar fires suspended along the walls to give off some heat. The twins were playing among a stack of zinc garden chairs, while Horace sat in his playpen and grizzled tremulously.

Mary noticed his blue fists: 'Isn't he cold?'

Clara swept him up. 'Nonsense, just hungry like the rest of us. He wants some tit.' She pulled open her shirt.

'You're still breastfeeding?' Mary had not produced enough milk to sustain Bella for more than two months.

'Obviously. Now why don't you lot bring up the food.'

'We've got to toast the goose first and I say it will hear us from here,' put in Fred, who had put a sugar lump in each glass and splashed them with brandy which he then topped up with champagne.

Clara continued to motorise the day. 'There is smoked salmon to start with. We should have it now. Can't someone bring it up?'

They drank the cocktails and ate the salmon, and then Clara marshalled everyone to carry up the dinner.

'I'll keep an eye on the children, so Stefan can concentrate on the heating,' said Mary, meaning to sound helpful.

Clara looked exasperated. 'It's not that cold and you've got Bella so thoroughly wrapped up, I'm surprised she can breathe.'

She marched off and Mary muttered, 'Don't tell her. I can't stand it, just don't tell her.'

Juliet was irritated. 'Bella was fine, remember? Slept right through it. It was your shrieking that woke her up.'

'I still don't understand what happened. How could the smoke from downstairs end up in her room?'

'A down draught, I think it's called. The flues connect and sometimes the fire isn't strong enough and the air is so still that the smoke can't rise, so it has to find another way out.'

'How do you know that?'

'It happened before, ages ago, on the same kind of

175

night. Dad lit a fire in the hall and a while later Tobias came spluttering out of his room, swiftly followed by . . . what was her name? They had practically nothing on. It was hilarious!'

'You knew?'

'About Daisy? Of course. You did too, didn't you? I mean she was before you.'

'Not about Daisy, about the hall fire and how it could do that.'

'I suppose so, now that I'm reminded of it.'

'You knew the room could fill with smoke?'

'Not really, I –'

'And that Bella was in there?'

It was you who shut the door, thought Juliet.

Fred appeared with a heap of plates and Mary asked him, 'You knew, too? About the fireplace in Tobias's room? The down draught?'

He looked from one to the other. 'I've heard the story.'

'You lit the fire.'

Juliet said it: 'You shut the door.'

Frightened, angry, they all spoke at once: 'How could you not think!', 'Why did you shut the door?', 'She's your baby', 'It's your house', and then Fred yelling: 'It's Tobias's room and I didn't think of it because it didn't matter because he's not here!'

'His daughter is,' said Mary.

'Yes,' said Juliet, 'and sometimes that just makes it worse.'

Clara's goose was plump and bronze, but it tasted of feather and bone. It was served with cranberry-and-date stuffing, puréed potatoes and swede, glazed carrots with caraway and sprouts sautéed with nutmeg – all babyish, burnt and cold. The children were bored and disappointed.

Bella strutted round and round, slapping every chairleg she passed, which was startling then amusing and finally annoying. Told off by Juliet, she retreated to a corner and stood regarding them all, her scarlet cheeks and wispy orange hair flaring against the tea-green walls. Mary would not concede that the child was over-dressed but eventually unbuttoned her cardigan. The twins disappeared and because neither Stefan nor Clara appeared to listen out for them, Mary felt obliged to. Horace wheezed as snot drooped from his nose and crusted on his upper lip. When Clara went to fetch her homemade plum-pudding ice cream, Mary leant over and wiped Horace's raw face. He began to yell.

'What set off roaring boy?' asked Clara as she came back in. She whisked Horace into the air. Only Juliet could see her face in the bleaching winter light and how tired she looked.

Cold, drunk and swimming inside, Juliet missed her mother and felt a burst of protective love for her sister.

'He was fine until Mary decided to scrub his face.'

'I only gave his nose a wipe,' said Mary.

Juliet had always liked her before, but she was beginning to sound peevish.

At this point Bella fell hard on her face and began to cry.

'You see?' said Clara, 'If you weren't so busy with other people's children, yours might not be concussing herself in the corner.'

'If you knew . . .' Mary rushed to pick up Bella, who thought her mother was shouting at her and cried harder.

'Knew what? That my brother died? I know that.'

'We all know that,' added Juliet, looking savagely at Mary. 'What you can't take is not having someone to look after you, that's why –' and she knew she should not say this but at last the stone laid on her heart by Tobias's

177

death was starting to move, 'you're after the nearest replacement.'

Fred, who had been plucking at the tablecloth gave it a yank so that plates, glasses, bottles, bowls, cutlery, candles and vases of holly rattled and slopped. Stefan took Horace from Clara, and went to find the twins. Fred stood up but kept looking at the tablecloth where he was dabbing at a puddle of red wine. 'I'll make another round of cocktails shall I? To go with the pudding? This is going to stain. Where's the salt?' He unscrewed the top of the mill so fast that it spun out of his hands.

'What on earth do you mean?' Mary could make no sense of this.

Fred had upended the mill and was shaking it over the spilt wine.

'I mean Fred,' said Juliet.

'Oh shut up!' said Fred and Clara simultaneously, which so annoyed Juliet that she went ahead and said it: 'Mary made a pass at you, didn't she, Federico?'

Wax hardened on the white cloth. Thick water oozed from an upset vase. Fred threw the salt mill at Juliet hard enough for it to have hurt her, and walked out.

'Why would you say something like that?' asked Mary.

They looked at her as if they had forgotten she was there.

Here they were: Mary in the corner with Bella simmering in her arms, Clara still standing, still looking up into the light and Juliet sitting back in her chair, as rigid as her sister. They had reached the edge of something.

'What is this about?' asked Mary.

Clara explained: 'Fred told Carlo that when he was babysitting for you, you made a pass at him.'

'I don't understand.'

'That he was holding Bella and you ran your hand, um, stroked his thigh.'

'His thigh? Why would I stroke Fred's thigh?' As she said it, Mary remembered the moment – reaching for Bella stretched out across Fred's knees and running her hand up and down the child's back just as she constantly, thoughtlessly, touched her. Fred's thigh. Her full, sudden blush as she realised what she had done convinced the sisters.

As Mary stood up, pulling Bella after her, something fell into her mind with the words already in place as if she had been wanting to say them for years. 'When I sing at the club, I realise afterwards how much of the audience I've taken in – someone's red hair, say, and their green dress, and the man next to them.'

'Mary, I think that's the longest sentence you've ever uttered,' Juliet remarked. This was interesting; troubling and interesting.

'Could you explain the point of this little speech?' Clara would not look round.

'Can you explain why you go down to London so often?' Mary was not sure that this piece of information belonged with the other, but nonetheless decided to cobble them together.

'You're being ridiculous,' said Clara turning round to the table and beginning to stack plates. 'I know you're embarrassed about lunging at Fred but you don't have to contrive more mess.'

'I'm not –'

'Who do you see in London?' asked Juliet, only because she was relieved to have found a way into a different conversation.

Clara fumbled the greasy plates.

This got Juliet interested. 'Clara! Have you got a man? A man in black?' She was following her sister round the table, jabbing her finger at her playfully; it was meant to be playful. 'That's a bit Eighties, isn't it? A throwback in black?'

Clara hurried out and her lack of response convinced Juliet that she was right. She turned back to Mary. 'I go off for a few months and you're seducing Fred and Clara's got a man in black. Well, well . . .'

How dare you, thought Mary and took another step: 'Who do you know who wears black?'

Even the shock of realising what Mary was suggesting didn't stop Juliet blaming her for this as well. 'You bitch, Mary George, you bitch.'

It took some time for Juliet to make her way down the three flights of stairs that led from the library to the kitchen. She took a wrong turning in one corridor, heard someone coming, panicked and slipped into a room where the twins were torturing their soft toys. She knelt down as if to play with them and they ignored her politely.

Juliet waited until she could breathe evenly and then set off once more, rehearsing her lines: 'I hear you're fucking my cast off.' Too direct. It left nothing to be said. 'Clara, a word . . .' Too smug. 'Seen anything of Jacob?' Not tough enough.

She strode into the kitchen: 'Clara, I –' but she wasn't there. Fred was doing the washing up. He had to stand on tiptoe to put the plates in the draining rack. His emphatic presence, his wispy hair: 'Bella, have you seen Jacob?' Where did that come from? She gave a painful, pleading laugh; Fred didn't even turn round.

Juliet walked through the kitchen and along a corridor, opening and then slamming each door she came to, more in protest than in hope of finding Clara. Here was the scullery, the pantry, and the laundry with its monumental washing machine and institutional boiler; rooms given over to fishing rods, photographic equipment and demi-johns, creosote, whitewash and pesticides, and jars of fading fizzing jam made from the pears and plums that overwhelmed the orchard each year.

At the end of the corridor, Juliet turned a corner and walked into Clara. Unprepared, she gestured at the row of doors behind her. 'Playing at it, playing at everything.'

Clara responded as if she too had been rehearsing. 'It's not what you think.'

'What isn't?'

'Me and . . .' She decided something. 'I can show you.'

Juliet was sufficiently curious to follow Clara up to the top floor where the ceilings were low and the rooms plain and chill. 'It's like Khyber Road up here,' she said. Clara seemed gratified.

They continued on to the end of the corridor and up a steep set of steps into an attic so large that it seemed to Juliet more like a barn. It was empty, apart from at one end, a rack full of paintings. Clara was taking one down, pulling off the plastic wrapping, setting it against the wall under a window so as to catch the dregs of after-noon light, and then she stood back and looked at Juliet while Juliet looked at the picture.

'Well?' prompted Clara, after a minute or so.

'Well what?'

'You can't see it?'

She could see that it was a face, or parts of a face. See what?

'You need to find the right perspective.' Clara shuffled her sister to the right, 'Can you see it now? Perhaps a little closer . . . no, not too close . . . now?' The elements of the face composed themselves and there was Jacob, as he had appeared the first time, when Juliet had attributed to him all that you might hope for in a beautiful stranger.

'It's true,' she said.

'Do you think so?' asked Clara. 'The plane of his nose, the way it flares and flattens so that the light broadens and sinks at the same time. That was hard to get.'

Juliet was slow to react. The small white pill she took each day kept her in suspension. There was no blood, no pain, just a spongy thickening. Her thoughts thickened into what to do – lift the axe, say the words – rather than why. But now she felt something rise through the thickened chemistry of her saturated body.

Clara rattled on: 'So of course I've been seeing Jacob. How else could I get this done? And that night we worked late, had something to eat and then dropped in at the club for a drink. Of course Mary saw us, she was meant to . . . I was going to say hello but you know how she scuttles off . . . oh for god's sake, I only painted him!'

'You paint landscapes not people.'

'It was a commission.'

'Who?'

'The point is now you know that whatever Mary was trying to suggest is nonsense.'

'Who commissioned it?'

'Barbara Dart.'

Juliet continued to look at the painting. 'Why didn't you tell me?'

'I thought you'd be upset.'

'Why?'

'Because you weren't here, because it's for his wife, I don't know . . .' Clara, so rarely nervous, pushed on: 'He has such a complex face . . .'

'And now you're for hire?'

'I couldn't really say no. She's done a lot for me.'

'Didn't it occur to you that she is only interested in you because of who you are?'

Clara looked blank.

'My sister?'

'That's insulting and absurd.'

'Why not?'

'You mean why. That thing you had with Jacob was hardly –' Enough.

'Would you have done it if it hadn't been Jacob?'

'It was a commission,' Clara repeated and went to switch on the lights, as if to prove there was nothing hidden in her or this room or this picture. 'And if you must know, yes, I wanted to do it. I haven't painted a human being since art school and I felt like having another go. And yes, perhaps I did it because it was him. He's an interesting subject. I'm a painter, he's a subject, she is writing the cheque. I didn't mention it because I knew you would read something into it. You always make something out of nothing. Always.' Whether or not this was an accurate observation did not bother Clara; with it, she felt sufficiently restored to leave.

Juliet remained. Why had Jacob agreed to this? She tried once more to find the exact point from which the portrait demanded to be viewed but kept losing it, as if Jacob were moving her in and out of place. The coherence of Jacob the glimpsed stranger broke down and she saw in his image what she had never seen in his presence: his struggle to become and remain his idea of himself.

Mary insisted on leaving and was persuaded to accept a lift from Stefan only here they were, still in the garage while he tried to get the car to start. Each time he turned the key in the ignition, the engine made less noise.

'I'll have to leave it a while, it'll only flood.'

As two quiet people, they were comfortable sitting in silence but Mary had something she wanted to say: 'I've given up singing, you know. I've left the band.'

'That's a shame. I've always meant to come and hear you. Why?'

'Because no one will look after Bella.'

'You can't find a babysitter?'

'I shouldn't have to. They are her family, Tobias's family, they should help me. Don't you think?'

'Well, I . . .'

'Forget it. I'm just fed up. You go in. We'll wait here.'

'Shall I bring you a blanket? Some tea and cake?'

Everyone adored Stefan. He took them seriously, distracted and consoled, but did not offer a view. Most of what he heard, he set aside. Mary knew she already looked foolish and would have to go back in because Bella would get cold and wake, but she was still too angry and frightened to trust herself.

Stefan decided to have one last try and the car started. He eased out of the garage and switched on the headlamps which revealed Fred, trying to look as if he had just emerged from the house. Stefan drew up alongside him.

'If you're heading back to Allnorthover, I might as well come too.' Fred got in the back next to Bella and when they arrived at the Clock House, carried her up the steps. In the time it took him to free a hand and open the door, he and Mary had been standing close together for too long. Each felt it and stayed there, as if put in place.

Fred spoke to the door. 'You know I didn't say it, not like that.'

'*They* made it into something more than it was, not you.'

'The thing is . . . of course it wasn't what it seemed, not at all, but it sort of raised the idea.'

'The idea?'

'Of us.' He could hardly speak.

*   *   *

When everyone had left or gone to bed, Clara returned to the attic. She wrapped up the painting and put it away. She had finished it the day after Jacob had come to her studio for the last time, when they left together and he stopped in the doorway and waited, inviting Clara to press past him. As she did so, she looked into his eyes and thought how difficult that fractured yellow-green was to get right and how the shadows either side of his nose ought to be bluer and deeper. Jacob permitted this scrutiny, and this moment of intimacy might have passed with grace had he not suddenly dug his fingers into Clara's bottom. His face was blank, as if he had stopped knowing and thinking, and later Clara decided that the Jacob who rubbed himself against her with such animal honesty was not conscious, and so was not the real him. She was more troubled by her own confusion. It was he who stepped back, although she had meant to.

SIXTEEN

Fred and Mary stayed on in Allnorthover, while Juliet returned to London. She was flying back to Littlefield on New Year's Day. She sat in the cold and the dark and did not venture out, unable to envisage anything beyond Khyber Road and its trapped echoes. If she went into the kitchen she saw Fred weeping, in her bedroom Jacob turning away, and everywhere, anywhere, she wanted to see Tobias. She felt the loss of him now as if he had taken something into his death that belonged to her and which she needed. She wanted his advice (when had she ever asked for his advice?). If she asked Carlo, he would say something encouraging; Fred would say something irrelevant and now she couldn't ask Clara because Clara was trying to take over.

Sara phoned and they met for a drink. She let Juliet tell her stories about Rogen and Merle, Terence and the sports bar, Buckie and the axe, and listened to her complaints about the snow. Eventually, she told Juliet that she was getting married and Juliet was taken aback to find that she could not think whom to. Later that night, crouched in front of the fire at Khyber Road, Juliet realised that she was more miserable and uncertain than she had ever been in her life. She phoned Ritsu.

'I feel awful,' she said by way of greeting.

'Juliet? What's happened?'

'I just feel awful.'

'I'm sorry for you, I really am, but can this wait till the morning? It's very late.'

'Is it?'

'You must still be on American time.'

'I am?'

'Not to worry. Let's speak in the morning.'

'Did you know Sara was getting married?'

'Isn't it great?'

'I don't even know him.'

'No, but –'

'Nobody tells me anything. It's as if they've all decided to punish me. Why do you want to punish me?'

'I know you're upset but I really have to go. It's late and I've got –'

'How would you feel if your brother was killed and your parents decided that instead of helping you get through Christmas, they would bugger off?'

'I don't have a brother, nor indeed any parents.'

Had Juliet known that? She couldn't remember. 'But what about me?'

'This isn't about you. Your parents going away, your brothers and sister – it's not all about you. I am hanging up. It is the middle of the night, and I've got someone here.'

'You've got someone too?'

'Go to sleep, Juliet.'

Juliet decided that she had been so emotional because she was unwell and the next day developed a fever. She shivered, sweated and ached, and lay in bed detailing the ways in which people were punishing her. All she had done was

187

go away and not because Tobias died – she had been planning to go already. She had got involved with a married man, but he had already left his wife and anyway she ended it by going to America. And once she had gone, everyone – Clara and Jacob and Barbara, Ritsu and Sara and Hannelore, Mary and Fred – had moved closer together. They were going on happily without her, as if all it took was a little shuffle and things were once more complete.

Had she ended things with Jacob? She thought about him all the time in Littlefield and he had phoned, even if he hadn't said anything. Perhaps he was waiting for her to speak. Why not speak? Why not speak now?

She went to sleep like someone in fear of falling – braced and clenched – and in her dreams she did fall so that the plummet of her body woke her and then she was sleeping and falling again, and someone was banging on her skull and demanding to be let in.

It was Carlo, at the front door. 'You look terrible . . . and I have to say, disappointed. Were you expecting someone else?'

'Of course I was!' Juliet shouted and began to snivel.

Carlo ran her a bath and made a pot of tea. She drank a cup standing up, as if to prove that she was fine after all.

'How did you know I was ill?'

Carlo had returned from Thailand to a flurry of calls from Fred and Clara, who said that Juliet looked awful and he had to find out why.

'You're a doctor,' was Fred's argument.

'So is Dad.'

'But we don't want to worry him.'

'Perhaps she's just put on weight,' said Clara, 'although it looks more like water retention.'

'She's on some kind of pill,' said Fred, 'I've seen her taking them.'

Carlo wanted to eat, drink, sleep. 'She doesn't say anything about her backache or bleeding any more, so whatever she's on must be doing her some good.'

'But you haven't seen her!'

'Everything has its side effects.'

'Just make sure that she's taking care.'

'She could try cutting out salt,' Clara said.

On the morning of New Year's Eve, Carlo paid Juliet a visit.

'You could try cutting out salt,' he began.

'What for?'

'Water retention.'

'Charming. I know I'm a bit puffy but these pills have made such a difference.'

'What pills?'

She told him.

'I haven't heard of them.'

'The doctor who gave them to me is in America.'

'What about your doctor here? What does he say?'

'The Americans are terribly efficient. They've got my treatment all lined up.'

'You didn't say you'd had any treatment.'

'I haven't yet. Just a few tests.'

'Which showed . . . ?'

'That I need some treatment, which I'm going to have as soon as these pills have calmed things down.'

And meanwhile you're alright, are you?'

'Maybe I'll try cutting back on salt.' She looked at her watch. 'I have to go out,' she said, and hurried him back into the street.

'It's New Year's Eve, remember? Do you want to come dancing?'

'No, I'm sick, remember? And I fly back tomorrow, remember?'

She refused his offer of a lift, saying that she had her bicycle and hadn't ridden it for ages. She cycled off, then turned back.

Carlo wound down the window.

'Thailand,' Juliet said, already wheezing.

'What about it?'

'Did you have a good time?'

'Oh, you know.'

'Oh?'

'You know.'

Juliet cycled towards the river. For the first few minutes she found it hard to adjust to being back on the left-hand side of the road and then she was used to it again. What surprised her more was that in four months she had lost all sense of London traffic and its strategies. She had grown used to broad lanes and straight lines. People rarely overtook in Littlefield and braked if they saw someone waiting to cross the road.

Juliet thought of London drivers as mad, visionary lateral thinkers. They judged space via their wing mirrors and thought they could see three opportunities ahead. They saw off hazards with minimal reflexive shifts or obliterating swoops of speed. They cut corners and parked with violent precision. They got as close as they could to one another without touching and hated one another on sight. All this took place at a visceral level. The London driver's mind was on other things – applying lipstick, putting on tights, eating breakfast, cleaning ears, reading letters, dabbing at toothpaste stains, changing radio stations, singing, and shouting at someone who could not hear them.

The icy air scraped Juliet's lungs but she pushed herself on, afraid to stop and find out what she was doing. The sun swept across the city like a searchlight, blinding everyone and making the traffic lights all three colours at once. At junctions drivers hesitated, squinted and lunged, while those on the pavement started to blunder and wander.

She was soon crossing Albert Bridge and then cycling along the north embankment pavement. At Lambeth Bridge, policemen in yellow jerkins stood around trying out carrying guns. With talk of war and more bomb scares, the roads leading up to Parliament Square had been cordoned off. Juliet decided to turn back south and only then, as she picked up her bike and carried it down the steps to the river walk, did she admit that she was heading for the Shipping Office. From here she rode straight there, afraid that if she crossed the river again she would not be brave enough to come back over.

In Jacob's memories of Juliet, she was speaking, frowning or turning away. He had no idea of her as she arrived that day. Her skin was flushed, her eyes muddled and inflamed, her nose was raw and her mouth, which Jacob had found so incongruously coquettish, was colourless and dry. Her hair had been allowed to grow as far as its first full curls, which bristled from her clammy scalp. She looked worn and yearning and to Jacob, less beautiful and more possible than ever before.

By the time Jacob got to feel something, it absorbed him so violently that afterwards he could only remember himself as lost and the thing as the agent of that. From the moment he put his hands on Juliet's shoulders to steady her, he was overwhelmed.

They sat side by side on the edge of his camp bed.

'I can't breathe,' she said, wiping her nose with her sleeve.

What Jacob was about to say was overtaken by a cough.

'You're sick too.'

'Tea?'

'Bed.'

They took off their clothes as if they hurt and lay down gingerly, tensing at the weight of the sheet, quilt and blanket as if those hurt too. Even in that narrow space they found enough room to lie apart, each stunned by the apparition of the other. Juliet laid her head on Jacob's chest and listened to the catch in his lungs, the flight of his heart. He fingered the damp new curls at the back of her neck and was encouraged when her sticky breathing lapsed into a moan.

The heater rattled as it churned air into hot dust. Jacob's hand moved from Juliet's throat, between her breasts and under, following the path of her sweat. She turned and raised her hand above her head, exposing the damper, hotter skin under her arm and bringing her nipple to his mouth. She tasted of salt and rust.

'Christ,' he said, as someone would only to themselves, 'Jesus.'

His body was in such a state of weakness that Juliet's touch provoked the most acute lust he had ever felt. Her hand moved downwards and as it reached his hip, he caught and pressed it against his cock and then his balls, which felt even more tender and susceptible than the rest of him.

He tried to kiss her mouth but she slid to one side, gasping. Then she turned away while reaching back with her hand to tuck his cock between her thighs. He found her wetness confusing; everything about him was sore and dry, and he pulled away and pushed a hand between her legs instead, wanting to be more accurate and gentle but

192

finding her so aroused that he rubbed hard till she came, painfully it seemed, and turned towards him crying, really crying, as she said 'Fuck me, fuck me now.'

He held his body apart as she gulped and sniffed, then found his way deeper and pressed harder, feeling her temperature rise still further so that the nape of her neck and the dip of her lower back from her high waist down to the long cleft of her bottom grew slippery, and as the spasm of his cough tipped him out of her, she turned in his arms and slid beneath him, melting. She kissed him roughly. His lungs hurt, his head hurt, his groin and back and hands and eyes hurt. He gave in, lay with his full weight upon her and buried his face in the sour, sticky mess of it all.

Jacob was deep in a congested sleep and from time to time began to snore and then turned onto his other side, resettling himself and his breathing. At one point he asked, 'Are you awake?' and she began to talk, telling him how much she enjoyed their telephone conversations, 'Silences, really. It meant a lot to me to know you were there.'

'Where?'

'There. At the other end.'

'The other end of what?'

'The phone. Your calls.'

He opened his eyes. 'My calls? You didn't give me a number.'

'I left a note in the hole.'

'The hole?'

'The hole in our wall.'

'Our wall? What wall?'

'Over there. Where we used to send each other messages.'

193

'We did? Oh, yes, we did. The hole. Yes. You left me your number?'

'You didn't get it?'

'No.'

'Did you think it was someone else's number?'

'I didn't get a note. Or a number.'

'But you called.'

'When did I call?'

'Are you still asleep?'

'Sleep.'

Juliet felt many things and with her body as confused as it was now, this seemed only natural. It had not been Jacob who phoned. She had known this, really, since the last call came and she heard a voice she could have recognised had she wanted to. While she was holding the receiver to her ear mesmerised by the idea of him, the person at the other end of each long silence had been his wife. Ask him now, she said to herself, ask him about the picture. But she did not want to share this moment with Clara or Barbara, and there were ways of looking at it and seeing that it did not matter. And what could he say? That he had done it for Barbara? It did not matter. He had not gone back to her.

Although there were a few more minutes to this day than there had been to the last, no one would have thought it any longer or lighter. By the time Juliet crept out of Jacob's room, there were fireworks already and she was glad that neither she nor Jacob had mentioned New Year, and that she hadn't stayed on with him to find out whether or not he marked it. Anyway, she had to fly.

Twilight had flattened the city, which now depended upon lit windows to explain itself. Shallow clouds picked up a smear of oily mauve from the river and low in the west the sun set in a fresh glow which might have been described as apricot or peach had such things come to mind at that time of year.

Juliet cycled over every possible bridge, not admitting that this was all just a matter of dirt and light, and that nothing was as charged or as consoling as it seemed. Perhaps if she had not been feverish or slowed by the small white pills, or if his touch had not exposed the effect of months alone, Juliet might have woken Jacob and questioned him further; she might also have wondered at herself.

SEVENTEEN

In the morning, Juliet returned to Littlefield. Terence met her at the airport in Boston, and she was overcome by how pleased she was to see him.

'How did you know which flight I'd be on?'

'The Dean's office.'

'Well, it's incredibly nice of you. It must have taken hours.'

'Five hours. The thing is –'

'I am glad to be back. Isn't that absurd?'

Only when they were settled and driving west towards Littlefield, did he manage to explain why he was there: 'Your jape with the axe.'

She had gone back up to her apartment and had waited for the police to turn up or for Buckie to come back and shout, but nothing happened and so she flew home and forgot all about it.

'It was a joke.'

'You put an axe through the windscreen of his car.'

'I slipped on the ice.'

'And the axe just flew out of your hands?'

'Well, yes. It was amazing.'

'You expect the college to believe that?'

'It was a joke. His face when I produced the axe was so comical, I couldn't resist. So I marched outside and then I didn't know what to do.'

'You slipped?'

'I really did, and I was holding the axe as if I meant to throw it so –'

'Didn't the old man go berserk?'

'That was the wonderful thing. The axe flew out of my hands, circled perfectly in the air and straightened out just in time to slice through his windscreen. Have you seen a windscreen shatter? It's remarkable, quite beautiful. Buckie just stared. We both did. Then he turned and ran, only he couldn't because of all the snow, so he sort of hopped and skidded away. I didn't see him again.'

'He went to the Dean. Which could have meant big trouble for you, except that he's sleeping with her.'

'Is Merle the Dean?'

'What's this got to do with Merle? The Dean is Janka Foord, the physicist. Didn't you meet her when you arrived?'

'There was some reception I was supposed to go to.'

'Buckie is nailing the Dean and everyone knows, so she can't be seen to take up his cause. You're really lucky, because apparently he has been making noises about dangerous weapons, criminal damage and assault.'

'If he wanted to press charges, wouldn't he go to the police?'

Terence laughed. 'You don't understand this place. He'd sue. He's been talked out of it for now. I think Merle had a word, but you still need to make a case for diminished responsibility, something like that. You've got to go to see the Dean.'

'But I wasn't diminished, I was drunk.'

'Don't tell them that. The Dean's talked to Merle. They've put together a pretty good explanation. You'll have to pay for the car repairs, though, and Buckie won't have you next door. They've moved you.'

'Where to?'

'Lucky again. A history professor has gone on sabbatical, leaving one of the college's nicest houses empty.'

'A house?'

'A very small one. It's old and rickety but it's up on the hill.'

'I didn't know Littlefield had a hill.'

'It's a trick hill. You can't see it and you don't know you're climbing it, but at the top, you find yourself above town.'

'Above the trees? That doesn't sound too bad. Would you be able to help me move my stuff?'

'They've done that.'

'They?'

'The college.'

'Moved my things without asking?'

'Their apartment, their house, their hill.'

'Their axe, too.'

'Exactly. That's where you're luckiest of all – their axe.'

A few days before the axe shattered Buckie Buckingham's windscreen, someone had suggested to Dean Foord that she might not be his only lover. Before she could confront him, he had disappeared to his wife's house in Connecticut, leaving his car in the garage and a letter addressed by hand to 'Janka', which he nudged under her office door. The Dean was full of forgiveness as she tore the envelope open but the letter was only a formal account of what he referred to as 'Miss Clough's assault', demanding action and recompense, and placing the matter in her hands. So when Juliet arrived in her office in January, Janka Foord was not in the mood to do Buckie Buckingham any favours.

'You must have been under a lot of stress,' she began encouragingly. 'Did the department give you too many students?'

'No.'

'What about your supervisor ... been working you hard?'

'No, not at all. If anything, not hard enough.'

'I see.' This girl did not look well. She was sallow and watery, and possibly a bit slow. 'And your health?'

The Dean's kind voice elicited a full account of her condition and the forthcoming operation. Juliet gave her permission to request a statement from her doctor: the severity of her pain, the level of medication, the lack of familial support – it all added up.

The Dean knew more and wanted to be told. 'Any recent, um, trauma? Anything else that might have contributed to your being so ... sensitive?'

'No.'

Dean Foord paused and then admitted that she knew that Juliet had recently lost a brother in a terrorist attack; Merle had mentioned it. She received Juliet's permission to add this information to her report.

Teaching began immediately. 'No such thing here as adjustment,' Terence explained. 'On, on!'

'The land of moving on,' Juliet said, now in the habit of competing with him in the field of pronouncement. 'They're so good at it that they even clear up after themselves.'

'Don't be patronising, especially as they've just cleared up after you.'

Juliet meant it; she was grateful and impressed.

Carlo's hospital was near Fred's bank and they sometimes met for a drink in one of the City's cellar bars, which were raucous for an hour or two at the end of the day and then deserted. It was eight o'clock, and they were almost alone.

'I'll buy another round,' offered Carlo, 'but will you go? My back's killing me.'

'What have you done?'

'Let my boyfriend give me another massage.'

'Can't you say no?'

'He'd be hurt. Besides, he needs the money.'

'You pay your boyfriend?'

Carlo ignored him. 'The other night, we were supposed to go out for dinner but I fell asleep in my chair and you know what? He went out, bought stuff and made soup.'

'Did you pay him for the soup as well?'

Carlo pushed a note into Fred's hand and told him to fuck off to the bar. He wanted to dwell on that evening, how Jonathan had fed him and worried about him and how, for the first time, he had spent the night with a man without having sex.

Fred returned with two pints of bitter – something they only drank when together because it was what they had drunk in Allnorthover – and changed the subject.

'I've got to move out.'

'Why?'

'At the last co-op meeting, the committee voted to expel me because they thought it was immoral of me to take advantage of cheap housing when I earned so much.'

'But half of them are raking it in, paying ten pounds a week rent and saving up for a deposit.'

'Which is what I've done, only without realising it, well not completely. Anyway I had a look and they're right and while I'm working for the bank, I can get a good deal on a mortgage and prices are dropping, so –'

'The end of Khyber Road. What will Jules say?'

'She won't mind.'

'She'll be back in June.'

'And I'll have a new house for us by then.'

'You want her to live with you there as well?'

Fred didn't know what to say; he hadn't imagined anything else.

In Littlefield, the same snow was on the ground. It lined paths and roads in scuffed slabs, and hid the fact that the world would be green again. The students returned, the snow remained, and Juliet was content. She spent several hours each day avoiding getting on with her work but there was still enough time left in which to do it. She slept well and wrote calm, cheerful postcards to her friends.

This life was simple. Her little house was warmed by hot air blown through grates in the skirting boards, and an open fire for which she found a pile of wood in a shed. The two compact downstairs rooms were filled with antique couches and bureaux. What space was left between bookshelves was hung with samplers, botanical prints and posters for county fairs. Feathers and seed-heads were tucked into their dusty frames. In the kitchen, orange and green gourds sank into themselves on the windowsill and three shrivelled corncobs, once red, white and blue, were nailed to the back of the door. Once Juliet might have taken them down. Now she accepted their presence as a sign that this was not her home.

'I have no home,' she said, more often than she knew, until Terence grew annoyed.

'Your family seat?'

'It's still there, yes, but I couldn't go back. Not to live. It's not waiting.'

'And why should it? You talk about your parents as if they were employed to keep the dust down.'

'Hardly. They couldn't wait to get away – ignored Christmas and set off to do exactly what they wanted.'

'So?'

'That's right,' she said. 'We're all going to do just what we want, which for me means being this far from them.'

'Was Christmas that bad?'

'Awful, but I learnt a thing or two and I reminded someone.'

'Of what?'

'That he wants me.'

'And do you want him?'

'How should I know?'

Terence laughed.

'No, really,' said Juliet, 'how do you, I mean . . . how should I know?'

Juliet returned to the hospital to discuss her progress and the doctor proposed a second scan. To Juliet, it all looked the same as before – clouds and shadows.

'Why does it all keep moving?' she asked.

'Because you keep breathing.'

'When you do the next operation, I'll be in and out in a day like before, right?'

'Not this time. You will require a fairly large incision and afterwards several days' bed rest; no lifting. Do you have someone to look after you?'

Juliet explained that no, she was alone and that it had been a difficult year what with the death of her brother in a terrorist attack, and eventually they agreed that she should remain on the hormone treatment for another five months and have the operation once she got home.

'I have no more pain thanks to your marvellous pills, perhaps I won't need the operation after all.'

'You can't take them indefinitely and the pain will come back. You need to address this through surgery.'

She would remember that first month back in Littlefield as a time of peace. She had worked and slept, and felt quiet and kind. Her days were routine and her conversations, other than those with Terence, were functional. She wrote another chapter of her dissertation.

One day in early February, Jacob Dart knocked on her office door.

'How did you find me?' God but he is the loveliest thing on this earth. All the heat in her body collected in her face.

He shrugged.

'Have you come here to see me?'

He smiled.

'Where are you staying?'

'With you?'

That someone would act, would risk acting, for her. That Jacob would act. She stood up, crossed the room and put her arms round his neck. A moment passed and then his arms were round her.

'With you,' he said, kissing her eyes and her mouth and covering her ears, 'I've come to stay. With you.'

Clara arrived at the back of the Shipping Office and as her arms were full of a wrapped painting kicked at the door, trying not to think of Jacob as she did so. The door was padlocked and her kicking at it set off an alarm.

Tania appeared from round the outside of the building. 'Oh, it's you. I've only just got here, haven't had a chance to unlock. I thought it must be Jacob forgetting his keys as usual. He's still camping out here; some of the time,

203

anyway. I was getting quite worried – all that coughing – but he must have found somewhere warmer, haven't seen him for weeks.'

'But what if he's in there?'

'You mean dead and half eaten by rats?' Tania laughed and Clara felt ridiculous so laughed too. In the gallery, she unwrapped the painting.

'It's extraordinary,' said Tania. 'It's him, absolutely.' She kissed Clara on the cheek, 'Congratulations!'

A bell rang and Tania went to bring through Barbara Dart, dressed in her usual finely tuned palette of blues. I would like to paint her as well, Clara thought; it would be like painting a painting.

Tania chatted on: 'I haven't seen you since all those Christmas parties. How was Cornwall?'

'Fab,' said Barbara, not looking up from the picture. 'I went to this dear cottage we've rented for years. I'm thinking of buying it.'

Clara was nervous. 'The face only coheres when observed from a particular angle,' she explained. 'It dictates the position from which it is looked at; otherwise it refuses to be seen.'

'He is a powerful subject, no? Difficult.' Barbara became still. She had seen him. Here was a Jacob who had withdrawn himself from her years ago. 'It's interesting,' she said and then, 'but it doesn't work.'

Clara did not understand. 'I'm sorry?'

'It doesn't succeed, as a portrait. It's not him.'

'Other people think it is.'

'Which other people?'

Clara floundered. 'Tania, you think it's him, don't you? You said so.'

'It's all so subjective . . .'

'No it's not,' said Clara and Barbara together, and braced themselves to resolve the matter.

'I can't do it again.'

'I wouldn't expect you to, and I'm sorry. It was my idea but it hasn't worked. I will pay you the rest of the fee, of course.'

'Please don't,' snapped Clara, already wrapping up the painting.

Barbara made a note to send Clara a cheque in a month's time.

'What does Jacob think?' Tania wondered.

He had not asked to see the painting while it was being done; nor had he discussed it with Barbara.

Barbara looked towards the back of the building.

'He's not there,' Clara said, enjoying Barbara's surprise. 'Isn't that right, Tania?'

'Haven't seen him for days.'

Barbara paused and thought and when she spoke again, her voice was reinforced with calm: 'He does keep odd hours. Have you looked, Tania?'

'I didn't like to and he's so often been gone before.'

'Perhaps we ought to.'

Tania found herself giving Barbara the key.

It was snowing again in Littlefield as Juliet led Jacob back to the house on the hill. They slipped and crept through the soft white world as if they were about to do something ridiculous or dangerous. The steps up to the house were glazed in ice, and Juliet had forgotten to sprinkle them with grit. Jacob climbed the packed snow to one side, stamping footholds with his boots, and then reached down for Juliet. With the determination of someone who conserved their strength for such moments, he lifted her up and into his arms and held her like a bride as she fumbled the key, such was her hurry to unlock the door.

EIGHTEEN

For a while, the talk in the city was of neither expansion nor decline. Although there were things that had to be played out, this was not an age of commitment and so it could not become one of risk. There was nothing to fear, even when talk of war became war; for London, this was more or less the same thing. London did not know the people who went to fight. They did not live in the city, but in barrack towns and other, smaller ports.

This war entered the language as military acronyms, sporting analogies, government patois and the variable pronunciation of Middle Eastern place names. Around the time the first jokes were coined, people stocked up on mineral water and candles. They watched the news, cried by their sleeping children and talked about moving to the country. It passed.

Money was being spent in unlikely places. Khyber Road was awarded a twinkling slick of tarmac edged with yellow lines, and a red brick pavement. The last corrugated-iron fences were replaced with hoardings and the illustrated promise to rebuild. Every other house in the street had been renovated, and someone had planted three saplings, which remained and grew.

'Our street is being coloured in,' Fred said to Juliet, whom he phoned from his office thirty floors above the river. 'And there are growing things. Thank god I'm off.'

'You mean it's no longer picturesque?'

'You should see this view.'

'Tell me about it, please. We've got more snow. Jacob left the shovel out and it disappeared into a drift, so we can't even dig our way to the car.'

'It's getting dark already, and the sky is sort of plum coloured. Everything else down there is bony, chalky, I don't know. I can't really say, but it looks wonderful.'

Juliet knew exactly what it looked like and almost said yes when Fred asked her to come home.

'I'm going to have five bedrooms in Botolph Square,' he said. 'That's more than twice as many as Khyber Road. Come home.'

I am home, thought Juliet that evening as she drowsed by the fire in the house on the hill. She had come in sneezing and Jacob had directed her to an armchair, tucked her up under a quilt and built a fire. He made hot toddies and read to her, stopping now and then to urge her to drink up.

'Do you like the cinnamon stick? I had to go to Mount South to get that.'

'It's lovely.'

'And the nutmeg? It has to be freshly grated. I grated it.'

'Freshly,' she said, meaning to tease him because he sounded so sweetly anxious, only Jacob did not seem to get the joke. He read on until she fell asleep, then carried her to bed.

He liked to watch Juliet sleeping and sometimes stayed up all night to do so. When awake, she toughened. Only at Christmas when she had arrived like a visitation, in a fever, had he believed that he held all of her and that was

207

why he had come to Littlefield. After his mother's second stroke, which ought to have killed her, Jacob and Sally had installed her in a private nursing home, which had been paid for by the sale of her bungalow and the advance on Jacob's next book. He had handed the sum over to the home intact.

The arrival of Jacob Dart, the author of *Foucault's Egg*, caused a stir in Littlefield. Merle asked Juliet what he was working on now, but Juliet did not know because she had not asked. One day when Jacob answered the telephone, Merle elicited the information that he was writing a book of essays called *The Disappointed Bridge*, about the self-limiting connections between modes of cultural theory.

'Jacob's new project sounds fascinating,' Merle said to Juliet.

'It does?'

'The disappointed bridge! So clever.'

'Isn't that a joke about piers?'

'I'm sorry?'

'Piers?'

Merle switched subjects by rummaging in her bag. 'I nearly forgot. Here's the key for Jacob. He's welcome to use it any time. And you must come to dinner again. Soon.'

Juliet took the key home and gave it to Jacob. All the way back she had been persuading herself that she was not going to ask what it was for.

'Thank you, sweetie,' he said and kissed the tip of her cold nose. 'Tea and cake? I found some madeleines in that little French bakery.'

'What's the key for?'

He had taken off her coat and gloves, and was warming her hands in his. 'A place to work. They have this cabin up in the woods behind the house and when Merle found out I was working on another book –'

'About piers . . .'

'Bridges. Anyway, they're terribly kind and it means I won't get in your way.'

'You don't.'

'Not yet, but once you get down to any serious sort of work . . .'

She thought she had. 'Why didn't you tell me about this new book?'

'Because it's not important; besides which,' he said, smiling so lovingly, 'you haven't read the first one.'

If Juliet felt troubled, she was too lulled – by treats and pills and snow – to pursue it. These days her worries flared softly, flickered and went out.

She and Jacob slept well. They rose late and ate a good breakfast. Jacob ground coffee-beans and squeezed oranges, and went out to the French bakery for croissants or brioches. Juliet had little interest in food but learnt to enjoy what Jacob presented. He was right, it was all delicious and she learnt to say so. He would wake her each morning when the table was laid and they would sit for an hour reading the *New York Times,* the *Littlefield Fencepost* or the weekly English news digest to which she subscribed.

Sometimes Jacob would alight on an article about a politician, a book or a war, and force Juliet into debate. 'Well that's obvious but do you really think . . . Don't you see . . . Everyone knows that he . . . Why agree with her? . . . Why agree with me? . . .' It became clear that while she scanned the papers for an anecdote that might amuse her, Jacob, who appeared to read equally casually, was absorbing names, statistics, issues and facts. He couldn't help it.

Jacob's mind was so acute and energetic that he had

learnt to exist in a state of semi-consciousness, otherwise he would wear himself out. This meant that he was averted, absent-minded and often estranged from what he felt and did. From time to time, his mind demanded proper exercise and what Juliet took to be a need for conflict, was a need to be in opposition. These discussions, which could go on for hours, wore her out even though she was attracted to their rigour. Afterwards, Jacob would look as relieved as a racehorse who had thrown his rider and galloped over the downs full pelt, on and on, until he had exhausted the accumulation of his unused self.

One day, she couldn't stand it. 'Why are you attacking me?'

Jacob looked bemused. 'I'm not attacking anyone; I'm just talking.'

He would suggest a walk and they would make their way down the hill and through the woods to the reclaimed railroad, where the trees were so thick that even in winter they made a low roof and sometimes a tunnel. In better weather, the railroad was busy. The locals ran, cycled or skated, properly dressed and equipped, and overtook Juliet and Jacob with a polite bellow, 'Passing on the left!'

'I hate this,' said Juliet. 'Having to walk in a straight line is bad enough but why does it have to be so organised? Why don't they just wander or stroll? Even their hiking trails are full of arrows and fences, colour-coded, tarmacked and stepped. There's no . . . no . . .'

'No what? Difficulty? Danger? Perhaps it's because they know how tough their landscape is. They have to be tough with it. You're spoilt, Juliet. The English countryside is ingratiating – it flatters people into thinking they're exposing themselves to something grand and wild.'

'I'm cold.'

'Then you should be pleased. That's just what the

English hope for in a walk – difficulty and discomfort. Nothing they hate more than a smooth path and a clear day.'

'You're English. More English than I am.'

'Am I?' To Jacob, the idea of belonging anywhere was preposterous.

Juliet sniffed. 'I want to go home.'

'But we're nearly at the river. Come on.' He took her hand. 'Listen . . . A woodpecker . . . There, no, to the left, up there, look! Look!' He held her as they watched the bird bounce from one tree trunk to the next. Had she been alone, Juliet would barely have raised her head, let alone stopped. She would have come back from her walk complaining that there was nothing to see.

They followed the track out onto an old wooden bridge over the Connecticut River and Jacob pulled her to one side, towards the broadening valley to the west. Without Jacob she would have turned back home an hour ago, or if she had reached this far would have hurried across, complaining about the wind or her wet boots, the pain in her face and fingers.

There were no rivers this wide, no bridges this long and high, in England. Girders rose extravagantly. Slow water, thick with ice, carried sun and cloud away from a silver horizon which folded into soft blue mountains.

Juliet stared. 'That is further away than I ever thought my eyes could reach.'

Jacob held her in place. 'Do you like it? Really like it?'

'Yes,' she said. 'Oh yes,' but having to speak tore her away from a thought, something to do with depth of field. She shook herself free and leaned forward so that the rail propped her up instead.

NINETEEN

On her thirty-fourth birthday, Clara woke up alone. She had been staying at Carlo's flat for three days while working at the Quondam Building. She would have come to London just for this – to sleep without interruption and to wake at a time she chose.

Carlo banged on the door. 'It's your babies on the phone, wanting to wish you happy birthday.'

So she listened to the twins sing Happy Birthday while Horace's voice enlarged into a sob behind them. The twins passed the phone between them, Mabel saying, 'Not to worry, Mummy. He's fine, really. You do your work,' and Sidney adding, 'You do your work. Really. He's fine. Mummy. Not to worry.'

Stefan got hold of the phone, 'Happy birthday, darling.'

'I'll skip today and come straight home. *Mummy's coming home.*'

'Maybe you should.'

'Really?'

'Maybe.'

'It's been alright the other times, hasn't it?'

'I suppose so.'

Carlo gave Clara a lift to her studio. It was a damp

212

day. A flabby white sky drew the yellow from the old stone edifices of the city, and the bare trees shone brown and looked less alive for it.

'I'm exhausted,' Carlo said. 'And I have to spend my days among the lying down.'

'Do you talk to them?'

'Sometimes.'

'The way people talk to their pets?'

'No, more like the way people talk to the mirror.' He threw the car round a corner and said, 'One day someone will ask me how my day has been – my day, not that of whomever I've been cutting up.'

'Doesn't Jonathan?'

'Jonathan is sweet, but he likes a good story.'

'Doesn't everyone?'

'The thing is, it's not all I do. I spend quite a bit of time behind a desk or in the lab; no one's interested in that.'

'Jonathan is rather beautiful.'

'He cooks and cleans, too.'

'If I had a man who looked like that, I wouldn't waste him on cooking and cleaning.'

'There's more to a man than a man like that. Oh god, are you going to start crying again?'

'I've failed. Sidney is neurotic, Mabel has no human feeling and Horace is a changeling.'

'Sounds like Fred, Juliet and you respectively.'

They said nothing more as Carlo concentrated on finding a way off the main road. All the sidestreets were gated or marked No Entry.

'A sign of gentrification,' said Clara when Carlo grumbled.

Carlo pulled over on the corner by a re-opened factory: 'I thought that place was derelict.' Two men were pushing a rail of summer dresses out into the rain. Another,

213

sheltering under a blanket, stood shouting by the back of a truck. A young woman called Kate, who also had a studio in the Quondam Building, wobbled past the men, stroking the dresses. She saw Clara, leant down to mouth hello through the car window and drew a smiley face on the glass. She had just left a nightclub and was on her way to her studio, to sleep.

'The party's over,' said Carlo. 'Off you go. I'm late.'

Clara walked off down the alley. Kate made her feel old and Carlo made her feel bad. The children gave her life peace and meaning but when she was with them, each tug at her attention got in the way of the completion of a thought. Stefan had always allowed her to turn away, but the children became anxious and tried to follow her. When it got to the point when she could neither speak nor hear, she came to London. After a day or two, she felt empty-handed and went home again. She only felt at ease when she was neither at work nor at home but on the train between.

That evening, Juliet phoned to wish Clara happy birthday.

Stefan answered. 'She's been in town and is on her way home. She'll be sorry to have missed you but you can celebrate next month.'

'I'm not coming back till June.'

'I know. I mean New York, the show.'

'What show?'

'She hasn't told you? She probably means it to be a surprise. She's got some work in a group show – something the Arts Council are organising, new British artists. I know she's really excited about seeing you.'

'Really?'

'Of course,' he said.

*   *   *

Fred's new house was tucked under the rim of the city in a part of north London that was attracting attention and would soon be given its own name. Botolph Square had lost half of itself in the Blitz, and was now triangulated by a main road. To the north, strings of Edwardian villas were subsiding into earth perforated by sewers, tunnels and underground rivers. To the south lay some of the last tower blocks to be built in the city. They were hostile and austere, and were talked about as landmarks.

Fred had taken Mary and Bella to see the house before he signed the contract. Mary watched her daughter run along the hall through the kitchen and out into the garden, and could not stand the idea of taking her home to their small rooms and the concrete square. The estate agent who was showing them round made an assumption and pointed out that there was an excellent primary school at the bottom of the road. Living this close, Bella was bound to get in.

'Well,' said Fred. 'What could be more important than Bella's education?'

Mary was tired. The house was lovely. Bella was happy. Fred persuaded her to move in.

At the end of her first week in her new nursery, Bella Clough was asked to bring in a picture of her home. The next Monday, she unrolled her drawing and began to explain it to the class: 'It's some of my homes. This is the door to Botolph and this is the door to Khyber.'

'Are those roses in the front garden?' asked the teacher.

'No, that's the dog shit.'

'We don't –'

'Khyber doesn't have a front garden. It has a gutter. I didn't have room for the gutter.'

'What's this under the stairs?'

'The living room.'

'You've made it rather dark.'

'It is dark, but the fire is darker. See? I drew all the coals.'

The teacher was relieved; she had thought they were more dog shit. At break, she stopped Bella on the way out and asked her to tell her more about the drawing. She pointed to a large room with big windows: 'And this? What's in here?'

'The living room at Botolph. The new house. Uncle Fred bought it for us.'

'You call him your uncle?'

'He's my uncle. This is the sofa.'

'How pink.'

'It's atrocious.'

The teacher pointed to the figures crouched on the floor. 'Why is no one sitting on it?'

'Because it's sharp and they are keeping warm by the fire.'

'Well,' said the teacher. 'Perhaps your Uncle Fred will buy you a nice new sofa.'

'He says he will, but Caroline made him forget to.'

'Is she your aunt?'

'No. She came to stay at Khyber when she got tired.'

'Tired of what?'

'Her husband. They live in King Kong.'

'Does she like the sofa?'

Bella shook her head, 'Oh no, oh no . . .'

When Mary moved into Botolph Square, she was unsettled by the quiet. She was used to hearing people carry out their family lives. Here, they withdrew into separate rooms behind solid doors and if there was any noise, it was of a lawn mower, a burglar alarm, a piano or a violin.

216

On the estate there had always been people around when Mary walked home, no matter how late, but here you turned off the main road into an enclave of swept streets that were empty after dark.

Their house, too, was quiet. In Khyber Road, everyone had gathered round the fire, even in summer. Here she, Fred and Bella had cobbled together a kind of family life from pre-existing timetables, habits, vocabulary and rituals, but the house easily swallowed up what little of this there was.

The people who lived there before them had installed wooden shutters reinforced with metal bars. The front garden was covered in decking edged with zinc buckets full of sharp plain plants, and the windows to the basement kitchen were protected by wrought-iron climbing roses.

'Prince Charming would need a blowtorch to get in here,' Fred said to Bella one day when he had lost his key and they were waiting for Mary to let them in.

'No,' she replied. 'Charming doesn't kiss Beauty. He dances with Cinderella.'

'So what's Sleeping Beauty's prince called?'

'He's called . . . he's called . . . Prince . . . Prince . . .'

'Prince Prince?'

'Exactly!'

'Like he's all princes rolled into one?'

Bella wasn't sure what this meant. 'Exactly,' she repeated and then, 'Oh no!'

'Oh no what?' asked Fred looking round but Bella just went on shaking her head.

'Oh no . . . Oh no . . .'

In the city, millions of people are pulled past one another night and day. From time to time they will touch or maybe

217

only breathe in someone they could discover they loved. If they did so, they would have a story to tell about how it was the city that brought them together, and when it went wrong about how it had all been down to chance. Fred and Mary might have got on with a life together had they been more determined and not just prompted by a misunderstanding; had they lived elsewhere.

Mary carried the piece of paper around in her pocket for a week and then decided to ask Fred for advice: 'Do men mind if we phone them?'

'Who's we?'

'Me, I suppose.'

'No.'

'I don't mean you, I mean men. And women. Do they mind?'

'Could you be more specific?'

'If a man gave me his phone number, could I ring him and if so how long should I wait to do so?'

'Who?'

'Shall I ring him?'

'Who?'

'Oh for god's sake, I'll just ring him.'

'Mary?'

'What?'

'Do you like the new sofa?'

'Oh. Yes. I hadn't noticed. Sorry. Why are you sitting on the old one?'

'I suppose I'm used to it.'

'Things change, Fred. Go and sit over there.'

He got up and went to sit on the new sofa, feeling a little thrilled because Mary had told him to do so. He had been meaning to throw the old one out. Under these high ceilings, the furniture from Khyber Road looked like the contents of a run-down dolls-house. Mary took the cordless phone from Fred's study and carried it up to the top of the house. She shut the door behind her and sat in a corner. 'Hello. Alexander Strachan? It's Mary George. The one who'd got on the wrong Tube . . . Yes . . . You were very kind. Stupid of me. Would I? Oh yes. No, I can't do Tuesday, Saturday's tricky. Wednesday week? Fine. Next Wednesday. Charing Cross at eight. Yes, under the clock. See you then.'

Mary went to Charing Cross to meet Alexander Strachan. She tried to remember what he looked like. Tall, but that was relative. Tall compared to her, yes, but not compared to Tobias. She felt sick. Was this a date? When had she last gone to meet a boy? A man. Alexander Strachan was at least her age, if not older. She was thirty-one. Wasn't his hair receding from his temples? She remembered a large and shiny forehead. Was it really shiny or was she making that bit up? Was it really large or had that been just the angle from which she looked at him? She had been sitting on a bench and he had been standing. She probably should have stood up, too. That would have been polite. He could hardly have sat down. He had been wearing a sober coat and a suit, but perhaps that was just for work. What was wrong with suits? He might have looked good in his suit. She couldn't remember. Nor could she find the clock, as the station was masked by hoardings and scaffolding. She tried not to be seen glancing at her reflection, which she did whenever she could as her fine hair, which she had wound into a knot, was coming loose and several strands now flapped about her face. She had something stuck between her front teeth, she knew it, and the most persistent sensation of having got her skirt caught in her tights. Oh god. Her left hand kept tugging at her skirt, while her right hand touched her front to check that her shirt hadn't burst open. Her throat was hot. Was she red? Was her shirt too undone? As she left the house she had hugged Bella, who examined her mother's chest and did up an extra button. Mary's body felt hot and damp. Her hands were damp. Her sweat smelt. Her breath smelt. She knew it.

'Mary?' Alexander Strachan. Tallish, fairish, nice. 'I thought we might go to a place I know in Covent Garden. Do you like fish, it doesn't matter if not, they do other things, I mean meat and things, unless you are a vegetarian, but then I'm sure they can do something, you know, with vegetables. Anyway. Is that OK? It's not far.' They set off, walking unnaturally far apart, smiling, amazed.

The waiter guided Mary into her chair and gave her a menu. She looked directly at Alexander for the first time: 'I have a daughter. Bella. She's thirty-two. Her father's dead. He was called Tobias. He's dead. I'm three −'

'Would you like some wine?'

'I used to sing.'

'Red or white?'

'White, please. Oh dear . . .'

Alexander laid his hand on hers. 'I was going to ask you to tell me about yourself.'

Carlo considered the body in front of him. The man had been an alcoholic who bled to death when one of the enlarged veins in his oesophagus haemorrhaged. His yellow skin and distended gut told Carlo that the liver would be shrunken and knobbly, and his spleen the size of three fists instead of one. His body had kept a record of sorts – an appendectomy scar and another on his arm which looked to have been caused by glass or a knife, stained index and second fingers on his right hand, a nose in bloom, a pierced ear, although the hole had grown over, and an oriental tattoo hiding someone's name.

It seemed to Carlo that this man had long ago decided that his body did not matter – these sooty lungs, this angry liver, the clogged heart and guts. In a way he was right but he was dead now, and dying was something only the body decided.

One morning Clara arrived at her studio to find a letter waiting. *Dearest Friend, I am watching a pair of cardinals dance in the snow. He is absurd, of course, all chatter and fancy moves, and his red – more than fire-red, sun-red, copper-red or blood-red, it is red-red, without depth or variation, unbroken tone. The red doesn't seem to belong to him, but to her – she is powerful and concentrated enough to dignify it. As if he had felt the cold and made a fuss, so she slipped off her coat and lent it. Such plumage. He does not deserve it.*

How are you, friend? Ready to bring your red to New York? The city will chatter and make its moves and plead with you to let them, us, try on your colours. What you said about my essay. So sharp and true. I was talking to you. I talk to you. Friend, my eye is on the eastern horizon watching for the snowbird, the firebird. Come burn us down. À bientôt, xJ.

A letter from Jacob; a hand reaching down and lifting her into the rare air above, where she could be her higher self. She could allow herself this much if she did not write back.

TWENTY

Clara phoned Juliet and insisted that an invitation to the exhibition had been sent to her weeks earlier.

'Did anything arrive from Clara? About her show?' Juliet asked Jacob.

'I don't know.' He did not look up from his book.

'But if you'd opened it, you'd remember.'

'Not necessarily.'

'Surely you'd . . . Was it addressed to me?'

'I don't open your letters.'

'Could you try to remember? Or have a look for it?'

'Why? You know about the show, when and where it is.'

'Yes, but she sent me an invitation and I didn't receive it.'

Jacob continued to read and Juliet sat beside him feeling troubled and ashamed. She did not think he was telling the truth and knew that the next day she would look, as sparingly as possible, through his papers. She found it – an envelope addressed to 'Juliet Clough and Jacob Dart'. He had not opened it.

*   *   *

The snow disappeared and the town of Littlefield enjoyed a brief, bare spring before the trees closed in once more.

Jacob proposed a trip to Boston. 'We could visit my old friend Patrick Hyde.'

'The architect?' Juliet was impressed.

'At last, someone you've heard of!'

'Isn't he based in London?'

'Yes, but he lectures at Harvard part-time.'

It was the week before Clara's show opened in New York and so Juliet suggested that they combine both in one trip.

'I'm not coming to New York,' Jacob said. 'You go, do, but I'll stay on in Boston or come back here.'

'Why not come with me?'

'I don't want to,' he said, so openly and lightly that Juliet could not think what might be wrong with that.

'Patrick Hyde is a old lech,' said Terence when he managed to persuade Juliet to come out to the sports bar.

'He's Jacob's friend.'

'Then I'm glad I'm not.'

'He does like you, you know.'

'Then why does he become utterly silent when I enter a room?'

'I don't know,' she said, 'but I'm sorry.'

Patrick Hyde had a warehouse apartment overlooking the Charles River. The world inside his building was hushed, subtly lit, and full of pleasing shades and textures. Juliet admired the sisal flooring, the brushed chrome light switches, the banisters wound with strips of leather, the smoky doors.

This apartment made her long to live in a place that

had not been home to anyone already. It took advantage of the plain lines and large dimensions of its space and every startling object in it looked made for its context. The overall effect was one of such balance that Juliet felt rambling and haphazard, like the kind of home she came from.

Jacob wandered comfortably off while Patrick guided her towards a corner where two low sofas were arranged under a vast arched window.

'What a fabulous window!'

'Bettina Urlicht, Juliet Clough,' said Patrick.

She had not seen the woman because she was sitting on the floor.

'And you're fabulous too!' Juliet improvised.

The woman rose and unfolded. Her features were so brilliant and enlarged that if she smiled, as she did now, she seemed to zoom towards you. Unusually for someone of twenty-four, Bettina had admitted her power and taken charge of it, softening her voice and drooping shyly so that all who met her thought how beautiful but also how unaffected she was. Juliet was pleased to think that she might like Bettina, especially when she pulled a handkerchief out of her sleeve and loudly blew her nose.

Jacob and Bettina greeted each other warmly, and the two women settled down to chat while Jacob wandered off again. Eventually, Patrick called them through to the dining room. He placed Bettina beside himself and Juliet opposite, next to Jacob, at one end of a table that could have seated sixteen. Juliet looked down into its surface, a welling green that swirled beneath the flicker of twelve tiny candles set in an iron spine. As her eyes adjusted, she realised that the walls were not black but a dry dark green that also shifted.

Patrick brought in bottles of icy white wine, a heap of

bread, a bowl of salad, and on a wooden board, a whole baked cheese. 'The cheese is from Bettina's family farm in Bavaria.'

'You're from a farm?' asked Juliet, with no idea of how it sounded.

'I am from Hamburg,' Bettina explained. 'It is my grandparents' farm.' Patrick smiled and ran his hand down her back in one thorough and familiar stroke.

They ate and talked and laughed, and Juliet tried to stop herself wondering. Patrick was not handsome but he was attractive. He was at least twenty years older than Bettina and he wore a wedding ring.

'My brother was going to be an architect,' said Juliet, hating herself for being so eager to find a place in the conversation. 'He got to his sixth year.'

'What happened then?' Bettina asked.

'He gave up.' Juliet couldn't tell them; suddenly she didn't want to. She could sense Jacob beside her, alert and detached.

'Just like that?' asked Patrick.

'Yes, just like that,' said Juliet and waited for Patrick to pursue the matter but he turned his chair towards Bettina, who was whispering in his ear. Juliet found it hard not to watch them, especially Bettina, who was scooping up runny cheese with her fingers. When Juliet reached forward to pass Patrick a bottle of wine, Bettina let her hand fall to his thigh and stay there. In this small light, Patrick's glutted smile gave him the appearance of a well-fed pet. Bettina continued to stroke him as she swivelled round to address Jacob.

'We could go to The Lily after dinner,' she said.

'Bettina's a member,' Patrick said. 'She knows the owner whereas I have only ever aspired to knowing someone who knows the owner!'

Bettina gazed into his eyes, and then pulled out her

handkerchief and blew her nose. Patrick blessed her and patted her back.

Bettina enthused about the clubs of Boston while Juliet tried to look impressed. When she could think of nothing to say, she decided to be encouraging: 'It's good to be reminded of what it's like to discover the nightlife of a city.'

'I've been here four years,' said Bettina, stretching her smile. 'I'm not talking about the obvious places. These clubs, places like The Lily, are more private, more . . . *authentic*.'

Juliet liked Bettina for being so obviously young and had to stop herself saying that when she had been 'your age', she had sought out those places too: the clubs that were staged in a different venue each week – a warehouse, a ticket office, a lock-keeper's cottage, a lying-in hospital, a gambling den.

'So you don't go out any more?' asked Bettina. She had a way of ironing out her English so that it was impossible to know whether or not she was being mischievous.

'I'm past it,' said Juliet. 'Thirty in a couple of weeks.'

'Oh, I thought you were older!'

Patrick raised an eyebrow but Juliet just smiled. 'So did I.'

Bettina switched tracks. 'So what's your subject – cities? Bridges?'

'Neither, at least not directly. I'm interested in frames, how we read their contents after the subject has, um, moved on.'

'Frames . . . ?'

'How we define them and what we bring to them, or take from one to the other so in that sense . . .'

'That could mean almost anything,' said Bettina, looking so innocently bemused that Juliet could not feel cross.

226

Patrick fetched a tray of grappa and coffee. He asked Juliet about Littlefield and she told him about the trees, but did so badly because she didn't want to share what she really thought with these people. Bettina sniffed and yawned until Patrick went back to the kitchen and returned with a bowl, which he set down in front of her. It was warm milk, and she wound one long arm round his shoulders and stroked his cheek to thank him.

'Oh,' he said turning to face her, his mouth almost touching hers. 'I forgot the honey.' Bettina shook her head, brushing her nose against his.

Jacob and Juliet watched as Patrick spooned honey into the hot milk and stirred. Juliet expected him to raise the spoon to Bettina's mouth, but he didn't. The girl wriggled and sneezed and one sleeve slipped down her arm revealing a nursery-pink satin strap on a broad brown shoulder. She lifted the bowl and with every sip she took, Patrick sank a little further towards her, as if slipping down into a warm milk bath.

On the walk back to their hotel, Juliet was speechless. She did not dare say a word and Jacob said nothing either until they were lying in bed, when he observed that Patrick was 'a bit of an arsehole, really', and she exclaimed over the bowl of milk and he remembered the nightclub talk and they giggled about one thing and another, and then made love like good friends.

Juliet fell into sleep and then woke an hour later feeling anxious.

'Jacob . . . Jacob?'

'Yes, darling?' He could sound affectionate and attentive with the barest effort.

'Did you think Bettina was beautiful?'

'I suppose so.'

'You were looking at her.'

'And at you and Patrick.'

227

'You were sort of licking your lips.'

'I was eating. What is this about?'

'I just thought . . . you were so *alert* . . .'

'Because I was with you. You're being very boring. Go to sleep.'

Boring. Juliet remembered how she had listened to his voice through the wall and thought that she had had a clearer idea of him back then when she couldn't see him. Now, listening in the dark, she began to remember what she had known all along.

Juliet caught a train to New York. After London, most cities seemed manageable, even provincial, but New York scared her. She liked to walk for the thrill of the light, which on a sharp March day was considerable. While her mind was on frames and clearings, loaded eyes and empty fields, she was being dazzled, captivated, overcome by the absoluteness of light sheared off by a grid of tall buildings and then hitting a plane. It was god and the city meeting one another conclusively, and it would only be like this for this hour on this afternoon.

Juliet arrived at the gallery in a state of exalted certainty. She had envisaged a large white space but found a low-ceilinged factory floor with false walls creating a serpentine trail of tiny rooms. Juliet pushed her way through the crowd.

In the third room, she saw two tall, colourful women. Clara was wearing an antique dress in a shade of pink which acted like a tuning fork so that her skin became warm cream, her hair cherry and apricot, and her eyes gooseberry jam. The dress was taut and smooth; she looked sumptuous. Beyond her, Barbara Dart wore her well-organised, innocent blues. She smiled with her eyes open wide.

Not for the first time, Juliet felt as if there were some higher adult world to which she had not yet been admitted. She turned and set off into another room where Clara caught up with her.

'I'm so pleased you're here!' she said, giving Juliet a powerful hug.

'Well at least now I know why Jacob wouldn't come.'

Clara looked at her carefully and Juliet explained: 'Barbara. I suppose if I'd thought about it, I'd have realised she'd be here.'

'And Jacob's not?'

'No, he's not.'

'Well that's alright then!' Clara bit her lip and twirled her sister round. 'Nice dress, but it could do with a belt.'

These days Juliet wore whatever Jacob approved of: over-sized untucked shirts, jerseys through at the elbow and nostalgic, wholesome dresses; clothes that reflected what he liked to call her – tomboy, crosspatch.

Clara was studying her intensely. 'Are you alright?'

'Yes, why?'

'You look a bit pale.'

'I've just walked the length of Manhattan and it's bloody cold and I've come to see my sister and look who's here: the former wife of my . . . my . . .'

'Lover?'

'We live together.'

'Boyfriend then?'

'I don't know.'

'Are they divorced?'

'Why is everyone so curious about the state of their marriage?'

'She's coming this way . . .' Clara hustled Juliet through several rooms and stood her in front of a familiar sky. It was one of Clara's early works – a study of the winter sun rising over the fields of Allnorthover. They were teenagers again, giggling and conspiring.

'Maybe I should leave,' offered Juliet.

'Where are you staying?'

'With a friend of Terence's, quite a way out, so maybe I ought to go.'

'I'm round the corner at the Lampen. You can stay with me.'

Barbara arrived. 'Clara,' she commanded, 'we must go to dinner.'

Clara put her hand on Juliet's shoulder. 'I have my sister with me,' she said.

'How nice.' She considered Juliet. 'I'm afraid there's simply no room . . .'

Clara tightened her grip and Juliet wasn't sure whether she was being brandished or protected. 'In which case please give my apologies.'

Barbara's smile snapped shut and she turned so swiftly that she might not have heard Juliet murmur: 'Mine, too.'

The sisters cackled their way through the building and out onto the street.

'I'm so glad you came,' said Clara once more as she let them into her room.

'Are you? I thought you weren't even going to tell me about it.'

'Oh that was just superstition, in case something went wrong.'

'One minute you're court painter and the next you're turning down dinner. Isn't that bad for your career?'

Clara was pulling bottles out of the mini-bar, opening a room-service menu. 'She's not god, Juliet, she's an arts administrator.'

'And Jacob's wife.' Juliet settled back against a heap of pillows and started to flick through television channels.

Clara passed her a drink. 'Then you should feel sorry for her. I do.'

'So does Jacob, that's why he sat for the portrait.'

Clara shook her head. 'I don't think so. I think he couldn't resist.'

'Resist what?'

'Himself.'

This notion delighted Juliet.

'Anyway,' continued Clara, 'it turns out that Barbara can resist him after all. She resisted the portrait . . . rejected it, actually.'

'But it was him! Entirely!'

'Not according to her, or at least not the Jacob she wanted.'

'But she can't do that, can she? Commission you and then when it's finished change her mind?'

'She still paid me.'

'But it's so whimsical. I hate them all so much.'

'Who?'

'Her and creepy Tania and that lecherous Patrick Hyde.'

'You met Patrick Hyde?'

'Patrick Hyde and his child bride . . .'

'But he's married to Valentina Zorb, the stylist. They've got about six kids.'

And so Juliet described the dinner in Boston, Bettina and the bowl of warm milk, and the more Clara laughed, the more she span it out until they all, Patrick, Bettina, Jacob even, were nothing more than the cartoonish inflations of a vicious joke about a world that she wanted nothing to do with.

Clara was worried that Juliet looked ill and Juliet was worried too – something had shaken Clara. As they fell asleep, she asked in the dark: 'What's wrong?' but Clara turned her back and let out a monstrous snore.

In the morning, Juliet came out of the bathroom to find Clara on the telephone.

'Please,' she was saying, 'I know I've been . . . Perhaps I made you, you're right, but don't just . . . please . . . can't we . . . I know it's the middle of the night there but this is important . . . please . . . just . . . don't go, say something, please . . .'

Juliet's initial reaction was to retreat but as Clara's voice broke down and she buried her face in a pillow, Juliet went to pick up the receiver and hang up. She even listened for a moment, in case whoever it was at the other end had relented and after all Clara's pleading would now speak, but they did not and so Juliet lay down beside her sister, placed a hand on her back and waited to find out what she could do to help.

TWENTY-ONE

Juliet finished the course of white pills. A week later she had a period but it was nothing; there was no pain, just a few days of thin bright blood. Two weeks after that she started to bleed again, more heavily. Her back seized up and she understood that the pills had stopped working and she was about to step out of their fog. Jacob remembered how she had been in Khyber Road and he looked after her. No one could have been more patient or kind.

When the pain got worse, she did not say so but she wanted her mother. Her parents had not been in touch for two months so she went off to phone them and came back in looking crushed.

Jacob sat down beside her. 'What's wrong?'

'My mother is becoming a nun. At least, she's spent another two months on retreat.'

'How interesting.'

'It's not, it's selfish. What about my father?'

'Isn't he in Salisbury?'

'That's the point. What's he doing spending all his pension, all the family money, on some run-down shack?'

'Perhaps they want to move there. It's got to be a better place than Allnorthover.'

'Allnorthover's alright; it's character-building. The thing is, my mother hasn't had anything to do with this cottage. She hasn't even gone there. What if they start leading separate lives? It could be dangerous.'

'You should feel lucky.'

'I don't. It makes me have to think about them.'

'Do try to calm down and remember that your body is going through a big readjustment.'

'You think I'm being hormonal?'

'No, I think you're being totally over-emotional. Now go to bed.'

Juliet obeyed. She loved being teased by him and told what to do. She missed her brothers and sister.

The next morning Jacob said, 'I'm taking you away next weekend – for your birthday.'

'Another treat?'

'Is that a complaint?'

'No, but there are so many . . .'

'Why do you have to qualify every good thing?'

'I don't mean to. It's lovely.'

He pulled her towards him. 'Let's just be.'

This sounded like the answer to everything and Juliet resolved to enjoy whatever Jacob had in store for her.

They drove north over the Connecticut River and then north-east up through New Hampshire and into Vermont, where the hills massed and the snow lingered. There were broken-backed barns, splayed picket fences, antique tractors and warehouses stuffed full of New England bric-à-brac for sale. Juliet found the plates, lace, cruets, knitted toys and tarnished silver depressing. She almost bought a stained patchwork quilt and a three-legged stool but remembered that in June she was going back to England, a place full of such things.

Jacob did not consult a map and brought them with nonchalant pride to their destination. Flagpole House was the oldest surviving building in the town of Nuthatch, and it was the most nurtured New England clapboard house Juliet had seen. The fresh paintwork was in muted greens and crimped icicles trimmed the edge of the roof.

The hallway was dark. No one appeared, not even after Jacob rang a bell which he found perched on a doily on top of a mahogany bureau. The bell was a souvenir from a cathedral in Europe, its handle an ungenerous cross. It made little noise.

'Hullo,' called Jacob, too quietly.

'Hello!' shouted Juliet.

'Oh, you must be the Darts.' A tall figure rose up in one of the shadowy reception rooms. 'Karen Courtney-O'Brien. So lovely to see you.' She was tall and spare and spoke in such a toneless chirp that Juliet made the mistake of thinking her welcome insincere. 'We took the place over from the Van Raans last year. Weren't they dear?'

'Yes,' said Jacob, 'terribly.'

'Yes they were,' added Juliet, wanting to be polite. Jacob frowned.

'We have everything ready for you in the Hinge Suite. Let's get you settled in.'

They bumped along into a severely heated room dominated by a four-poster bed. Jacob announced that he was going for a walk.

'I'll stay and explore,' said Juliet, a little dutifully.

The story of the house, its history and renovation, was on hand in a folder of laminated pages. It's a hundred years old, thought Juliet, so is Khyber Road. In London, it's hard to live in something that isn't. The room looked authentic, but was proving unfriendly. The armchairs, one too low, the other too narrow, eased her back out as soon as she sat down, and the bed was topped with a slippery fireproof coverlet. There were six books on a shelf – poetry, botany and local history – and perfume atomisers and bone-backed brushes arranged on the dresser. The room contained four mirrors, all warped and at odd heights. Juliet had to tug at the drawers, and the hangers in the wardrobe were skewed because it was so shallow.

On the sloping desk, a visitors' book had been turned to a fresh page. Beside it was a fountain pen and a bottle of ink. There was a log fire sealed behind glass in a brick chimney breast. Juliet thought it must be decorative until she turned what looked like an oven knob and flames appeared.

Jacob came in. 'I've booked a table for eight.' He unlaced his boots, sat on the bed and looked at her. 'Are you cold?'

'My brain can't make sense of this. It looks like fire and I can feel its heat but I don't believe in it.'

'You find the place unconvincing?'

'No, no, I like it. It's beautiful. You were so clever to find it. They've done it up very carefully, I know, but it's a little bit –'

'Chi-chi?'

'I suppose so.'

'More so than an English country-house hotel?'

'I don't know, I've never stayed in one. Really, this is beautiful,' and then knowing what Jacob valued more, 'and so interesting. I don't know about America on a domestic scale. Every idea we've been given of the place has been epic, hasn't it? All about adventure, battles and quests.'

'You're making it sound like Arthurian England.'

'But we've had kitchen-sink England, too. And kitchen-sink Europe: clocks ticking in drawing rooms, *Madame Bovary*, Vuillard, Ibsen, provincial entropy . . .'

'Entropy? It is a fashionable word but I'm not sure you know what you mean by it. Besides, there are countless American works about small-town life.'

'Oh. Yes. Of course there are. It just seems different, to us, from the European version. Pioneering, for a start. And in Europe, one small town is only a hill or valley away from another. Here, they can be a detail in a wilderness.'

'A clearing in the forest? A circle of wagon trains on the prairie? The space that ceases to be a space as soon as you enter it with your gaze? Do you really think you're the first person to have thought about that?'

Juliet had been thinking and writing about it for years. She felt cautious now, knowing that if she pursued this conversation, Jacob might say something that would unravel her ideas to the point where she would throw out thousands of words and want to start again.

'I might have one of those muffins to keep me going. Do you want one?'

'Hardly.'

Juliet poured a cup of thin coffee from a plastic thermos jug, toyed with a shrunken red apple in the fruit bowl and examined the basket of muffins. There was a card pinned to the frilly cloth: *Welcome back to Flagpole House Jacob and Barbra!* Juliet dropped it in front of Jacob who glanced and said, 'She hates it when people misspell her name like that.'

The irritation of a missing 'a'. There had been other times when Jacob reacted with a sidestep like this, forcing Juliet to adjust to his angle. This, though, was the time that it did not surprise her. She managed to say only that she thought she'd have a shower and went through to the bathroom, where she sank to her knees. There was a sharp pain in her belly and she thought it was her old pain but then realised that this pain was a feeling; not the kind she was used to, but something absolute and raging. I want a real life, not baskets of muffins and bowls of warm milk, not this entropy, and yes that was the right word, this over-invested, under-lived version of the good life. Fuck it, she didn't even want a particularly good life, so long as it was real.

Dinner was elaborate and delicious, but Juliet was finding it hard to disguise her pain. Jacob moved his chair round next to hers and put his hand on her back, but for once it made the pain worse.

'Please . . .' she began shifting her body away from him.

Jacob observed how pain roughened her features. If he could not cure her of this then it happened without him and when Jacob saw the world turning away from him, he tried to get ahead. He stood up and walked out.

Juliet, unsurprised, watched him go and wondered if he had ever been fully present. Just three months had passed since Jacob had arrived in Littlefield and lifted her up to the snowbound door. Was she going to stop believing in him already?

The bathroom's plumbing had been modernised so discreetly that Juliet couldn't work out how to turn the water on. Jacob found her. He twiddled the dials and adjusted the taps while Juliet, ashamed now more than angry, took off her clothes and then his.

She said it: 'This is not real life.'

He looked so sad, 'I know.'

They stood under the falling water and embraced with the seriousness of people who know what they are and are relieved to be able to hold onto something.

Clara lay beside her husband in countryside darkness. She could not see her hand or his back, and was in any case too scared to reach; such a gesture might tip the matter irrevocably.

'Why has this happened?' she whispered. 'Am I too old? Too familiar?'

'No,' said Stefan, 'you're not here.'

'You go to Geneva.'

'Where I work, and when I'm here, I'm here. For months you've been completely absorbed by something else.'

'My work.'

'Really?'

'Are you trying to suggest that you have been playing around with what's her name because you thought I was doing the same? Is that your excuse?'

He would not speak.

Of all the things Clara might have said next: 'Are you in love with her?'

'Don't be so vulgar.'

Clara felt the machinery of her life, all that squeezed and tugged at and propelled her, give way: the twenty-two rooms of the house were dust; the children, with their laundry, games, illnesses and noise, hurtled into space; and memories of a train to London, a plane to New York, a painting, a letter, a pink dress, rose in her mind as proof that she had been turning away and that Stefan was right about her being full of something else, not someone though, not really someone.

This pain was as black and clean as the pain she had felt when Tobias died. It cut through the surface of life – its features, polish and grime – and lit up the fundamental, majestic shapes that were ordinarily lost from view. Clara had thought that they would all learn from having lost Tobias. But she had been distracted and Stefan had too, and now it seemed that pain was only pain and that there was simply more or less of it.

*　　*　　*

There were days when Carlo looked forward to going home. He had given Jonathan a key and liked to find the place lit up and full of his singing. Jonathan sang as he flitted around the kitchen making something intricate for supper; his mealtime chatter was a kind of song and later he might sing Carlo to sleep, too.

'How were the bodies today?' Jonathan said as he put down two plates of foamy courgette soufflé. 'You take yours apart while I put mine back together. You'd have thought my work was the more demanding.'

'You had a client today?'

'One of my regulars,' said Jonathan. 'Eat up, it's collapsing.'

Carlo hated the regulars, the men who wanted so much to be touched by Jonathan that they endured his catastrophic massage again and again.

'You can't have regulars, can you?' said Jonathan. 'Do they seem the same or different?'

'Different. Often I know what I'll find but –'

'Tell me a story,' Jonathan interrupted. 'Go on! I'll tell you one of mine.'

'I did a post-mortem on a baby this morning. My first one.'

'How did it die?'

'In the womb.'

'No I mean technically, or whatever.'

'Nothing obvious. They'll run some tests and maybe we'll find a cause, maybe not.'

'You mean it could have died for no reason, just like that?'

'We don't always find out why.'

'But that's your job isn't it?'

All Carlo could think of was the list he'd chalked up on the board:

Spleen	*1g*
Kidneys	*10g*
Heart	*12g*

It had looked like what it was – something and nothing.

Going to bed had become about trying to get Carlo to sleep. He did not resist when Jonathan anointed him with lavender, ginger and juniper oil and arranged him in a yoga position known as The Corpse – on his back, arms outstretched, hands facing upwards, legs loosely apart. 'You'll snore like a hog, but you will achieve deep sleep.'

If Carlo stirred, Jonathan would jump up and fetch camomile tea or a hot-water bottle and would offer to read, or do anything that might help. Carlo wanted to be helped but sometimes the only thing to do was to lock the bathroom door and masturbate, thinking about men he had glimpsed or imagined, too tired to think about the man who was actually there.

One morning, Jonathan ran his hand down Carlo's body until it rested on his cock, 'Remember?' Carlo smiled and pushed himself into Jonathan's fingers then began to stroke Jonathan's balls, arse and thighs, and Jonathan rocked and sighed, 'Yes, yes,' but stayed soft. He twisted away from Carlo's roughness and took his cock in his mouth only Carlo's need had trapped itself, leaving him stalled and numb. Jonathan's mouth was too much and not enough. They tried but neither could calibrate his touch to the other.

'It's ridiculous,' said Carlo. 'I'm so hard, I can't.'

Jonathan withdrew his body into a curl. 'Never mind.'

'We mean well.'

'Never mind.'

*   *   *

Mary went out to have dinner with Alexander Strachan, and Fred babysat. As he kissed Bella goodnight, she looked up. 'Egghead.'

Fred smiled.

'Good?'

'Yes, it means clever.'

'I thought it meant bald.'

Fred hurried off to the bathroom mirror. He believed that he was as he had always been and did not expect to change. It's the worry. Looking after them all. They're making me lose my hair.

He planned to open a bottle of wine and sit out on the terrace at the back of the house to think about the garden. He liked the idea of land, even more than that of owning a house, and made plans for getting rid of the slugs, for stopping cats shitting in the flowerbeds and for mowing the lawn, but then he had another glass of wine and thought about Caroline. It was only a week since she had gone which meant he might not see her for months but that was alright because it took that long for things to calm down.

Several times now, Caroline had come back from Hong Kong and spent time with Fred. She accepted his devotion as a cat might, according to her own needs and mood. She tidied up, joined in and looked after Bella. When Fred and Mary moved to Botolph Square, Caroline spent three days helping them to unpack after which she was off, heartless and serene. Fred knew no one who lived so evidently in the present moment. He saw it as a gift.

The doorbell rang and in the end he decided to go and see who it was. 'Caroline!' Fred was horrified. 'I almost ignored it. I thought it must be someone wanting something.'

Caroline brought several bags into the hall while Fred

stood and watched, so astonished that he did not think to help.

'I do want something,' she said as she walked past him into the living room.

'Me?' He made a joke of it, rolled his eyes and then rushed over and threw himself down beside her on the new sofa, his legs getting caught up and kicking against her. She ignored him as she ignored all digressions and surprises.

Fred offered her a drink, jumping up as violently as he had sat down. At times of great excitement, Fred's mind sped up, his body too. He had been about to run and compromised on a sort of skip.

Caroline followed him. She was concentrating. 'What if I did want you?'

Fred sloshed wine into glasses and began to drink from one, forgetting to offer her the other. He was supposed to say something now, the words that would make it happen.

'You don't want me.' It was not what he had thought or rehearsed, not even what he meant.

'Why should I not want you?'

'Because things are fine as they are.' He didn't mean this.

'You don't mean that,' she said just as he thought it, which startled him so much that he retorted, 'Of course I mean it. I wouldn't have said it otherwise.'

He drained the first glass of wine and picked up the other. 'Anyway, you're supposed to be in Hong Kong. With your husband.'

'Oliver likes you.'

'Then he can't know that you have slept with me.'

'He does. We tell each other everything.'

'That's disgusting!' Fred finished the second glass and poured two more.

'Is it? Well, I've told him that I have to be with you.'

'Really? You haven't told me . . .' He had no idea why he felt so cross.

'Why else do you think I've come all this way?'

'Why do you ever come?'

Caroline was offering herself to him and he was spoiling it. He looked hard at her, meaning to show that he felt different to how he sounded, that he meant Yes, of course, yes!, but she startled him by saying, 'I love you, Fred.'

He had never seen her like this. His vision of Caroline was of a monument, all firmness and heft.

'I don't like your hair,' he said. Her highlights had been gauged according to the Hong Kong sun. 'Or that orange stuff on your skin.'

Unphased, she moved on to her next point: 'Is there someone else?'

'You said that like a line you'd been given.'

'Please. Say.'

For the first time since she had arrived, Fred felt that he could breathe. 'Yes,' he said, 'there is.'

'I knew it. It's Mary, isn't it?'

He laughed. 'Yes. You're right of course, I am in love with Mary.'

'Why then have you pretended to be in love with me?'

He was enjoying this now: 'What's my line? I've forgotten my line.'

'What line? This is real.' Her voice was not attractive.

The front door opened, which meant that Mary had come home. Fred slowly poured more wine, hoping that she would reach the kitchen before he had to respond.

Mary was pleased. 'Caroline! What a –'

Caroline yelped, as if she had trodden on something sharp.

'How nice,' offered Mary.

'What happened to what's his name?' asked Fred.

'I couldn't find him.'

'Couldn't find who?' asked Caroline.

'I had a, well, I was meeting someone and I couldn't find them.'

'Did you not agree on a time and place?' Fred asked. 'I suppose you thought you'd just wander around the city until you bumped into each other.'

'No. We were to meet at Chevreuil.'

'Chevreuil!' said Caroline. 'He must be keen. Rich and keen. Who is he? How did you meet?'

'By wandering around the city until we bumped into each other. Now I must go to check on Bella.'

'He stood you up.' Caroline still put things together out loud.

'I told you, I couldn't find him.'

Mary had not been to Chevreuil before. It was a converted garage on the King's Road, which she remembered as derelict and then for a year or two as a market where fashion students sold their designs. Now it was two floors of canteen tables laid for intimate dinners on a mass scale. Alexander had said they should meet in the bar, which was so full that the crowd had spilled out into the reception area. Mary could barely get through the door. Everyone was taller and younger than she, and knew how to stand and what to say. She spotted a woman in a white shirt carrying a clipboard and tapped her on the shoulder.

'Excuse me.'

The woman turned – heavy blue-black hair, frosted eyes, thin white mouth. 'Mary George!'

'Theresa. Hello.' Mary was back in Allnorthover, trying to dissolve into the place and to avoid the attentions of mad Tom Hepple who said she could save him. Theresa and her gang sought her out for fun; they had her surrounded.

'So,' said Theresa. She was smiling as if there were no reason not to. 'You still with the doctor's son?'

'No.'

'Shame,' Theresa responded flatly. 'Says you had a kid. It was in the paper.'

'The paper?'

'You know – births, deaths.'

'Tobias must have been in the paper, too.'

Theresa clapped her hand on her mouth and gasped. 'Silly me. I forgot. Shame.'

'No you didn't,' Mary said.

'Sorry, what was that? It's so bloody noisy in here.'

'You didn't forget!' Mary shouted. People nearby went quiet and turned to listen. 'You didn't forget.'

Theresa's mouth grew thinner and whiter. Her brief black eyebrows shot up and she raised her right hand. She's going to hit me, Mary thought, only Theresa was brandishing her clipboard.

'Do you have a reservation?' she asked, dragging a marbled fingernail down her list. 'I can't seem to find your name.'

Mary thought about this. 'Says I've come here as someone's guest.'

'Ooo . . .' said Theresa. They were at the bus stop in Allnorthover and someone had just said that Mary had a lovebite on her neck. 'So you've managed to move on.'

Mary considered Theresa's face and how little adjustment she had made to her teenage snarl to produce an effective expression of welcome. 'And now I'm leaving.'

TWENTY-TWO

One afternoon, Juliet came home to find Jacob sitting very still.

'My sister telephoned. My mother died last night.'

Jacob had never taken her to see his mother and now she would never meet her or know her as Barbara had.

'Don't worry,' she said. 'I'll make some calls, find us a flight. If I can get seats tomorrow, I'll cancel my class. No one will mind.'

'I've booked a flight.'

'When do we leave?'

'Tomorrow afternoon. I'm going alone.'

'What about me? Shouldn't I be there?'

Jacob silenced her with his red, wet eyes. 'Sweetheart, what for?'

That evening, they sat outside on the porch step.

'Would you stay here if you could?' he asked.

'With you?'

'Yes.'

'With you and half a dozen children and a dog?'

'If you like.'

'We can do that anywhere.'

'Not London, we're too poor.'

'Are we?' Juliet had no idea.

'We could live by the sea, in a stone cottage with a big garden. From the bedroom window, you would be able to see the sea.'

'How would we live?'

'I don't know. How do we manage to live now?'

'Tell me more about it.'

'About what?'

'Our home.' The night, Jacob fucked her with such energy and ambition that Juliet feared he might use up all the desire he had left.

Monica Clough had her third stroke at the age of seventy-eight, and died in the presence of her daughter and daughter-in-law. She had not seen her son for five months. He arrived two days later, after Juliet had driven him to Boston in time for the afternoon flight. She got up in the American dawn to do this and Barbara drove across London in the English night to meet him. She took him back to her flat and ran him a bath.

Juliet waited for Jacob to get in touch. She reminded herself that someone had died and that she knew what that felt like and understood that he would want to go away, or go back and in any case, he had to. He had said that he would stay with his sister. She and Juliet had exchanged greetings when Sally rang up every week or so. Juliet would move into another room, but then listen. Most of their conversation appeared to be about Monica but every now and then Jacob would say something else, often something he had not told her.

'I'm so sorry I wasn't here when you called. I was in Vermont . . . Yes, lots of snow still . . . Actually, I saw something amazing, an indigo bunting . . . No, not the lullaby, the bird; it was the bluest thing I have ever seen. I was walking towards a wood, and there it was on the snow . . . the male, I think . . . all show . . . but unearthly, you know? . . . As if it put its all into its brilliance, made itself a gesture, a declaration . . .' This was not for Sally, who never knew what to say when Jacob spoke like this, this was for himself. 'Yes, tell Monica, do, an indigo bunting . . . no, Vermont . . . and give her all my love.'

Juliet knew that with a little effort, she could find Sally's number. It would be on a phone bill, or in a diary or address book. Jacob left everything lying around so openly that she never snooped. She had never gone into the cabin, even though the key was right here on a hook in the hall. He had told her of Barbara breaking into his room at the gallery, and suggested that she routinely rifled through whatever of his she could. Juliet, only just thirty, had been shocked; nothing had yet cost her so much that she could understand.

Jacob was full of the freedom of grief and he craved a stranger. He wanted to remember what it was like to be potential. Each day, he walked to the British Library and sat in the Reading Room not reading, and then he would go out to the old gardens of a nearby square to walk under trees, to smile at girls, and to make something of the pink-and-white unfurling of the magnolia, and the candy-coloured cherry.

Which stranger? He was captivated by a woman's ankle, the back of a man's neck, the roll of this one's hips and the weight of that one's hair. He fell in love with a smell, maybe sweat, maybe roses, a cracked lens in a pair of spectacles, a shaving rash on a white chin, the way a belly creased and folded. He adored one who bit her nails at her desk and another who sat beside him on a bench plucking at a whisker on her chin. Each was innocent to him and innocent of him. If he found the right one, he might be saved.

Juliet Clough had not been forgotten. Jacob needed everything he could muster in order to rise out of his mother's death and the depths of himself. He would not betray Juliet. This was for her.

Clara heard that Jacob had come back for Monica's funeral, and that he had not returned to Littlefield, but did not want to speculate on what this might mean. This was a fragile time and Jacob, the idea of him, had proved dangerous. In any case, she had no time to think. Stefan had been spending three weeks in Geneva and so she was alone in the country with the children. She took them to see her parents, hoping that everyone would benefit from their energy and noise, but the doctor was shut up in his study with plans for the renovation of his cottage, and while Francesca fed them all, she chose not to speak. Clara wondered if her mother had been silent throughout her childhood and she had not noticed. She couldn't remember.

When Stefan came home, she watched him kiss the children without any of the urgency of a disappearing man, and hoped that she was safe.

That night when they talked, they lay closer.

'I haven't been unfaithful,' he said. 'I haven't actually slept with her.'

'Then why tell me about it?'

'I had a duty to.'

'And you wanted to hurt me.'

'That is absurd. I could have slept with her but I didn't, so as not to hurt you.'

'She must be very young to be so patient.'

'She understands that I need time to think.'

Clara began to cry: 'I am thirty-four which is different, you know, to being thirty. There is no time, no time at all.'

'According to the rules, you'll live longer than I will.'

'Maybe, but I don't get to go on choosing. You can just go along with whatever and try out something else, and for all sorts of reasons remake your life. You get to go on choosing and that is why men are so –'

'So what?'

'Romantic.'

Clara agreed with Stefan that she would go to London for a week and that afterwards they would both spend the rest of the summer at home. Tucked under her studio door was a note from Jacob: *Dearest Friend, In John Evelyn's time, whales were found in the river. One was stranded at Deptford. Shall we get on a boat and go look for whalebones? I'm here now, I think. xJ.*

They didn't get on a boat or travel to Deptford. Jacob turned up at her studio at the end of a day and they went to a bar that had just opened round the corner. Clara noticed that he looked out of place among the fluttering young – a man who did not appear his age but upon whom gravity was now exerting itself.

Jacob, too, was thinking about age. Clara looked tired, as if being and carrying herself required more effort than it ought. Her curls were cooler and drier than he had remembered, the reds settling down.

'Why are you looking at me like that?' she asked.

'I was thinking about when we first met.'

'In Khyber Road.'

'Yes.'

'You opened the door as if the house were on fire . . . no, you *were* a fire, at the height of your blaze.'

'A pretentious way of reminding me that I'm getting older. I'm still ten years younger than you.'

Jacob did not flinch. He was content with the way he was ageing. There seemed to be no imminent expansion, depletion or collapse; no jowls, paunch or thinning hair. He knew, though, that his texture was less fine, and Clara could see it breaking down into its component parts, as it had in her picture, so that while his beauty was still remarkable, it took longer to have its effect.

When they had finished their drinks, they walked to the Tube station. Jacob took Clara's hand and turned her towards him. He leaned forward and kissed her on the mouth, meeting her eyes.

'Don't worry,' he said as she pulled away and tried to speak. 'We never will.'

'No.' She relaxed.

They were not wise or careful or good, just exhausted.

Mary was picking up Bella's toys in the living room when Caroline appeared and in her useful way, began to help.

'It's been very nice having you here,' said Mary, thinking how much she liked this woman who was of a type that she felt she ought to despise. 'Why are you looking through the rooms-to-let pages still? Fred seems very happy. Why not stay?'

'Fred has made it clear. I'm in the way.'

'If anyone's in the way, it's me and Bella.'

They were on their hands and knees, collecting together the pieces of a jigsaw puzzle which had been incomplete for years. Bella seemed to think that one day the missing pieces would be in the box and she would be able to complete the picture.

'Only in my way,' said Caroline, nicely.

'Fred's too. The pair of you are finally together –'

'Are we?'

'I thought you were.'

'We're in separate rooms.'

'I thought that was quite romantic.'

'It's not. He's terrified and besides he's still in love with you.'

Mary sat back and shook her head vigorously, 'Oh no, oh no,' she said.

Juliet was walking along Main Street when someone ran into her. He came upon her as an impression of terror – his face creased, his mouth wide open. He was not running as people in Littlefield usually ran, but with real urgency and no thought.

'Theo Dorne – I'm so sorry, are you alright, can I buy you a cup of coffee?'

'You run as if you were escaping a bear,' Juliet said as she sat down.

'Oh. I was trying to catch a bus.' A girl with whom he had had a fight was leaving town. He had seen her in the street, ran to catch up and just as he did so realised that he wanted to let her go, so he had kept on running until he lost his footing and collided with Juliet.

'No, a bear came to mind, not a bus.'

'You're right, it was a bear.'

Theo Dorne was a research assistant in the history department. He was shorter than Jacob; broader, darker, younger and more . . . coherent. Had he really not seen Juliet before? He would have remembered. For one thing, he had thought for a moment that she was a boy. Her curly hair was neither short nor long, and her clothes gave little clue as to the details of her shape. Theo studied her

253

dark eyes and dry mouth, set in a face that looked plain at first sight but from then on became intriguing. She had the large, flat ears of an Indian goddess and a goddess's golden skin. She bit her lip and frowned, and Theo took a breath and asked her out.

Three days later, he walked her home after an evening in the sports bar, and they sat on the porch step and drank beer.

'You live here alone?'

'I do now.'

He was close enough for her to breathe him. The night was cooling and her skin prickled. He was raising a bottle to his lips. Their bare arms were about to touch.

'I'm going back to London at the end of June.'

'And meanwhile . . .'

He leant against her conspiratorially, she leant back and they stayed there, shoulder to shoulder, each giving up their weight to the other. Theo said nothing; he was waiting for Juliet to decide.

He cannot touch me as deeply as Jacob, she thought, which means that Jacob is safe. She rehearsed the words, Come inside, and reminded herself that she was young and abroad and had been left alone. Not everything had to have consequences.

There was something about this formulation that she had learnt from Jacob and which made her uncomfortable: a way of connecting and disconnecting parts according to the point to be made, as if everything could be broken down and rearranged and would work just as well.

Such thoughts were for later. Juliet stood up and held out her hand. 'Come inside,' she said.

'Sure?'

'It's getting cold.'

'No it isn't.'

'Come inside.'

Their sex was wonderfully straightforward compared to the fine adjustments of Jacob, so multiple and imperative that Juliet strained to make her body answer all his questions at once.

Juliet did not intend to see Theo Dorne again but when he called and asked if they could meet, she said yes; she wanted to. Then the telephone rang once more.

'Hullo.'

'Jacob? How are you?'

'I don't know.'

'And how was the funeral?'

Silence.

'Jacob?'

'Yes?'

'Where are you staying?'

'I'm not sure. There's been a lot to sort out.'

'When are you coming back?'

'I think I should stay, sweetheart, and in any case, you'll be back soon.'

'But your stuff . . .'

'You could ship the books and chuck everything else. Just leave it.'

'We were meant to go back together.'

'I know and I'm sorry, but I'm here now. What can I do?'

He had been speaking so quietly that if he said goodbye, Juliet didn't hear him. She looked around the room and realised that even though this was not their house, she could not imagine living with Jacob anywhere else.

Furious and heartbroken, Juliet walked to the cabin and saw through the window that it was heaped with books, bottles and clothes. He had taken everything of himself from the house and had put it here, as if in storage. It looked like his room at the Shipping Office. She did not open the door, and returning back along the path remembered how Theo's smile had become laughter as she came on his fingers and how her noise, too, had taken shape as laughter. She threw the key to the cabin into the trees.

Alexander Strachan found his way to Botolph Square. The sun shone, his head hurt, and the drifting pollen had brought on an attack of hay fever. A child was raking gravel in front of the house.

'Hello,' Alexander said, and sneezed.

'Bless you,' the figure straightened up, turned and took off the scarf tied round its head. It was a boy – grubby and foreign-looking, with curly hair set back on his head like a slipping wig. 'Sorry?'

'Oh, I'm so sorry.'

'Sorry?' Fred couldn't understand why a stranger would stop by the wall, say hello, sneeze and then apologise.

'I thought . . . I'm looking for Mary George. Is this her house?'

'Yes.'

'Is she in?'

'No.' Fred tugged at a root.

'Oh.'

Alexander wondered where to start. 'Alexander Strachan.' He sneezed again.

'Federico Clough, bless you.'

'You don't need to, it's hay fever. The thing is, can I leave a message?'

'Why?'

Alexander was tired. 'Are you her gardener?'

Fred looked down at himself and smiled. 'That's right. Miss George's gardener.'

Alexander felt in his jacket and found a pen and a piece of paper. 'I tell you what. I'll just shove a note through the letterbox.'

'You do that,' snapped Fred, picking up some secateurs. 'You do that and I'll do this.'

'Sorry?'

When Alexander had gone, Fred let himself back into the house and picked up the note. *Dear Mary, Please don't mind that I came to find you. I hope very much that you might like to find me. Yours, A.S.* Fred meant to put it on the hall table but thinking it might get overlooked, decided to take it up to Mary's room only on the way he went into his own room and left it there.

Mary did not know what to do about Alexander so meanwhile decided that something had to be done about Fred. One evening as she leant over her sleeping daughter, she ran her hand down her back and not for the first time, blushed as she remembered her hand on Fred's thigh. Enough.

She found him in the kitchen and as she had rehearsed, came straight to the point: 'You ought to know that Caroline has told me.'

'Told you what?'

'How you feel about me.'

'What?'

'Why it isn't going to work out with her.'

'Who says it's not going to work out with her?' Fred remembered the hem of Caroline's night-dress and how it gathered and slid up to her hip as she tucked her legs beneath her.

'I adore Caroline,' he said. 'Always have. You know that.'

'Then why did you tell her you liked me?'

'It seemed a good idea at the time.'

'You used me to make her jealous?'

Fred was relieved. 'That must have been it!'

'You used me?'

'Did she sound jealous? Do you think it worked?'

It didn't matter. He was himself again and so was she.

'I've been working on something for her birthday.' Fred opened the freezer. 'Come and look.'

The top shelf was packed with trays in which tiny flowers had been set in cubes of ice.

'They're beautiful,' said Mary. 'When's her birthday?'

'No idea.'

'And you did it before you knew she was coming back?'

'Seems that way.'

'When will you give them to her?'

'I can't. They'd melt.'

'So what will you do with them?

'Nothing. Do you really think she sounded jealous? What exactly did she say?'

TWENTY-THREE

Theo Dorne turned out to be as young as he looked – five years younger than Juliet. He was interested but not curious, and she felt no desire to tell him everything. She spent a lot of time with him out in the sun. Her body felt clearer as her skin grew darker and her hair had come to life now that it reached her shoulders. To Theo, she seemed more wild and golden each time they met.

The warm days extended into gentle evenings. People sat outside feeling the air on their skin, and were struck by life. The overall mood was one of contingency charged with the threat of electrical storm.

Theo found a bicycle for Juliet and took her out along the rail-road, over the Connecticut River and on into Mount South. She said nothing but she was excited to see things she had hoped for from America and which now, on this hot night, were revealed: the spill of traffic lights swaying over junctions, a bar called The Salty Dog, teenagers cruising in cars as long and low as boats and bare-chested men riding motorbikes as long as cars.

'Where are we?' she asked. They were pushing their bicycles down a street full of brash makeshift stores.

'Don't you know this town?'

'I thought I did. I come here for books, newspapers, the deli, the libraries.'

'What have you been doing all this time?'

'Not much.'

'Well let's get in here and have some fun.'

'Fun,' repeated Juliet, feeling uncomfortable.

The club was called The Covered Dish. Juliet had seen it advertised in the *Littlefield Fencepost* and recognised the names of some of the bands who played there. It had not occurred to her to go to see them.

'Didn't you go to clubs in London?' Theo yelled over the music as they leant against a wall and swigged bottles of beer.

'Yes, but mostly jazz.'

'There's a jazz band playing here tonight.'

Juliet was relieved, 'Great.'

She felt even better when she saw the band come on stage, a guitarist and a saxophonist, charismatically nondescript, who stood on either side of the stage as if waiting for someone to appear in-between them.

'I know them! They used to play with my brother's girlfriend. She's a singer and there's this great club in Soho called The Glory Hole. They're called The Natural Fringe.'

'The what?'

The guitarist approached a microphone and said in an unnecessarily drab London voice: 'Hello Mount South. We are Smokey Vanilla and the Pirouettes.'

'They're not Smokey anything!' protested Juliet. 'They're The Natural Fringe.'

The band played the same refracted songs they had performed with Mary, only now they were about absence instead of expansion. The audience loved it but Juliet couldn't stand it. When they came off stage and wandered over to the bar, she went up to introduce herself.

The guitarist was pleased. 'We miss Mary.'

'Has she left the band?'

'Well, after the business of Tony –'

'Tobias.'

'Sorry, yes, Toby, terrible business. Anyway, she said it was too hard, what with the little girl and being on her own.'

Juliet felt terrible. 'Did you try to persuade her?'

'She moved, didn't she?'

'Yes, but I can give you her number. You'll get in touch?'

'Sure, maybe.'

When they left, Juliet and Theo bumped into Merle and Rogen Dix coming out of a restaurant.

Merle greeted her avidly: 'Juliet! I didn't recognise you. How's Jacob? I was so sorry to hear.'

'About what?'

'His mother?'

'Oh. Yes. He's fine, actually.'

Theo was right beside her. She ought to say something but couldn't think what and so said goodnight and got onto her bike and set off so fast that he had no choice but to nod apologetically and hurry after her. They swooped through the dark, back under the leaves, their lamps skimming over a nocturnal world they could only imagine from its sounds of call and fright.

At the house they got into bed, and hesitated.

'Who's Jacob?'

'The one who lived here. Jacob Dart.'

'Foucault's Egg?'

'Have you read it?'

'Sure.'

'I haven't.'

'So where is he?'

'London, I think.'

'How old is he anyway?'

'About twice your age.'

'Really?'

'Maybe. He makes me feel twice mine. And what about you?'

'She's gone, too.'

'Where?' Not who.

'London.'

Both were amused by this.

'So we're safe for now.'

'We are.'

They kissed and slept well.

At six, Carlo turned off the alarm. He drove across town, stopping for coffee which he sipped and spilt as he swung the car through the already sunny streets, enjoying the fact that he knew this route so well. He opened the sunroof and turned up the radio when a track came on that he had been dancing to a few nights before. He sang along as he jumped a red light and wiggled his hips as he waited for a lorry to back out, and then accelerated into the pleasingly empty road, turned a corner and slammed on his brakes because here was a zebra crossing and a woman waiting with a pram. She smiled at Carlo as he gestured for her to go ahead and he smiled back just as another driver came round the corner behind him as fast as he had, with the same confidence and in the same mood, and hit his brakes but not as quickly, or maybe the brakes weren't as good, and although his car slowed it did not stop until it hit Carlo's, not hard but forcefully enough to propel it forward and into the woman and her pram.

By the time the ambulance came, Carlo knew everything was going to be alright. The woman could not get up, her thighbone was broken, but he had brought her the baby, who had been spilt from the pram and was bruised and screaming but otherwise fine. She stared at it and stared at him, as the other driver sat on the kerb with his head in his hands and the police surrounded them all, asking questions nobody could answer.

After the police reports and the hospital (not, thank god, his hospital), Carlo called in and explained, and then went home. Jonathan was in the bath, singing. Carlo walked in, took off his clothes and joined him and Jonathan stopped singing and washed his lover's body, wrapped him in a towel and took him to bed. Carlo endured all this tenderness, but knew he was doing so for the last time.

The driver who had crashed into the back of Carlo's car spent the rest of the day in a pub. When the barman refused to serve him any more, he tottered outside, gained momentum and stepped into the street. With the next step, his foot wavered, his body sank and he rolled into the path of a car which veered round him and into a set of traffic lights.

It was an everyday ballet of the near miss, in which the smallest adjustment to position or timing might turn a casual encounter into one that changes lives. The sequence leading up to such events is so intricate and casual, who is to say where fault lies?

On this early summer evening, one man stood and shouted at another who lay in the street wondering if he was dying and wanting to sleep. At least someone was turning the lights out, he thought, as the buckled traffic lights fizzed. There was a pause, just long enough for anyone who was watching to understand how one thing led to another, before the other lights at the junction went out too; a further pause and the streetlights dissolved; a slight delay, and the windows above them emptied of their full white, the deeper yellow and then the flat green light within.

*   *   *

This ought to have been a local affair, a power cut in a sub-section of the London grid, but within that area was Paddington Station where Alexander Strachan was expecting to arrive on a train that had left Cornwall eight hours earlier.

Two weeks after visiting Botolph Square, he had phoned Mary at the bookshop. 'I expect my note didn't impress you much.'

'What note?'

'The one I put through the door at your house. Your gardener said it would be alright.'

'My what?'

'The bald boy with the hair.'

'I didn't get a note, but thank you for going to such trouble to get in touch and I'm sorry about dinner. I got stuck.'

'Can we try again?'

Alexander was so glad that she said yes that he wanted to see her as soon as possible, which meant the evening he got back from Cornwall. His train was due in at seven o'clock and he would have been at the pub by eight, only the train ahead of them hit a cow just outside Truro and there was some confusion over a red signal at Bristol, after which the driver had to make an emergency stop and the woman sitting opposite Alexander scalded herself with her tea. He fetched ice from the buffet car and they got chatting. She was American, an historian at a college called Littlefield, which he had heard of and knew to be good.

She wondered about the cow. 'It took them over an hour to move it.'

'We like to do these things properly,' he said, and she had laughed prettily and dabbed at her slender, angry wrist until he offered to go back to the buffet and get more ice and while he was there, something to drink.

While Mary waited in a bar in Camden Town, the train drew into Paddington two hours late, just as the power cut wiped all the electronic information boards clean. There were no times, platform numbers or destinations. People gathered around a car parked on the concourse, engine running and headlamps on, in front of which stood a station-master holding a torch and reciting timetables from a thick book.

Alexander helped the American with her bags and thought for a moment to ask for something – what? A number. Why? She appeared to expect him to say something of this kind and when he didn't, shook his hand and walked off into the dark. She turned and waved or maybe blew him a kiss, Alexander could not quite make it out, and he was relieved but also knew that there would be times, years hence, when he would be stirred into sleeplessness by the memory of the American blonde he had met on a train on the night of the Paddington power cut.

Mary waited, determined to believe that this time they would meet. And Alexander would have made it if his taxi had not sat in the still coagulating traffic until he thought surely she'd have given up by now, and there was nothing for it but to walk his way out of the gridlocked streets and into a part of town where things still worked and moved.

On her last evening in Littlefield, Terence asked Juliet to go for a drink. She insisted they go to the sports bar, 'It's what we do,' she said, and ordered White Russians, even though it was only five o'clock and so hot. 'It's what we drink.'

Terence drew on his cigarette. 'Where are you going to live?'

'I'll stay with my brother for a bit. He's got this huge house.'

'Room for Jacob?'

'Jacob? I shouldn't think so.'

'You sound cross.'

'I know his mother died but I've no idea where he is. It's as if he's fallen off the edge of the world.'

'Perhaps that's what it feels like to him.'

'If that were the case then he'd need me, wouldn't he? He'd get in touch.'

'Perhaps he wants you to go and find him. After all, he came to find you.'

'You never go back to England, do you?'

'Never.'

Terence had exchanged his flannel shirts for cream linen. His cufflinks were gobs of silver and his houndstooth jacket was lined with silver silk. The shaved hair at his temples was greying elegantly.

'You look older than you are; it suits you.'

'You look older too.'

'I'm waiting for you to add that it suits me.'

Terence shrugged: Jacob's sidestep. Juliet was provoked. 'Well I can't be ageing that badly, I've got a younger man.'

'Another man?'

'No, a *younger* man. Theo Dorne. You know him?'

'A little. Isn't he working on the emergence of empiricism? Seeing is believing?'

'He is certainly straightforward.'

'What about Jacob?'

'I offered to go with him to London and he said no. Then he called to say that he wasn't coming back.'

'He ended things?'

'He said he wasn't coming back.'

'But why should he? You're about to go back too.'

'I suppose so.'

Terence spent a long time grinding out his cigarette. 'Another drink?'

When Juliet got home, she went through a heap of paper and found some of Jacob's notes for his new book. This one of Jacob's voices made her restless. She could not follow a sentence or scan a line, so shut her eyes, opened it at random, and put a finger down: 'The bridge is a means, a way. It is not a place and so when we stand on a bridge, we do not inhabit, we do not have a place to stand.' Too charming.

It was only nine o'clock. Jacob would have taken hold of these hours and would have marked them. They would have lain together in a cool bath or walked out to find the moon, which at this time of year was as orange as an evening sun and twice as large. They would watch for the mother raccoon and her baby who emerged from the trees to pick over the bottles and packages in the recycling bin. Jacob would make lemonade or margaritas, and would arrange something unusual – smoked macadamias, caper-berries, sugared almonds – on one of the pretty, chipped plates he had bought on the way to Vermont. But the pleasure of such things was in their arrangement and Jacob had always looked a little disappointed by the unobservant way in which she ate.

Juliet fetched a plate now and laid on it a little of the three foods she had been living on since Jacob had gone: peaches, corn chips and orange sherbet. She ate some of each, and lit a cigarette. She had no idea what to do next.

An hour later, she called Theo. 'I know I said I wanted this night to myself, and I think I do in the end but could you come over for a while? I haven't even gone and I miss you.' Would she have dared to speak to Jacob as simply as that?

Theo came, and they spent an hour on the porch. They agreed to swap addresses and phone numbers, hers in

London (Botolph Square) and his in San Francisco. She pulled a book from his jacket pocket (Montaigne's essays) and wrote her details in that, and so he went indoors and found a book on her desk and did the same. They held onto one another for a long time and then kissed as if it were almost too much for them, which it was and so they did not kiss again.

When Juliet thought she might sleep she let herself think about Theo, not with any formed interest but for the pleasure of something as fresh as his attention. He would be a distraction when she was back in London, and was once more facing the swirl of her old life – Jacob's disappearance, Fred's house, Clara's marriage, Carlo's bodies, Mary's singing, the doctors waiting to operate and Tobias's refusal to be felt. Her parents rose to the surface, drifted and receded, and Juliet watched them go, calm now because she could cross any bridge and see Theo – or someone like him – on the other side, waiting for her in a new and empty city.

TWENTY-FOUR

To Juliet's surprise, the time she spent in Littlefield set itself aside so neatly that soon she could not imagine herself there. She had lived in the middle of a forest in a foreign country where she did not have to travel far or work hard. It had been a pleasant existence, and Jacob had enlivened and complicated it in ways she still could not make sense of and so these too were set aside.

London remembered her. As she walked along Piccadilly, the number nineteen bus passed, taking her home to Khyber Road. When she went to see her tutor at the Institute, she met herself on the fourth flight of the tightly wound stone stairs where for years she had paused to look down over the low banister with the same shiver. She was greeted everywhere by details she knew intimately: the loose corner of a wall, a missing railing, the greening and flaking bark of a plane tree. There were certain views, too, in which the rhythm of windows or the graph of the skyline were unnervingly recalled.

She had flown back into London at dawn and arrived to see the sun shining on Fred's new house, which was a real house, solid and white with high ceilings and tall windows. Juliet soon learnt that it had begun to change those who lived there. They had straightened up and separated out. Even Fred looked taller; older too now he had lost so much hair.

Botolph Square was calmer than she had expected. Fred, Mary and Caroline had established a routine which meant that they saw little of one another. Juliet was alone all day and by evening was eager for company, but Bella was fretting about being teased at school, Fred had to call brokers in New York and Tokyo, and Caroline was busy. Juliet phoned Clara, who was either in her studio or putting children to bed, so she sat alone by the empty fireplace and told herself stories about Khyber Road.

Juliet called her parents and promised to come home the next weekend, then set about finding someone to go with her. No one would, so she went alone to sit with her mother at the kitchen table and to walk with her father in the woods. The countryside around Allnorthover was at its most open. The hedgerows crept, every garden frothed and insects trawled the flowery, fumy air. Yet compared to the green of Littlefield, this landscape looked thin-skinned and easily exhausted.

She searched the village, the house, even her old room but found nothing to make her feel better, so caught an earlier train than she had planned to, back to the city, noting the landscape's shift from a kind of countryside to the beginnings of a town – warehouses among cottages, shabby brambles giving way to slippery green brick and then the first scattered tower blocks, and among them the occasional tree, always one alone, overshadowing a patch of grass and reaching fraily up, sometimes beyond the fourth or even the fifth floor.

From Liverpool Street Station, she walked down to the river. On the embankment, she met herself with Jacob and understood that it was not over. She did not allow herself to think further, or to admit that she needed time to

270

accommodate what had happened with Theo; and there was also the matter of money and her thesis and a place of her own. Everything she recognised made it clear that certain matters had now to be thought through and acted upon. Some things, love and work and the body, did not take care of themselves after all.

Clara found him. His sister Sally had become worried when he left her house in Bath and did not get in touch. She had thought of asking Barbara, and then Juliet, but wasn't sure what was going on and would have hated to cause any upset. She remembered Clara's name from talk of an exhibition, and worked out that Clara and Juliet were related. So she wrote a note to Clara Clough, care of the Arts Council, who forwarded it to her studio.

Clara had thought all morning about what to do. She did not know where Jacob was. That was all she needed to say. She phoned Sally: 'I don't know if I can help.'

'Your sister hasn't said anything?'

'She's only been back a fortnight. We haven't really had a chance to talk. What about Barbara?'

'He stayed with her when he first got back and then he came here after the funeral and then –'

'How is he?'

'I couldn't really say.'

Clara persuaded Sally that there was nothing wrong in her phoning Barbara and asking where Jacob was. Sally did this and called back.

'She says she found him a room, with an old friend of theirs, that architect Patrick Hyde.'

'He knows Patrick Hyde?'

'Oh yes, in fact Patrick and I once –'

'Do you have a number?'

'I didn't like to ask, but I have an address. At least I

hope it's still his address. It must be more than ten years old. He invited me to a party to celebrate the birth of his third child, or was it his fourth . . .'

'So you'll go and see your brother?'

'Me? I don't know if that's what he wants.'

'May I have the address?'

'You won't give it to your sister will you? It's just that Barbara might get a bit upset if she knew I'd passed it on.'

'I'll contact him myself.' A note, she was thinking, I'll give him the number at Fred's house so he can reach her. She did not like to think of Jacob as up in the air.

'Forty-eight Chacony Villas, SE1.'

'It's only a few streets away from my studio.'

'Perhaps you could just pop round? I'm sure Patrick wouldn't mind. They insist on being informal.'

'I'll make contact.' She would write a note.

'Thank you. I hope you don't mind, I know we don't really know each other but you know Jacob a bit, I think, the art world and all, so I'm sure you understand.'

'Understand?'

'Let me know how he is, will you? Give him my love.'

Clara tried to write a note but could not strike the right tone. Written down, the information she had to give, Juliet's phone number, looked so slight that the note declared itself an excuse, which it wasn't. She really did not want to see him. The trouble was that if she sent a note, she wouldn't see him and so couldn't tell Sally how he was. If she went now, it would be done. She worked on the corner of a painting till she would only have an hour to spare before catching her train.

At first she thought the man who opened the door was Jacob – mid-forties, making the most of his hair and asserting the poignancy of his failing good looks. He was wearing an apron and holding a glass of wine, and somewhere behind him, far away, she could see sunlight, glass and steel. A child flitted past, then another.

'I'm looking for Jacob Dart.'

Patrick Hyde smiled, as if remembering something pleasing.

'Jacob? He's upstairs, or at least I think he is. Come in, come in. Drink?'

'No, thank you. Would you mind letting him know I'm here?'

The architect grinned. 'Oh I think you should just go on up, sorry what did you say your name was?'

'Clara Clough.'

He looked as if this might be even better than whatever he had envisaged. 'It's the top floor. Do please go on up. I'm sure he'll be delighted.'

Like a teenage son, Jacob had been given the attic room of this four-storey townhouse. He stood in doorways, said nothing at dinner, finished the whiskey and slept till midday. The three children of the household, aged eight, ten and twelve, were impressed and then unnerved.

Clara made her way upstairs through the brutally converted house and on to the top landing, where Jacob was standing in a doorway. He kissed her with slow-motion formality on each cheek and then retreated, which she took as an invitation to go in. The room had been punched out of the roof and extended into a glass slope under which all the heat of the day and of the house seemed to have gathered. Jacob, in pyjama bottoms which ended above his delicate ankles and a girlish sweatshirt that did not quite cover his softening belly, did not look warm. Clara was finding it hard to breathe. She glanced around at the floor covered with paper and books, the jam-jar lid heaped with cigarette butts, the half-eaten bar of foreign chocolate, the wads of tissues and the milk bottle half full of yellow liquid.

273

'Are you alright?'

Jacob looked behind himself and back at her, and shrugged.

'It's just that your sister's worried. I wouldn't have bothered you only she wanted to know that you were alright. And Juliet's back and doesn't know where you are.'

Clara wrote the address for Botolph Square on a piece of paper lying on a desk, but in the end did not give him the number.

That night Clara dreamt that she walked into the architect's house and Jacob reached out and touched her hair and the place went up in flames. She cried out and woke Stefan, whose question, 'Let go of what?', entered her dream as her own.

Two postcards arrived from San Francisco. In spacious, connected writing, Theo told Juliet that if she were truly interested in bridges, she could come to see the Golden Gate, and that he missed her. The second postcard said that she could come and see fog if she preferred, and that he missed her. Juliet was so perturbed by how one feeling distracted her from another (Theo from Jacob, instantly) that she set herself a single task and saw it through. It took her two hours of flicking through all the books she might have left on her desk that last evening in Littlefield, to find the page on which Theo had written his number. She waited until he ought to have been waking up and called, but got an answering machine with a girl's voice on it, a brisk lilt, 'No one's home.' Without being prompted to leave a message, Juliet found that she could not.

Those postcards had brought back his voice and now she needed to hear it. She called every hour until it was midnight in London and he picked up the phone.

'Juliet? That's so great!'

'Hello.'

'It's good to hear you. Did you get my cards?'

'Yes.'

'So you called. I gave you my number and you called.'

'Yes, I did. I miss you.'

'Sure. I miss you.'

'So.'

'So . . . how's London? Have you seen Jacob?'

'No, not yet.'

She didn't want to ask about Theo's girl; she didn't want to know her name or if it was her voice on the machine.

'I have to tell you something,' Theo said. 'I might be coming over. I've been offered a junior fellowship at University College.'

'You might come here?'

'Maybe.'

'That's wonderful. When did you apply?'

'Before I met you.'

'Oh.'

'I should have said something but I didn't want to scare you.'

They both passed this off as a joke.

'We might get to see something of each other.' He sounded as if it had only just occurred to him. Juliet was finding it hard to grasp. Everyone else seemed so far away whereas Theo actually was far away and didn't, at that moment, seem so at all.

Jacob turned up at Botolph Square the next Saturday afternoon. Caroline answered the door and they both tried to hide their surprise at seeing one another.

'Go on through,' she said, gesturing rather formally towards the back of the house.

Jacob reached the brim of the garden, six steps up from the kitchen, and hesitated unseen in the steep shadow of the house. Juliet was standing in the long grass with her hands over her eyes, counting. She had her back to him. Bella, hiding behind a bush, signalled to Fred who had crept up behind Juliet with a garden hose in his hand. Sun toppled down through the leaves of a neighbour's chestnut tree. Fred grinned and put a finger to his lips, Bella clasped her hands and stretched up on tiptoe as water arced from the hose. Drenched and squealing, Juliet ran at Fred and fought him for the hose till they both fell to the ground in a growing pool. Bella hurried to throw herself on top of them, but stopped short and yelled: 'A stranger!' She stood pointing at Jacob like a sergeant choosing a volunteer, and he shrank down onto the step so that the only way Juliet could greet him was to put out a hand and pull him to his feet.

She took him through to the living room and shut the door behind them. She did nothing about her wet clothes and dripping hair, and did not resist when he pulled off his shirt and used it to dry her face. She leant against his chest but when his hand rose from her waist to her ribs and onto her breast, she drew back.

He whispered, 'We lived together.'

'Like babes in the wood.'

He held her head against his chest and she was startled by how fast his heart was beating and then annoyed to think that he had positioned her to make sure she would hear it.

'We had a nice time,' she added. *Nice.* She stepped back, and saw that his shirt had three buttons missing and one sleeve rolled up, and felt irritated.

He was running a finger up and down and round her arm, and his touch made her skin panic.

'Please,' she said, moving away. 'You got on a plane

and went back to England, leaving me alone in the forest.'

'I telephoned.'

'Days and days later, and even then you didn't tell me where you were staying.'

'With Barbara and then with Sally. You had only to ask.'

'But why not tell me?'

'My mother died. I was finding it hard.'

'My brother died but I didn't go off to stay with some ex.'

'You went to America. I'm sorry I disappeared, I realise that's what it must have seemed like, but it wasn't about you. My mother . . .' She had not remembered that his voice could sound so weedy and fake.

If she felt sorry for him, she would have to feel bad about Theo. 'I offered to come back with you.'

'You couldn't, you had to teach. What difference would it have made if I'd flown back just to leave again?'

Juliet was furious that he couldn't tell. 'It would have changed everything,' she said.

He sat them both down. 'We want a real life together. That's what we said. This first year hasn't given us much of a chance but now, we can choose. We can make a home and do our work. It's all that's real – love and work and a place to be.'

'And overdrafts and illness and unfinished PhDs . . .'

'We can manage all that. What we need to do first is find a place to live.'

'I thought I might stay here a bit.'

'I've started looking. There are some delectable streets north of here; a bit rough but up and coming . . .'

'I don't have any money.'

'I do. My mother left me a bit and I ought to get something out of Barbara after all I put into our place.'

'I don't know, the idea of it seems a bit strange.'

'Strange?'

Juliet still could not imagine them living together anywhere other than Littlefield. 'I mean unreal.'

'My feelings about you are real.'

'Yes, but your feelings about yourself are more real.'

'You are real. I believe in you.'

There it was, the problem: 'But I don't believe in you, Jacob.'

'That's alright, I don't believe in myself either.' His voice was swollen with feeling. He lifted her wrist to his mouth and she felt nothing.

'What are we doing, love?' he said. 'We mustn't waste us.'

'I'm jetlagged, I've got a chapter to write by the end of the month, and I've got to see my doctor.'

'I'll come with you.'

'No.'

'Please let me come. I look after you, remember? That's what I do.'

Jacob was still courting her, but she resisted. She knew that once he had had his effect he would step aside so as to observe it.

'I'm not sure you ever felt very much,' he said in a more familiar voice.

'Fuck off, fuck off, fuck off,' she screamed, not caring how childish it sounded because at least then he stopped talking and would soon be gone.

Carlo thought that Juliet was looking wonderful but could see that the pain was back. One day, when she was alone in the house, he phoned.

'What's happening with your innards?'

'They're going to be sorted out.'

'Which hospital?'

'I don't know.'

'You'll go and see your doctor then, chase it up?'

'I said I would, didn't I? Only he's not my doctor any more, now that I don't live in Khyber Road.'

'Sign up with another practice.'

'But I don't know where I'm going to live.'

'Then go back to the Khyber Road doctor and don't let on.'

'Can I do that?'

'You're not supposed to but the point is you ought to see someone.'

Juliet wasn't sure. She felt herself again, and part of herself was this pain.

TWENTY-FIVE

The next day, Juliet was sick. There was pain, although it was not the time when it usually came, and it was different, a stabbing in her right side. She vomited, and then returned to bed feeling empty and hungry. At lunchtime she wanted an omelette and went down to the kitchen but the melting butter and broken eggs made her retch so she took a piece of bread and went back upstairs. In the afternoon, Fred came up with some news. Their parents had sold the Clock House.

He sat on the end of Juliet's bed in a huddle, and rocked back and forth.

'They're going to live in Salisbury. Carlo says it's fine, a bit basic and remote but fine. Are you alright?'

'Jet lag.'

'Still?'

'I suppose so.'

Juliet did not think further about her parents but she fretted about the house. Objects she had scuffed and stained and left behind now appeared beloved and endangered. What would happen to the walnut bureau, the chaise longue, the Chinese dragon mirror, the brass kitchen clock? Her sickness stayed with her as a hollow

280

queasiness, and although she chewed dry bread and oat cakes, and drank mint tea, it would not go away.

The sickness and pain came and went, and her stomach was bloated. She was tired in such a profound way that she stood apart from herself and watched what she was going through with only the slightest interest.

She continued to work and managed to establish a kind of routine as she picked up the threads of her research. The images she had been working on spoke to her differently now: nothing within a frame could be empty, not even an empty frame was empty, and there was always a frame. She tried to explain this to Ritsu over lunch one day, and went home wanting to write her seventy thousand words again.

Another postcard arrived from Theo: 'Will be seeing you in September, take care, T.' Juliet felt only vaguely excited. September was months away.

Barbara Dart was calm. She knew that Jacob was at Patrick Hyde's house and that Juliet was at her brother's. It could not be said that they had split up, but only because Jacob would not have made clear an ending, and the girl would be too unsettled to make anything clear herself. He would hide from Juliet and then rush towards her, and would always be too little or too much. It would not occur to him that a girl like that would go on making her life, and of course she would.

Barbara had asked Clara to sit on a panel which discussed arts promotion. She had said almost nothing during the meeting but the others were pleased to have an actual artist there, and one at such a promising stage of her career. Afterwards, Barbara suggested a cup of tea in her office.

'How is your sister?'

She sat behind her desk with Clara opposite, as if this were an interview.

'It's hard to say.' The sun was full in Clara's face, and she raised a hand to shade her eyes.

Barbara swung round in her chair and lowered a blind. 'She strikes me as the type who gets over things.'

Clara was startled. 'She's quite frail at the moment.'

'Really?'

A tray of tea arrived, but Barbara made no move to serve it.

'Yes, and we're all a bit worried.'

'I'm sure she'll be fine. Jacob proves surprisingly easy to live without . . .'

'She isn't lovesick; this is real.'

'No it's not, she'll see that soon.'

'I realise you must dislike my sister but she's not well and I think –'

'Oh no,' Barbara insisted, 'this isn't personal. I rather admire her, actually. You have to remember that I know Jacob better than anyone. It wasn't her fault. She's just the one who said yes.'

Clara closed her eyes. She wanted a moment to make sense of this, only Barbara had the conversation in her grip: 'Never mind all that. I'm so sorry to hear that she's unwell, what on earth's the matter . . .'

The emptying of the Clock House was to take place immediately. In this settled weather, Doctor Clough arranged for the contents of the cellars, attics and barn to be turned out into the garden where his children could choose what they wanted. He had an inventory drawn up and furnished each of them with a copy when they arrived together one Saturday morning. There was a second list of the few items that the doctor wanted to take to the cottage near

Salisbury. Francesca Clough was as indifferent to her grandmother's cherrywood cabinet and fur coats as she was to the table-tennis table. She had decided to take only what she could fit in her car.

The journey made Juliet nauseous and when she saw all their junk and treasures laid out on the yellow lawn, she blinked and retched. She had no home of her own, nowhere to put the cherrywood cabinet or to hang the fur coats, and no need for pearl-handled opera-glasses, mildewed trunks and a hundred brittle paperbacks, but she wanted to save them all. Things that had given the Clough home a sense of substance and achievement looked shabby and useless in such daylight – split cardboard boxes of school exercise books, plastic bags leaking mouldy toys and clothes, records beginning to warp in the heat, a chair with no back and a desk with three legs. The doctor had arranged five bicycles in order from Fred's tricycle to Tobias's racer, and a series of wellington boots, red child size one to green adult eleven. Inside the house, the pictures and mirrors had been taken down so that the walls were reduced to flat surfaces and hurt the eyes of those who glanced towards a place where for years there had been something into which they could travel.

At first, no one ticked anything on their list. Then Clara sat down in her Welsh grandmother's rocking chair. 'Didn't this used to be in Tobias's room?' she asked and stood up again. Juliet sat down.

'If you want it, do say,' said Clara.

Juliet jumped up. 'Not if you want it.'

'Please, no, you have it. Unless Fred? Carlo?'

In the end, Juliet ticked the chair on her list.

The brothers had started a game of table-tennis but the table was more warped than ever so they gave up and hauled it off to the bottom of the garden, where they decided to make a heap of things for a fire.

By the end of the afternoon, each child had acquired some furniture, one or two paintings, some glassware, crockery, linen and a few useless but significant objects, some of which were of real value. They ate supper with their parents and walked across the garden to start the fire. It was a mucky, unreliable enterprise as the things on it were either too dense or damp to burn, or so synthetic or aerated that they went up instantly in noisy white flame, giving nothing else time to catch. Carlo retrieved the last of the winter's wood and coal, and soon the fire was a clean blaze, which inspired them to find more to feed it.

Clara ran back to fetch a box she had put in the car and began to throw on her early sketchbooks.

'What are you doing?' screeched Fred. 'That's your juvenilia!'

'If I keep them then one day someone might see them,' she explained. 'I'd hate that.'

'You have a point,' said Juliet. 'I'm going to throw in my diaries.'

'What about those books that have gone green?' Carlo encouraged.

'You're right. The pages will crumble if I ever try to open them again. And you?'

Carlo fetched a sheaf of photographs, 'Do you want anyone to see what you looked like in the Eighties?' and they danced for the mischievous joy of watching themselves bubble and disappear.

Carlo stopped when he realised that he was holding a picture of Tobias, aged fifteen, sitting on his first rebuilt motorbike.

'I should give this to Mary, for Bella.'

'No,' said Clara. 'Let's keep him.'

Fred was avid, 'He's ours!' He snatched the photo and threw it in.

When the others went inside to find more wine, Clara

284

got something else from her car. It was a canvas she had taken down from the attic of her house that morning. She stuffed it quickly into the fire, pushing at it with a stick so as to make sure that it did not unfold before it had turned completely black.

Clara tried to persuade them all to stay, but when Carlo said that he felt like driving back to London, the others were quick to persuade him to do so. They wanted to leave Allnorthover behind in flames and darkness.

It was two in the morning when they arrived at Botolph Square and Mary was in the kitchen, making tea.

'You look all dressed up,' said Juliet.

'I've been out to see a band. Caroline looked after Bella.'

'How was it?'

'Great.' She had gone to see Smokey Vanilla and the Pirouettes, and had talked to them afterwards. They were to try something out the next weekend.

'Well we've burnt half the furniture and plundered the heirlooms,' said Fred. 'Who wants cheese on toast?'

Juliet grinned. 'Lord knows what we're going to do with all the stuff we said we wanted.'

'You just felt sorry for everything,' said Fred.

Mary looked agitated. 'What about Tobias's tools?'

'I don't remember,' said Juliet. 'There was so much stuff. I'm sure Dad will have set them aside.' She made a note to phone her father in the morning.

'There should be something for Bella,' Mary said.

'Of course!' said Fred.

'We thought of that,' said Juliet. 'It was meant to be a surprise, but you know our Welsh grandmother's rocking chair that used to be in his room?'

Mary smiled. 'I used to feed Bella in that.'

'It's yours, hers, whatever. And there's the patchwork quilt, Tobias had it the longest I think, although Carlo nabbed it for a while, it's American, really old, you can have that too, oh and the opera-glasses . . .'

'Opera-glasses?'

'For Bella. I'm sure she'll go when she grows up, she's just the type.'

'Thank you,' said Mary, 'for thinking of us.'

'And what's more,' said Fred, 'we thought that before this house fills up with all that junk we ought to have a party because once the dining table arrives, we'll have to give dinners instead.'

'We used to give dinners without a dining room,' said Juliet.

'Did we? I don't remember.'

'And it's your birthday next Saturday, Fred. You've reached a quarter of a century and we've lost our home. It's the end of childhood. We can celebrate it all.'

'Don't you mind?' Mary asked.

Fred shook his head. 'After Tobias, losing the house isn't so bad.' It was not a convincing equation, but it was one that, with variations, had become of use to them all.

Barbara was right. Things between Juliet and Jacob were not yet clear. He turned up again, as he used to at Khyber Road, and asked her humbly if they might go for a walk. It was a fine evening; Jacob had chosen it especially.

They made their way to the Heath and up the hill, past the last of the families kicking footballs in the dusk, the last sated runners and dog walkers, until they were accompanied only by lovers, mostly couples but also those who were hopeful, prospective or off-duty.

'It's odd that we're still living in other people's houses,' Juliet said, trying not to show that she was out of breath.

'And now it's with other people.' Jacob took her hand and she did not object.

'Could we sit?'

He led her into the long grass.

'Not there,' she said, 'on a bench.'

A giggle, the chink of a glass, the strike of a match, the edge of a moan.

'Come and lie down with me,' Jacob said.

'Where?'

'Anywhere. I miss you.'

'I'm not well.'

'Then let me look after you.'

'That's not what I need.'

'Then come and lie down.'

His mouth was on her neck and she felt an echo of the explosion there had been when he first kissed her, but that was it. She did not trust his desire for her and because of her sickness, did not have the strength to be interested in what might lie beyond it.

'We'll never fill this house,' Fred had said when they made a list of people to invite to the party. 'Everyone will have to be told to bring someone we don't know.' So that was what they instructed their friends to do, and also why the next Saturday night, they found themselves surrounded by strangers. Some mistook Fred, in his suit, for a waiter, which he didn't mind as he liked to be thought of as a man who employed waiters.

'This is my house,' he said happily to a man leaning against the banisters. The man looked nervous and bent down to pick up a cigarette butt that he had just trodden into the floor.

Caroline was answering the door and taking coats. Clara was out in the garden shouting and making people laugh: 'So I burned them all! My great works!' Carlo introduced people he didn't know to one another. A severe architect lit the cigarette of a chubby banker, a defiant academic debated with a fractious doctor, and Fred listened, amazed by how the people he knew, or at least the people they knew, were becoming what they were.

Mary passed through each crowded room, drawing on the life and noise around her. She had invited several people from the bookshop (two turned up) and also the boys from the band, who arrived with their instruments.

'Maybe we'll have a session later,' the saxophonist suggested.

Mary shook her head. 'I'm just going to check on my daughter. Do go through and help yourselves to a drink.' She hurried upstairs with no intention of coming back down.

In the bathroom on the top floor, she found Juliet kneeling by the lavatory.

'I'm not drunk,' she said, wiping her mouth.

Mary looked at her green-ringed eyes, her watery face. 'You've been feeling sick a lot haven't you?' She busied herself fetching a glass of water. 'Are you at all faint?'

'It's not what you think. I can't be pregnant. I feel too ill.'

Mary helped Juliet onto her feet and gave her the glass of water. They sat side by side on the edge of the bath.

'Are you sure?' Mary ventured.

Juliet shook her head. 'Not absolutely.'

'What will you do if you are?'

'I don't know. It's ridiculously unlikely.' She saw something in Mary's usually guarded face that interested her. 'What made you have Bella? She wasn't an accident, was she?'

'No.' Mary decided to tell the truth. 'The year before, I lost one.'

'Christ, I'm sorry. I didn't know.'

'It wasn't his.'

'You had an affair?'

Mary shook her head. 'That sounds too grown-up. I just bumped into someone I hadn't seen for a long time.'

'Daniel Mort?' He was the only other man Juliet could imagine her with, the boyfriend before Tobias, an art-student friend of Clara's.

'Yes. When I went back to Allnorthover to help my mother clear out the shop, I went into Camptown and there he was.'

'Did he know about the baby?'

'No, but I told Tobias.'

'What did he say?'

Mary retreated. 'I can't remember, but I wish I hadn't.'

'Been unfaithful?'

'No, I wish I hadn't told him. I thought it was the honourable thing to do but it hurt him so much, and I offered to have an abortion, and then the decision was made for me.'

'That must have been a relief.'

'No, because then I couldn't show Tobias that I'd chosen him.'

'I always thought you two were quite simply happy, and that was why you decided to have a child.'

'It was all I could think of.' Mary did not like other people's curiosity any more than did Juliet. 'I don't know what's going on with Jacob,' she said, reaching out to touch Juliet's shoulder and then thinking better of it. 'But what with his wife, it's going to be complicated.'

Juliet felt dizzy and put her head in her hands. 'It certainly is,' she muttered, hoping that by the time she sat up again, Mary would have disappeared and that they would never have had this conversation.

*   *   *

One of the guests recognised Smokey Vanilla and the Pirouettes, and they were persuaded to play. Fred was so excited – A live band! In his house! – that he bounced round shouting for Mary, who came to meet him wondering what this evening would bring next.

'The boys want you downstairs,' panted Fred, tugging at her sleeve.

'The boys?'

'The Pirouettes!'

This was where Mary lived, not where she sang, and she hadn't sung for ages, at least not this year. Fred jumped up and down and clapped his hands – 'Ladies and Gentleman, Smokey Vanilla has been reunited with the Pirouettes!' Most had no idea what he was talking about but fell in with his enthusiasm, and stomped and cheered as Mary edged into view.

She could not imagine doing what she was about to do, but also knew that this was what she had been hoping for – not here like this and not yet, but here it was. A saxophone and an acoustic guitar; no mike, reverb, monitor, stage or lights, but something of a song she knew well. Mary followed one phrase and then another, took a breath, hesitated, and caught the refrain:

Might as well,
where have you been,
haunting me, too easily . . .

She sang to her shoes and then to the wall, and knew that people could barely hear her. The music took over once more, and she turned and looked up into Fred's face and saw how badly he wanted it to go well.

The one who knew, here again,
who knew me, here we, here again . . .

She had dropped out of key. The guitarist frowned and moved to meet her, which surprised the saxophonist who had to bend a note a long way to catch up. Mary could not hear herself, not even in her head, and was cut off from her voice by walls of panic.

You said you loved, might as well,
the cold begins to . . .

That first note wasn't so high; she ought to reach it easily, she usually did. Mary shook her head at Fred and walked away, relieved that the crowd let her pass and that no one said anything except one pat and a whisper, 'Well tried, very brave!'

The final shock came at dawn. Fred had woken up next to Caroline and hastened downstairs to find something to bring her on a tray. As he reached the hall, he breathed in the surprisingly fresh air and realised that the front door was open. The pockets of the jacket he had left hanging on a hook were empty. He walked from room to room, letting his eyes remind him of what ought to be there – his computer, fax machine and pager, the television and stereo, Bella's red plastic tape player. For days to come, those who lived there would reach for something only to add it to the list – the bicycle he had bought Mary, Caroline's camera, Juliet's grandmother's moonstone bracelet. At what hour had they all been so fast asleep? Or had someone passed through the house during the party, opening every door, cupboard and drawer, and slipping whatever they chose into deep invisible pockets to leave again unnoticed by these fools, caught up in their own small excitements and griefs?

TWENTY-SIX

Juliet lay in bed and looked around the room. Everything seemed slightly out of place, as if the world had tipped a little. She felt sick again, that strange combination of full and void. When she made her way downstairs, she found Fred and Caroline talking to a policeman.

'Method of entry?' he was asking.

'The front door I should think, like everyone else,' said Fred.

The policeman scrutinised the door. 'No sign of anything being forced. What makes you think they came in this way?'

'It was open.'

'On the latch?'

'No, open.'

'The windows were open too,' put in Caroline,' so some of them might have come in that way.'

'There was more than one?' asked the policeman.

'There must have been, what, seventy?' calculated Fred.

'Not including those of us who live here,' said Caroline.

'Or the band,' said Fred. 'There was a live band, you know.'

On the policeman's advice, Fred and Caroline paced each room, trying to remember what might have been where, and then sat down to make notes.

'You look like a couple preparing a wedding list,' said Juliet, who felt too rotten to care if everything she owned had been stolen. They just smiled.

Fred's bank had given him a deal on insurance, something he would never have thought of for himself, and the idea that someone else would pay him to buy new things amazed him. The loss adjuster who came to the house left Fred a pile of leaflets and he read every word.

'Do you know,' he announced, 'there are all kinds of insurance. The ordinary kind for the stuff in the house and for going on holiday; then there's insurance for when you're not in the house and not on holiday; and some for if you can't work because you're dying, or if you lose your job or just plain die.' A locksmith arrived and shook his head until Fred agreed to buy a new front door with three locks and a reinforced frame, and bolts for all the windows on the ground floor.

If Fred felt any fear about the dangerous world he had discovered he lived in, it was countered by the pride he took in his organised response. He was a man in charge of three women and a child, and enjoyed being able to provide what was needed in order to protect them.

Each night, when he had finished talking to New York and Tokyo, Fred would turn the locks and bolts, and only then would Mary feel able to stop watching over Bella, who could have been taken along with the camera and the bracelet, slipped into an invisible pocket while her mother sang so badly downstairs.

Fred would go up to Caroline and they would talk themselves to sleep listing the details of the different kinds of machines Fred might buy. Caroline spent hours in department stores, taking notes.

Juliet listened to the keys turn and the bolts slide, Mary's creeping steps and the amiable babble coming from Fred's room. It was already a different house and they were different within it.

Juliet went to see her doctor at the health centre on the estate near Khyber Road. She caught a Tube and then an overground train and then a bus, and found herself back in a different London, where all there had been to worry about was what Fred was giving his stupid friends for dinner and whether there was enough coal for the fire.

The doctor was not the handsome young man Juliet had seen before but a woman with a bad cough. She did a urine test on the spot. 'You're not pregnant, so that's one less thing to worry about. Now hop up on the couch and we'll take a look. I'm glad you came in at last. Did you not get a letter?'

'What letter?'

'It says here that we received a report from your American doctor giving the results of your investigations and treatment, and that you are due for surgery. In fact, looking at these dates, well overdue.'

'Are you sure I'm not pregnant?'

'Yes, sure. Now if I could just . . .'

Juliet lifted her hands away from her belly. 'Sorry.'

The doctor felt something, frowned and felt it again more deeply and Juliet screamed. The doctor concentrated for a long time. They both stopped talking. Then she returned to her desk, and waited for Juliet to get dressed and sit down beside her.

'What is it?' Juliet asked.

The doctor said that she would refer Juliet as an urgent

case which meant that she would be seen within a week. They would notify her of an appointment by letter, at which point Juliet said that she was just about to move and gave her address as Botolph Square.

She walked round the corner to Khyber Road, where she found the windows boarded up and the front door nailed shut. Looking through the letterbox, she could see a heap of envelopes, leaflets and fliers. People had gone on delivering things to the house as if people had gone on living there.

A week later, a letter arrived at Botolph Square offering her an appointment at the hospital that Thursday. She went along and queued up at a desk until it was her turn to hand over her letter.

The receptionist shook her head. 'Sorry love, but this was for last Thursday.'

'But I only got the letter on Monday.'

'That's been happening a lot lately – people getting their letters after their appointment time.'

'But my doctor said it was urgent.'

The woman clicked through a number of files on her computer. 'It says here that we offered you an appointment last October.'

'I was abroad. Can I see someone now? I feel so ill.'

At that moment, both the receptionist's telephones rang and she glanced past Juliet as if to indicate that this roomful of women were all feeling just as bad and their insides were just as monstrous. The waiting women looked at Juliet; she could not look back.

Like many English country houses, the one that Stefan had bought on his marriage to Clara Clough gave the impression of always having been what it was, whereas centuries of expansion and decline had made sure it never settled. A prosperous generation built a new wing, a fashion-conscious descendant covered oak panelling with silk, windows had been bricked up to avoid tax, the person who installed radiators had fireplaces boarded up, a lawn became a tennis court and then a lawn again. The house's weak foundations, and the thinning, tipping plane on which it had been built, meant that the Hawley brothers from Ingfield had to be kept on permanent contract to deal with subsidence. Expert and taciturn, they wandered the corridors, inserting gauges, braces and props. And because they never threw their hands in the air and announced that the place was about to fall down, Stefan and Clara relaxed and believed it never would.

They had agreed to spend August at home. She would not go to London and he would not go to Geneva. They would plan a new winter garden, oversee the renovation of the conservatory, and have something done about the tennis court. But today, Stefan was going to take the children out and give Clara time to work.

He stood by the open front door waving his car keys. 'Where's Mabel?'

Clara called up the stairs, 'Mabel, you're going now!'

There was no response.

Stefan rattled his keys some more. 'We're going to be late for the show. It starts in half an hour.'

'Mabel!' Clara yelled. 'The show starts in half an hour!'

'I wish you would stop fiddling with your laces,' Stefan said to Sidney.

'Unvn.'

'He says they're uneven,' explained Clara.

'Nn Mbl.'

'He says he doesn't want Mabel to come,' said Stefan.

'Ssn.'

'Oh not that again,' said Clara, 'They've been playing this game all week.'

'Who's Susan?'

'Mbl.'

'She wants to be called Susan and this boy here has decided that he is called John.'

'OK,' said Stefan genially, 'come on John,' and he shouted 'Susan!' at which Mabel came running triumphantly down.

Clara watched them, Sidney forgetting about his laces once his sister was there, Horace happily chewing on his father's collar, and Stefan looking as if he had about him all that he required and she was afraid for herself and then not, because he came back and kissed her full on the mouth.

'I'm so pleased,' he said.

'Not shocked?'

'No.'

'I was. But I'm pleased too.'

'So long as it's not another set of twins,' he said, stroking her hair.

Clara blanched. She hadn't thought of that.

She knew what pressures this new baby would bring but also knew that Stefan was really back, and she believed that he would really stay.

She shut the door and walked along the hall into the kitchen. Nothing demanded her attention; no one was sick and nothing was broken. She was free to work but couldn't bring herself to when the time was given to her so easily. She relied on the static that came from being cross or tired to reduce her focus. If she painted now, when her mind was clear, she would travel too quickly through an idea and it would be realised in its slightest form.

This was the argument that Clara had formulated

for use when asked about art and children. That the limitations they placed on you could become a way of reducing the aperture, of thinking deeply and of looking more closely. She knew that this was not the truth, or not all of it. The trouble was that if she did start now, with enough space and energy to see what should happen next, and if she began to approach it, then she would be caught by the possibility of something that she could not see through, not without stopping listening.

She walked up the three flights of stairs to the library, which was filled with an encouraging light. The one painting she had finished this year lay against the wall. It was a study of this room, its high green walls and north-facing windows, and what might have been a tear in the wallpaper, had there been wallpaper – an extruded figure leaning hard into a corner, the pattern of a dark green dress, bony empty hands and a lurid hank of hair. The picture frightened her; she had no idea what to do next.

She picked up a magazine and put it down. Beside it was a sketchbook, and a letter from an American dealer. It was ten o'clock. She would go down the three flights of stairs again and make a pot of coffee and by then, something would occur to her. As it was, the telephone rang. Someone had arrived to save her.

'Juliet? What is it?'

'I need to talk to you now. Are you busy?'

'What's happened?'

'It's hard to say.'

'I'll come to you.' That was it, the answer to her empty day. 'I can catch the ten thirty.'

Juliet did not argue. She was overwhelmed at having allowed herself to ask for help, and to have received it.

Clara drove joyfully to the station. She was going to

help Juliet. She wouldn't stay long. She'd be back in time for tea.

Juliet met Clara at Liverpool Street. She cried when she saw her sister striding down the platform towards her and stumbled as she rushed to meet her. These days, she was always about to fall down.

She had summoned Clara and here she was and now something had to be said. Why would talking help? Talking was what people did to thicken rather than to clear the air. Conversation was a strategy, like bricklaying or a relay race, full of overlaps. It was its own construction, its own journey. You didn't listen and wait, then think and speak; that took too long and made everyone uncomfortable. Talking without thinking, though, was how you found out what you meant.

They sat down in a café and Juliet began. 'I feel as if I'm being sucked into myself.'

'You're not *by* yourself though, you've got us.'

'I know you've all been worrying about me.'

Clara looked at her sister carefully. 'Clearly not enough. What is it?'

Juliet explained about the growths and the pills and the hospital appointment she had missed in October and the one for which she had been too late. Clara took charge and after briskly berating Juliet for letting things slide, she wrote down the name and number of Juliet's consultant and promised to get her an appointment.

'I should do this myself.'

'You're not well. Let me do it for you.'

'Thank you.' Juliet looked carefully at her sister. 'And how are you?'

'Pregnant.'

'Oh no.'

'I'm pleased.'

'So everything's fine with Stefan now?'

After the night in New York, when Clara had told Juliet about Stefan's affair, she had refused to say more.

'I hope so.'

'You think that a baby will make everything alright?'

'No, it was an accident.'

'Really?'

'What are you saying?'

'It just seems a strange time to have another baby.'

'There's never a time that's not, in one way or another. I'm sorry, I know what with all you're going through that you are bound to feel ambivalent about this.'

'That's not fair. Babies are the last thing I think about.'

Clara said nothing.

'What about your painting? It's going so well.'

'I'll keep it up.'

Juliet looked so delicate that Clara put her in a cab and told her to go home to bed. Juliet was glad to. She did not want to think any more that day, nor did she want to find herself talking about Jacob or mentioning another name, Theo Dorne, a name no one here had heard yet. Until September Theo Dorne was in San Francisco, far off in the west across an unarguable distance of land and sea.

Clara could walk to the Quondam Building from Liverpool Street in thirty minutes and she made herself do it. There was an hour or two to be made use of before she had to go home. She marched past banks and churches, decisive in her route through the forks and curves of the City. She unlocked her studio and sat by the window, and wondered when she would come back again.

Juliet was woken in the night by pain that passed like a blade through her body, leaving her struggling for breath.

She got up but the pain folded her in two, more pain than she had ever felt, as if all this time it had been collecting itself. She reached the landing and then lost consciousness and fell down the stairs, waking everyone. Mary fetched pillows, Fred fainted and Caroline called an ambulance.

This time no one answered the door at Chacony Villas. Clara walked across the street and looked up past the white steps and the studded black front door, the shuttered windows and the four generous storeys of the flat white façade. The house's exterior gave no hint of what had been done to it inside. It looked as if all the architect's alterations would one day be spat out into sacks and skips, and the house would reassert itself once more, long after this briefly coherent family had broken up and gone.

She could see a figure by a window on the top floor and he could see her. Wanting to remain clear about the purpose of her visit, Clara neither smiled nor waved. Jacob came down and opened the front door. Clara went through into the hall and then stopped. Jacob stopped too. She waited for him to try to show her in to somewhere where they could sit down and to offer her a drink, so that she could refuse, but he did neither.

'Juliet is in hospital. She had an emergency operation yesterday. One of those growths, a cyst, ruptured.'

'What growths?'

'I'm not sure.' Clara knew, in detail, but felt that it was a private matter.

'She had pain but –'

'She was supposed to have an operation last year.'

'I had no idea.'

Nobody had, but Clara did not want to console him.

'Why an emergency?'

'She collapsed. An ambulance took her straight in and they opened her up and found that this thing had burst and was poisoning her. She must have been in a great deal of pain. I don't just mean now but for ages. They said so. It was poisoning her.'

Jacob stood in the doorway.

'We nearly lost her.'

He looked up and then down. His eyes and mouth tightened; the screws were turned. The force and variety of his feelings might have been about to propel him out into the world but he stopped on the top step, looked at the houses opposite with their identical doors and windows, and shook his head.

TWENTY-SEVEN

Fred and Carlo moved Juliet's bed downstairs. She came home to Botolph Square and lay there with her hands on her stitched and bandaged belly. She had been in hospital for two weeks and Carlo felt sure that she should still be there now.

'You're the same colour as the old sofa from Khyber Road,' he said, leaning over to kiss her forehead.

She pushed him away. 'This is not a coffin.'

'I know that. I don't kiss corpses.'

'Whose was the most beautiful body you've ever cut up?'

'And I don't tell stories.'

'You used to.'

'How are you feeling?'

'Empty.'

Carlo laughed.

'It wasn't a joke. Now tell me what's happened to the angel Jonathan. We don't hear about him any more.'

'We split up.'

'Why?'

'I couldn't do it. I mean I couldn't be it.'

'It wasn't what you wanted?'

'It was everything.'

'Oh dear.'

Francesca Clough had gone to the hospital every day and stayed on when Juliet came back to Botolph Square. She slept on the floor in the next room, helped her daughter to wash and took her to the lavatory. When Juliet could do these things for herself, Francesca went back to Salisbury.

Juliet began to want things like buttered toast, chocolate and cheese, only nothing tasted right. Her mouth was dry, her tongue carried the taste of iron and her stomach was inflamed. She took painkillers and antibiotics, and found it hard to have any sense of recovery – they had already told her that there was another operation to come.

On what was to be the last day of summer, she sat in the garden relishing the chill and pulling her quilt around her. This time last year she had arrived in Littlefield. She could remember its weather, buildings and trees but not much human detail. She saw London in those terms, too, or had done when she had been light and quick and able to keep moving through it. Now she walked slowly and had time to look at people, and they took their time looking at her.

'Why do people assume that if you have any sort of physical difficulty, you must be mad?' she asked Caroline one day when she returned from the corner shop.

'You do look a bit like a, what are they called, those people who've been taken over, who have no mind and just sort of clunk about . . .'

'A zombie?'

'That's it.'

The first time Jacob came to see her at the hospital, they had not known what to say to one another and so he read to her. He came to the house and read there too, and she would fall asleep or pretend to.

He arrived one morning as she was about to go to the hospital, and she opened the door and continued past him into the street.

'I'm sorry, I'm on my way to the hospital for a check-up.'

'You're walking?'

She looked like paper.

'It's only ten minutes away. I should try.'

'I'll walk with you.'

He took her arm and they set off at a formal pace, stopping now and then as Juliet hesitated. She was not in pain, which led her towards a new kind of discomfort, that of being too light: she felt like nothing and couldn't understand how nothing could be made to move along the street.

'Thank you,' she said, holding Jacob's arm tightly.

She talked on, about the doctors and nurses, the drugs and machines and ward routine.

When they reached the corner by the hospital, Jacob slipped his arm free. 'Goodbye, sweetheart.'

'You're not coming with me? You said you were coming with me.'

He didn't want to think about what had been growing inside her or what was gone; nor about the people who were in charge of her now.

'You'll be fine,' he said, kissing her on the cheek. 'They'll look after you. They know how.'

'Coward,' she whispered.

He nodded; he had to agree.

As he turned to leave, Juliet grabbed his collar and with surprising force turned him back to face her. He looked down at her shaky fists.

'You are not exempt,' she said, remembering Fred's word.

Jacob shrugged and she let go.

*   *   *

Alexander Strachan lived in the far south-west of the city and worked for a firm of solicitors in Holborn. He avoided going home, at least at the same time as everyone else, and liked to walk through the less obvious streets of Covent Garden and Seven Dials, behind the theatres and the opera house where there were no coach parties or mime artists, just narrow houses where bars and restaurants eked themselves out over several tiny floors. Alexander strode through unlit alleyways, past overflowing dumpsters, phone boxes wallpapered with prostitutes' cards, puddles of fermenting vomit. He was used to the movement in shadows and doorways, the destroyed young who found their way, more and more of them, onto the streets and passed the time half awake or half asleep. Like many who lived in the city, Alexander was neither intimidated nor upset. He confused familiarity with being immune, and being immune with not being culpable.

It was raining, and for all Alexander's ideas of solitude, these streets were busy. Other people left work late and did not want to go home. He was not in a hurry and let himself be slowed or redirected by a couple opening an umbrella, or a procession of office workers emerging from a door.

It was eight o'clock and growing dim, mid-September. Some of those who passed by felt, as did Alexander, a loss of pressure: another meaningless summer was over.

A stiff man walked an old dog in a tartan coat. A mother wrapped her child in her jacket and lifted it up in her bare arms. A security guard pretended not to notice the teenagers who had moved their sleeping bags and flattened boxes beneath the roof of his hotel. A boy stopped to help someone unfolding a map. An elderly man pondered the last bunch of roses in a bucket at a florist's stall and a young man leant over to push his girl's wet hair out of her eyes as they went in through a door.

Alexander saw all this as he looked ahead up a rising, dingy street at the top of which he saw a pale face in a bundle of black and something in the walk, headlong and tremulous, that reminded him of Mary George; no, not reminded him – it was her, he was sure. To have met her by chance twice! If it didn't mean anything, he had to make it do so.

Caught up in this vision, he set off after her, forgetting that nothing had passed between them since he had been too late to meet her in the Camden Town bar; but that had been through no fault of his own. He ran along the slick pavement, reached the top of the road and thought to call out because there she was ahead, and then thought not to. He hurried after her again, dodging umbrellas and people who stopped for no good reason other than that they had seen something interesting or had reached a destination.

He followed her into a sidestreet, and hesitated. She might not want to see him; after all, she had not been in touch. So he watched her instead as she slowed down by the glass façade of a bar and seemed about to turn back towards him, but then stepped through the glass and disappeared.

Alexander made himself smoke a cigarette, and believed that in the time that passed he had considered what to do. He walked down to the bar. When he could not see her, he went in. What would he say? What if she were meeting someone? He took his time moving between the tight-packed tables and the standing throng. He had a glass of wine and smoked another cigarette, all the time looking.

There was a rasp of feedback through a PA and

someone was asking people to step back, which they did and a small stage appeared. A woman jabbed Alexander with her elbow, spilling his wine, and a large man in a steaming pullover blocked his view. When the band were announced, 'Smokey Vanilla and the Pirouettes!', Alexander thought it best to give up and leave. He recognised her voice as he reached the door.

Jacob sat in the room at the top of Patrick Hyde's house and waited. Someone would come. When the family were out, he would go downstairs and take some bread and cheese, and maybe a bottle of beer, and most evenings Patrick came up to urge him to join them for supper, which he always refused. Patrick took to leaving a tray and a bottle of wine outside his door, all of which was gone by the morning.

Patrick loved his friend and knew him well. He phoned Barbara.

'It's his version of protest,' Barbara said.

'What's he protesting about?'

'He thinks no one loves him.'

'But everyone loves him!'

'He wants us to prove it to him.'

'He's going to have to grow up.'

'Jacob?'

'OK, not grow up but at least find somewhere proper to live. My eldest has his eye on that attic room and to be frank, he's a bit of a black cloud – hard for us all to live under . . .'

'You've been so kind and patient.'

'You don't have to flatter me, Jacob ought to be doing that.'

'But I'm grateful, truly . . .'

'You are devoted, Barbara darling, but you also have

better things to do than act as an ambassador for Jacob Dart.'

Barbara shrugged. 'He needs one. Anyway, I have a solution.'

The next Friday night, Barbara collected Jacob and his bags from Chacony Villas and drove him out of town.

Juliet sat in the basement library of the Institute trying to decipher a Latin inscription on a seventeenth-century engraving of Vanity, who was depicted as a woman holding a hand mirror and paying no attention to the little dog, Fidelity, slipping from her lap. The animal was dissolving into the jagged, fussy folds of her skirts. It was a fading emblem which Juliet once believed had disappeared completely, but now glimpsed everywhere: sleeping in corners, crouching under tables, this creature haunted the emptiest pictures.

Every observation that occurred to her now was like a loose thread in her thesis waiting to be pulled. She had told her supervisor that it was as if someone else had written all those words and he said something encouraging about her gaining an objective perspective, and that she ought to stick to the position she had spent so long establishing and see her argument through.

Juliet didn't want to. The woolly autumn atmosphere was making her sleepy, so she left the library and went up into the courtyard where the tax inspectors whose offices filled the largest wing of this once grand house smoked and parked their cars. It was raining, so she stood under a colonnade and lit a cigarette.

'Juliet?' It was Theo. He stepped out of the rain and opened his arms.

Their embrace was not quite that of lovers, and involved some awkwardness.

'This doesn't happen,' said Juliet. 'I don't bump into people. Other people do, all the time, but I don't. It doesn't happen.'

'It hasn't,' he admitted with a powerful smile. 'I came here to find you. I went to the postgraduate secretary's office, she told me who your supervisor was and he said he had just seen you in the library. So.'

'When did you arrive?'

'A couple of weeks ago.'

'Oh.' Perhaps he had called at the house when she had been sleeping; or phoned and someone forgot to give her the message.

'Melissa came to settle me in, then went back.'

'The one who came to London?'

'Yes, but just for a month or so. We spent the rest of the summer on the beach and now it's time to work.'

Juliet suggested that they find a cup of tea.

Theo noticed that she walked slowly, and that she looked thin.

'Are you sick?' he asked as they sat down.

'I was,' she said. 'When you met me, didn't I seem a bit strange? I was not myself.'

He could not remember her body, just what it felt like to be touching her and inside her. 'Strange? In a way. Intriguing . . .'

She told him concisely about her condition, the pills, the investigations, her collapse. 'And there's more to come,' she concluded.

He stood up, drew her out of her chair and entirely held her.

Theo Dorne enjoyed the rain that came to London that autumn. It kept him indoors, with his head bent over a book, sometimes with a magnifying glass in his hand. He liked stepping out at the end of the day into damp and darkness; he was not someone to be so easily brought down. He got out of bed when he woke up, started work when he intended to, and swam each day in the university's neglected basement pool.

He and Juliet had exchanged numbers as he waited with her for her bus and she had phoned the next day to invite him to Botolph Square.

'We have a proper dining table now,' she explained, 'and so we're going to have a proper dinner.'

'Christ,' said the boy who answered the door. 'You look like you just stepped out of the sea.'

'The Atlantic,' said Theo, and introduced himself.

The boy reacted as if this was the funniest thing he had ever heard and ushered Theo in.

A big American in a big American jacket, was how Fred described Theo to Carlo later. He hopped about, taking Theo's wet things and arranging them on a radiator, then rushed off with the two bottles of very good wine Theo handed over, saying something about towels.

Theo turned right into the nearest room, where a small woman was sitting in an armchair with a large child on her knee.

'Hi,' he said. 'A real fire!'

'The one in Khyber didn't have flames, only smoke,' said the child, slithering to the floor from where she looked up fiercely.

'I'm Mary,' said the woman, rising.

'Theo.'

They sat down and smiled at each other.

After a while, Mary asked, 'Has Fred offered you a drink? No? I'll just go and see what's happening . . .' her voice trailed off as she hurried from the room.

'So!' Theo addressed the child, clapping his hands together enthusiastically.

She shook her head. 'Oh no,' she said, 'oh no, oh no.'

Mary did not come back. Instead, a blonde woman with a vibrant tan appeared, carrying a tray of bottles and glasses.

'I'm Caroline, you must be Theo. Juliet's in the kitchen, refusing help. Did you meet Mary? Where's Fred got to? Bella, don't do that!'

She poured several drinks, handed one to Theo and quizzed him energetically about his first impressions of London.

Fred arrived with the towels. 'You can mop yourself with these, and do give me those boots. I'll stuff them with newspaper and give them a chance to dry. Has someone given you a drink?'

'Perhaps he'd like to tidy up in the bathroom, darling,' said Caroline. 'And you could lend him some dry socks.' Theo looked from her to Fred to the child on the floor.

Mary reappeared. 'Bedtime, Bella.'

'Oh no!'

'Oh yes!' said Caroline, and Bella got up to go.

'She's delightful,' said Theo, 'a real force.'

'Who, Mary?' said Caroline.

'Not your au pair, your little girl.'

Fred and Caroline beamed, and neither rushed to explain.

The doorbell rang and this time Caroline went to answer it. She brought in a tall fair man in a suit, who presented her with a bunch of flowers and shook Theo's hand. 'Strachan,' he said, 'Alexander Strachan.' At first Theo thought he might be as much as forty but then he saw it was the cut of his clothes, the polish on his shoes, the exactness of his gestures. He appeared to have been untouched by the rain.

312

Mary came down and blushed, and Theo watched the man come forward and kiss her with a shy kind of passion. He liked Alexander and Alexander, who looked up and saw the smile on Theo's face, liked him.

'Can I go say hi to Juliet?' Theo asked.

'Absolutely!' said Fred. 'Along the hall and straight down. She can't cook, by the way, and she won't let you help.'

As Theo reached the kitchen, there was a crash of breaking crockery. He found Juliet in a heap on the floor.

'Are you alright?'

'That fucking child,' she was saying as he helped her up.

'I thought you'd collapsed again.'

'No, I slipped. On a banana skin.'

'Seriously?'

'My niece is a purist.'

'The little girl upstairs?'

'You met her.'

'And the balding excitable boy, the timid girl, the guy in the suit and the bossy blonde.'

'You met them all.'

'Who are they?'

As they cleared up the mess and Juliet retrieved what she could of the meal, she explained who everyone was, adding Clara, Carlo, Tobias and her parents to the picture.

'We're a bit much, aren't we?'

'Is that the same as being too much?'

'It depends. Too much what?'

'Let's stop this right now. We need to eat,' said Theo.

And so they did, and Juliet discovered what happens when a person who is good and who sees goodness sits down at your table.

* * *

313

As Barbara pulled up outside the cottage, Jacob got out unprompted to open the gate. He remembered just how to lift it over the stone and how to lift it back. He fetched the spare key from beneath the flowerpot in the porch and opened the front door, and together they carried in all the bags and boxes.

'You've changed everything,' he said and she frowned before he added, 'I mean you've brought out its character.'

Barbara led him through the sage-green hall, along the newly stained oak floor and into the raspberry coloured living room with its exposed beams and woodburning stove. He nodded admiringly at the chaise longue and the carved bookcase. In the kitchen he smiled at the pitted table, the narrow bench, the Aga, the chrome fridge and the set of expensive knives. She led him up the mustard stairway and into a bedroom where sparkling white walls surrounded a big brass bed. There was a tall iron candlestick on the floor and the windowsill was lined with old Cornishware of an irretrievable cream and blue.

Barbara crossed to a door on the far side and lifted the latch. Jacob followed her. He had to bow his head as he stepped through.

This room was also blue but navy, dark and compacted like dry powder paint. There was space for a single bed, a chair, a desk and a chest of drawers. Jacob pulled back the heavy red curtains and opened the window. He knew what was out there – a garden, a stone wall, a sweep of grass, the rise and fall of dunes, and the sea.

'This room is for you,' said Barbara, behind him.

He sat down on the bed and felt himself sink into this house at the end of a lane at the southernmost tip of the country.

'I'm tired.'

'I know,' said Barbara and stepping back into her own room, closed the door.

TWENTY-EIGHT

Three months passed. Juliet had grown stronger and continued to work. She found a job in one of the university libraries and started to look for her own place to live. From time to time, she phoned Theo and they went to see a film or had dinner or walked along the river.

She made him a promise: 'I'm going to take you over every bridge in London.'

'All in one go?'

'No.'

They parted at bus stops, in Tube stations, on street corners and at taxi stands, and always Juliet would lean forward to kiss him holding herself so that no other part of their bodies touched, and then she would be gone and Theo would remain as if the city had gathered itself around this scene and would not let him step back from it.

'What happened to Jacob Dart?'

'He was married.' As if that were the real reason.

The day before Theo flew home for Christmas, they met in a bar at the top of a tower. The weather forecast had warned of a record-breaking fog and while Juliet imagined a cloud descending, what happened was more as if the air gradually outweighed itself.

Juliet and Theo drank martinis and watched the domes, spires, towers and pinnacles of the city come and go.

'I thought there would be nothing to see,' Juliet said, 'but I've never seen it like this. And I do like this invisible drink. The only reason I can tell there's anything in the glass is because of how cold it is.'

'It could just be a cold glass.'

Theo wanted to bring Juliet's attention back to the room, and him.

'I hope it's cleared by tomorrow so I can get home.'

'If it doesn't, you'll have to stay here.' Juliet imagined Theo with them for Christmas at Botolph Square, playing Monopoly with Fred and hide-and-seek with Bella, or maybe the two of them alone in a cottage by the sea or on a hotel balcony somewhere hot . . .

'I have to get back. I have to see Melissa.'

'Of course.'

'You don't understand. I'm sorry, I mean I haven't explained but that's because she doesn't know. I haven't told her.'

Juliet sipped her drink and nodded. Theo relaxed. She waited but he said nothing more. 'I didn't quite catch what it is you have to tell her.'

'Like I said, that I want it to be over.'

'You didn't say –'

'So I shouldn't be telling you.'

'You want it to be over.'

'Yes.'

'Is that a different thing to making it be over?'

'I don't know. I have to see her.'

A waiter set down a bowl of olives and collected their empty martini glasses with a sweep of his hand. He raised an eyebrow to Theo who nodded, and two more drinks were brought.

317

Juliet drew back and looked out. 'Don't do anything because of me.'

'I'm sorry?'

'I'm not going to be the cause of something and I don't know what I –'

'You're not. What were you saying? That you don't know what you –'

'I'm not? Good. Not that I presumed, I just don't want to be the . . . not if otherwise everything would be . . .'

'Juliet,' he said, leaning across the table to take both her hands in his. 'I know you've been sick and that you've still got a way to go.'

'It's never going to end, not unless they empty me out entirely. They have a nice word for my condition – frozen. Everything is glued together and in January they're going to try to prise it all apart. I already have one scar, and that's not healing too well. It's quite purple. And I have to pee all the time. Doesn't that put you off?'

'You're going to be better.'

'Possibly. Better than this, but it's never going to go away entirely, not unless I have half a dozen children although from what they say, having one might be difficult enough.'

'Do you think about what happened last summer?'

'Oh yes,' she said, with no change of tone, 'all the time.' It was true. She went home from an evening with Theo and lay there remembering as much as she could of how he felt and tasted.

'Don't do anything because of me,' she said again, trying to be clear.

'I'm afraid I don't have any grand gestures up my sleeve, not like Jacob Dart, travelling thousands of miles to surprise you.'

'Maybe I was just the furthest place he could run to.'

'It doesn't sound as if you liked him very much.'

318

'I realised I don't believe in him.'

'So how can he exist?'

'Because someone else does.' She needed to be clear. 'I don't know what I felt about him. My brother died, I was full of pills, I went away – the whole time I knew him, I was never myself, so I don't know.'

'And when you met me?'

'I don't know except . . . you made me happy and with Jacob, even when we were at our best, I wasn't happy.'

'Are you happy now?'

'Are you?'

For a moment she thought Theo was about to shrug and if he had she would have walked away, but he was only raising himself to lean forward and whisper in her ear.

Without qualification, the word travelled immediately and deeply.

The Clough family did not spend that Christmas together. Clara and Stefan took the children to Geneva, Carlo went with friends to Miami, and Mary took Bella to visit her mother in the Welsh borders. The doctor and his wife served lunch to the homeless for a charity in Salisbury. No one missed Allnorthover. The Clock House had been sold to a Dutch scientist who turned out to be the new director of the nearby animal-research centre. The Cloughs, among others, had been trying to get the place shut down for years.

A week before Christmas, Caroline had taken Fred shopping and as he twirled in the green tweed coat she had picked out for him, announced that she was going away.

'I have to go back for a bit,' she began.

'I know,' he said, still twirling. He liked the way the coat flared and flashed its tangerine silk lining.

'Oliver's pretty low and there's a lot to sort out.'

Fred stopped twirling. 'Oliver? I thought you meant you were going to see your parents. You do that every Christmas, Caroline Twerp! You don't spend it with Oliver, or me, but with your parents; it's what you do!'

'Take the coat off. You're turning pink.'

She lifted it from his shoulders and handed it to an assistant along with her credit card.

On Christmas Eve, Caroline phoned from Hong Kong to tell Fred that Oliver was in hospital. In the six months that she had been away, he had done his best to drink himself to death and she did not feel able to return to London, at least not for now. Fred spent Christmas Day eating chocolate and drinking champagne cocktails while Juliet tried to work but kept falling asleep. Theo phoned from San Francisco and she felt light with happiness and then wondered about Jacob.

When everyone was back, Fred demanded that the family see in the New Year at Botolph Square. He even invited his parents.

The day began quite well. He got up early, put the champagne to chill, and went out to buy flowers. When he got home, there was a pool of vomit at the foot of the stairs.

'I'm sorry,' said Mary hurrying towards him with a bucket and mop. 'It was Bella. She's feeling rotten so I've put her to bed. I think she's got a fever.'

In the afternoon Francesca arrived, laden with packages and more flowers.

'Where's Dad?' asked Fred, taking her coat.

'He's hurt his back. Nothing serious, he just needs to rest. I've brought you your pan forte and chestnuts.'

'We always have them on New Year's Eve and I forgot, my god . . .'

'It's alright, they're here. So you can fill your stomachs before you all go out dancing.'

'No dancing.'

'What are you doing then?'

'Staying here.'

'But I've come to look after Bella so that you can go out, especially Mary.'

'I thought you'd come to celebrate with us. We're all celebrating together, here.'

'Actually,' put in Mary, 'I have been invited somewhere and if it's alright, I'd like to go.'

'Where?' asked Fred.

'Of course you can go,' said Francesca and seeing the look on the face of her youngest, her baby, 'and Fred can go too.'

'Go where?' he asked, excited, and Mary was about to say yes, of course, he could come along when Juliet appeared in a new dress.

'Is this alright?' She looked cross, or at her most shy. 'Is it really alright?'

'You look beautiful, darling,' Francesca replied, which did not count.

'You really do,' said Mary. 'What would you call that colour . . . honey? Caramel?'

'You make it sound sickly. Is the skirt too much? All that flounce . . .'

Fred was impatient: 'Well since you ask it might be a bit grand for where we're going. And where *are* we going, Mary? Will we have time for champagne first?'

Mary got changed and then went to find Fred, who was in the kitchen. 'The thing is that I don't know where I'm going because I'm being taken, by Alexander.'

'A New Year's Eve mystery tour, just the ticket!' He opened the fridge to admire the row of chilling bottles. 'Does Alexander like champagne? We could crack open a few bottles here and then take another along . . .'

'No, I don't know. Look Fred, you can't come. It's just us . . .'

He stopped fussing and rushing about and looked at Mary. 'That's not your black dress.'

'No, it's red.'

'Everyone's been out buying new dresses. It must be quite a night.'

'It usually is, or at least people hope it will be. I'm sorry.'

'You look beautiful.'

'That's your mother's line.'

They were alone; everything stopped.

Fred lifted his hand to her face, and she caught and held it. 'Have you heard from Caroline?'

'Oliver might die.'

'I'm sorry – for her, for him, for you.'

'She might never come back.'

'I think she will. She's tough and she's clear and in her own peculiar way –'

'She loves me?'

'She does.'

Fred nodded. 'Fuck it, let's start on the champagne.'

Upstairs, they found Alexander.

'We should wait for Carlo,' said Francesca.

'And Theo,' said Juliet. 'He's coming straight from the airport.'

'Carlo's always late,' said Fred, busying himself with glasses and a bowl of ice cubes. It was almost a party after all.

'Isn't it cold enough?' asked Juliet. 'It's been in that monster of a fridge all day.'

'Of course it is,' said Fred. 'The ice is ornamental.'

Only Caroline might have pointed out that it would dilute the champagne, but she was not there. The rest of them took the glass they were offered and raised it in a toast, and to exclaim over the tiny flowers that the ice was releasing.

Everyone made Fred happy for a couple of hours and then remembered their plans.

'I made a reservation for nine,' Alexander said to Mary. 'We ought to go.' Seeing Fred's forlorn expression, he added, 'Perhaps you and Caroline would care to join us, when she arrives?'

'She's not, she won't,' said Fred casually. 'But thanks, yes!' Mary caught his eye. 'But no. I think I'll stay put.'

Juliet was leafing through a phone directory. 'How do you find out if a plane has been delayed?' No one was listening.

'What's happened to Carlo?' Francesca asked. 'He's not answering his phone.'

'He said something about going to a club. Don't worry about him,' said Fred, who was cross with his brother. 'What time is it in Hong Kong?'

Juliet put the directory down. 'How many airlines fly out of San Francisco?'

'We're going to be late,' Mary said, taking Alexander's hand. 'Happy New Year, everyone.'

'You're not coming back for midnight?' Fred followed them into the hall.

At ten o'clock, Francesca left Fred and Juliet playing cards and went to bed.

'So what happened to the Dart?' asked Fred.

'It never really settled, I suppose.'

'Did you love him?'

'Yes, I think now that I did.'

'It sounds tragic.'

'Oh no, it was more comic than anything, a comedy of manners. Neither of us ever managed to say or do the right thing.'

'But that's not funny.'

'A tragedy of manners, then. Can we have another drink?'

Juliet went to the window and looked up at plane lights blinking in the darkness. It was impossible to tell where they were, let alone what direction they were headed in or how fast they were going. When you looked for them, and even if you could tell the difference between lights and stars, you saw more and more. Theo must be up there, stuck in the congested skies where people were forever arriving and departing.

As Fred opened another bottle of champagne, the telephone rang. He rushed to pick it up, 'That'll be –'

'It's Theo!' said Juliet, who reached the phone first. 'Theo?'

'Hi, we've only just landed. Is it too late to come round?'

Juliet surveyed the empty bottles, the single lit candle, the television on with the sound turned down, and Fred. 'Why don't we meet somewhere else?'

'Now?'

'I know a place from where we can see right across the city. We should go up there and watch the fireworks, if you're not too tired.'

'I'm fine. Just tell me where and I'll get there as soon as I can.'

When Juliet put the phone down she said, 'I love meeting Theo. It's always so simple.'

Fred passed her a glass of champagne.

'I shouldn't have any more if I'm going out.'

'And I'm not going to raise a glass alone at midnight so let's do it now.'

Juliet took the glass. 'Happy New Year,' they said and kissed one another formally on both cheeks.

'Things are getting better,' said Fred. 'Two years ago, Tobias died. This year you only almost died, so next year the most we have to fear is a serious injury.'

Juliet went upstairs and began to take off the dress, then decided to keep it on and added thick tights, a jersey, a scarf and boots.

'Do I still look alright?' She asked Fred on the way out.

'Surprisingly so. Like a ballroom dancer in the middle and otherwise a babushka. I tried to get you a cab but they're not even answering the phones.'

'That's OK, I can walk.' She wanted to. New Year's Eve was a time when bad things rarely happened; even bad people's minds were on other things.

Every house Juliet passed made plain its level of celebration. The fullest rooms were brightly lit, and some had their windows open; candles wavered behind paper blinds and televisions chugged away behind drawn curtains. Some houses were locked and dark and in others there was a single light in a top room. There must have been hundreds, even thousands, of people who were alone, but Juliet did not notice any. Knots and gaggles of people went by, and most exchanged greetings with her. People overflowed from pubs, restaurants were full and everywhere there were added lights and music.

Carlo had come home from the hospital exhausted. The problem was not, he realised, the long hours he put in, other doctors did far more; it was how he had to concentrate in order to see what he had been trained to look for, and so as to ignore the rest.

He had a shower and lay down before heading off to Botolph Square. He was only going because he had promised Fred. What he really wanted to do was meet up with some friends at a club. He shut his eyes and the world went out as if someone had hit a switch and he was more deeply asleep than he had ever been before. He would not stir till morning, when the celebrations would be over and he would wake from a number of senseless dreams.

Clara carried her glass of champagne to the bottom of the garden where she sat on the wall and looked back at the house; so many windows. Stefan was happy about the baby and it would be alright because, after all, they loved their children.

For years she had managed life as it had gone on expanding: more painting, more children, being here and in London, Stefan away. Then Tobias had died and it had been a relief to let slip, to allow life to come to her and happen how it wanted. Whatever had almost happened – to her, to Stefan – could happen again and end differently. She had to take charge.

When Barbara told Jacob that she was going back to London for New Year's Eve, he got in the car and came with her. They were going to Patrick Hyde's party, as they used to. Patrick called it his 'last fling' before the start of his six months in Boston. The house was fuller and brighter than anywhere else. Jacob followed Barbara into the crowd but slowed until he could not help but lose sight of her so that there was nothing for it but to turn and walk back out again.

Like others walking towards the hill that night, Juliet imagined that she and Theo would be alone up there. She envisaged the pale green slope up to the black bushes and the steeper green beyond, where they would stand at the top of the top and declare themselves to the city. Theo might build a fire.

As she crossed the footbridge she saw a group of people ahead, and beyond them more people. From every side of the hill, they were converging.

'Where shall I meet you?' Theo had asked.

'At the top, of course.'

She hurried to climb as the crowd thickened around her. Every time she looked up, the cluster of people at the top had concentrated and spread. She reached them, slowed and began to make her way through. There were several fires already and those who had found the spot they wanted, settled firmly into place. Others, like Juliet, made their way round and round, looking for a better view or someone they had arranged to meet. Everyone glanced at their watches or asked one another the time, but this was to be a celebration and so they smiled at whoever got in their way and those they let pass thanked them. Every contact meant something. It was that kind of night, when all it took to make a decision was brushing up against another person's actions or words.

At quarter to twelve, the hill was full and most decided to stay where they were and enjoy what they could. Some, though, could not do that yet. Juliet walked on round, each time more slowly. At five to twelve, she was at the front of the hill and stopped to look where everyone else was looking, across the city. She would not give up. Theo was back down here on earth and coming towards her.

'Happy New Year!' someone shouted.

'Two minutes to go!' shouted someone else.

'I make it forty-five seconds.'

And so an inexact midnight rippled through the crowd, who made the most of it and then set off cheerfully back into the dark.

Juliet lingered, wanting to know what it might have been like had they been alone, had Theo been there.

*　　*　　*

There are not many people left on the hill now. She turns and climbs further, looks down and sees him running. She shouts but he does not hear her and so she shouts again, this time loud enough.

They stand at the top, alone as she had imagined – above the city, below the sky. It is one o'clock.

'An hour west of here it is midnight and you made it on time,' she says.

'But we're here and I didn't.'

'That,' she says, 'is the absolute truth.'

They start walking and turn a corner, beyond which someone is coming towards them. Juliet will have only the time between the moment at which she recognises Jacob and the moment they meet, to decide how to move past him.